FORBIDDEN

F-BOMB: SEALS LOVE CURVES, BOOK 7

MARY E THOMPSON

F-BOMB: SEALS LOVE CURVES

Welcome to the world of F-BOMB where a group of former SEALs have come together to protect the curvy women they love and the country they call home from the dangers of the world. They have the training and the knowledge, and they have the ability to kick some ass when needed. And it'll be needed.

F-BOMB: SEALs LOVE CURVES
Freedom (free everywhere)
Fiancée (subscriber exclusive)
Forgotten
First
Failure
Friends
Family
Forbidden
Future
Finally

SUBSCRIBE NOW AT MARYETHOMPSON.COM

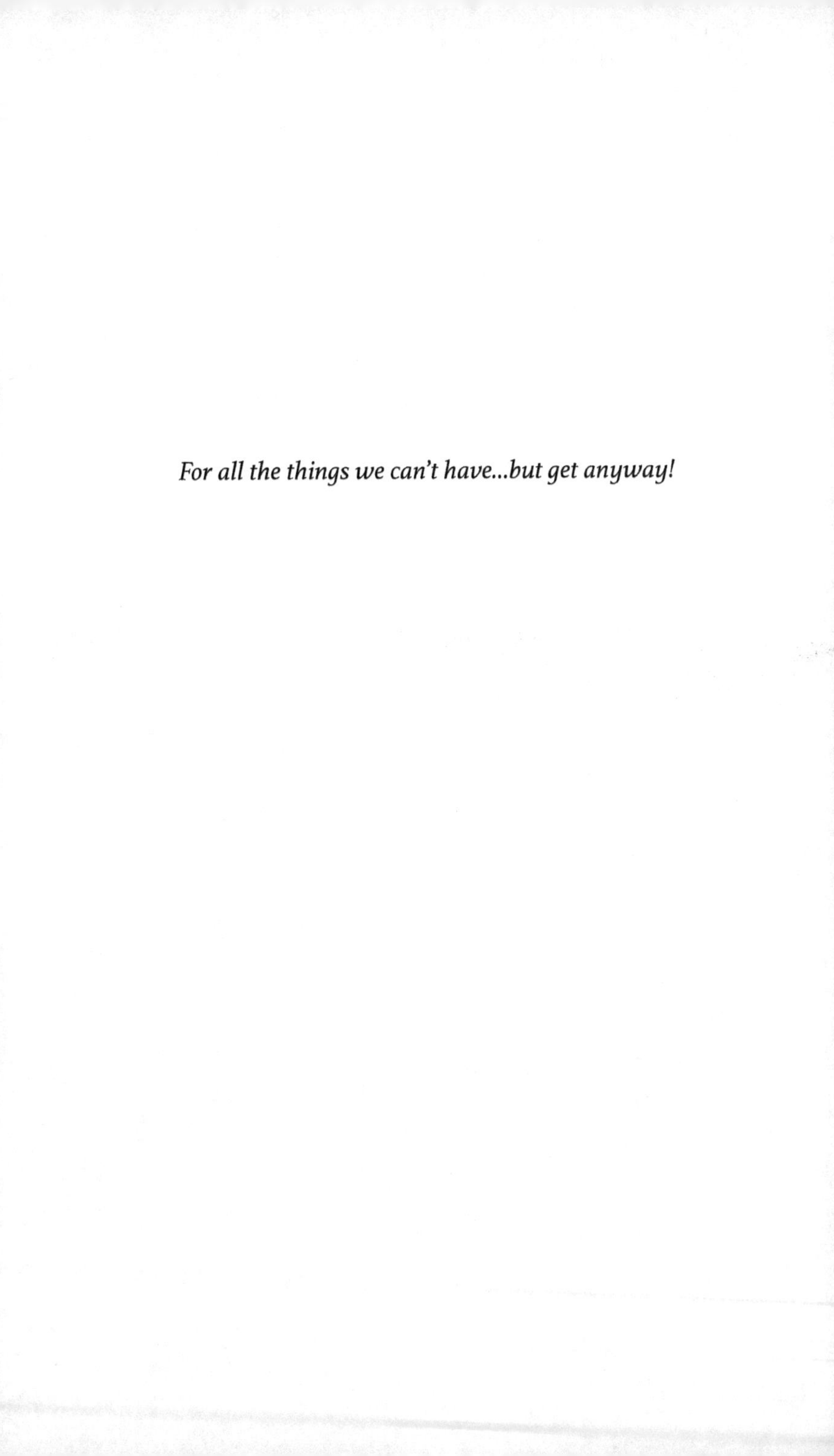

For all the things we can't have...but get anyway!

1

MEGAN O'KEEFE STEPPED OFF THE PLANE AND TOOK A BREATH of fresh air. Well, not fresh. Airport air. But it was better than the air on the plane. She was on the ground and ready.

The walk through the airport was quick, and she found her bags without any trouble. When she got outside, the line of cars waiting to pick people up almost brought tears to her eyes. She didn't have anyone there. But she could have. She was the one who chose to surprise her brother.

The cab dropped Megan off in front of Justin's house, Slade according to his friends, and for the first time since she came up with her plan, she faltered. Since she didn't tell her brother she was coming, she had no idea if he would be home.

"Crap," she said.

Instead of chasing down the cab that had left her at the end of the driveway, Megan grabbed the handles of her suitcases and headed up to the house. Maybe Justin and Kyra were there. Maybe she'd get lucky.

She rang the doorbell and was immediately met with a

loud barking that only got louder as she stood there. After a second, a voice, Justin's voice, shouted over the dog.

"Megan? Are you seriously at my house right now?"

"Hi, big brother! I wanted to come up and visit before your wedding."

"Why didn't you tell me?"

"It's a surprise! I wanted to meet Kyra and your friends and see what's so great about Niagara Falls. You know, besides the obvious."

"Awesome. I'm so glad you're here. Um, but I'm not home."

"Yeah, sorry. I should have called you. I really didn't think this through."

"It's fine. I promise. Listen, Kyra and I are just finishing up with work. We'll head out shortly. You can go around to the back and hang out there if you want. I don't have one of those doors I can unlock from here. We'll be there as soon as we can be."

"That sounds good. I can use some of this Niagara Falls sunshine."

"Because you don't get enough at home."

Megan forced a smile for her brother and chuckled. "Something like that."

"Okay, I'm gonna go so we can head out. See you soon."

"Yep. Bye!"

Megan wasn't sure if the camera thing in the doorbell was still on, but Justin was silent, so she assumed he signed off. She looked at the well-manicured lawn and the massive trees around the property. There wasn't another house in sight from where she stood. With how loud the barking inside was, she couldn't say she was surprised.

Megan grabbed her bags again and dragged them through the grass to the patio in back. It ran the length of the house and extended at least ten feet. There was plenty of grass beyond the patio before the tree line interrupted the open area for the dog to run around.

The dog. Megan turned to the full glass doors to see if she could spot the front door from where she was. He was looking back at her.

"Oh, you are the cutest thing ever, aren't you?" she cooed to him through the glass. He smiled and wagged his tail. "You know you are, don't you? Hi, Howler. I'm Auntie Megan. I can't wait to come inside and give you a big hug. But for now, I have to sit out here."

Megan left her bags next to the door and picked a chair facing the woods. She sat down, relieving the pressure on her back. Standing and sitting on an airplane for hours was murder on her body. She wasn't the healthiest person, even under normal circumstances, but it was worse when she was forced to cram herself into a tiny seat. Her oversized body was not built for airplanes.

After sitting for a few minutes, Megan kicked off her shoes and went out onto the grass. It was warm on the surface but cool underneath and refreshing to her tired feet. She stretched and moved her body, trying to work out the kinks. She took a deep breath and thanked God for delivering her there safely.

Megan went back to her chair and sank into it. The warm afternoon sun soothed her. She hadn't been sleeping well, and before she knew it, she was drifting off in the chair, not a care in the world.

"Megan," Justin called out, startling her awake.

"Hey. Hi. I'm here. I'm up." Megan swung her feet over the edge of the chair and looked up at her brother. God, it was good to see him.

"Come on, little sis. You need some rest and food."

"Are you going to cook for me?" Megan teased.

"Yep. I'm a pretty good cook. But you can help if you'd like. First, Megan, I want you to meet my soon-to-be wife. This is Kyra."

Kyra was standing at the door holding on to Howler's collar as he strained to get away. She waved and Howler lunged, nearly breaking her grasp.

"Dude, calm down," Kyra said with a laugh. "Sorry, he's even more excited that you're here than Slade. Are you okay with dogs?"

Megan nodded. "Absolutely. I told him I couldn't wait to give him a big hug."

"He's not going to wait long, either. I'm letting him go. Are you ready?"

Megan chuckled and nodded. Howler took off as soon as the resistance against his collar was gone. He ran toward her and made it about halfway before his hind legs gave out and his butt hit the patio. He didn't stop, though, just scrambled through it until he reached Megan.

Megan laughed and leaned forward to wrap her arms around Howler's neck. He panted happily while she rubbed his body and told him what a good boy he was.

"He's a spoiled rotten creature," Justin said playfully. "And he knows it."

Howler looked up at his owner like he was a god. Justin grinned at the dog. Megan knew she made the right choice coming early. She needed to see the life her brother had. Decide if it was a life she wanted. Not that she was telling him that. Nope. As far as he was going to know, she was just visiting. When she made her final decision, then Megan would tell him she planned to move there.

"Come on. Let's head in. We can start dinner. What are you in the mood for?" Justin asked.

Megan kissed Howler once more, then stood and hugged her brother. "I'll eat anything. You know that." She gave a self-deprecating laugh.

"Me, too," Kyra said, gesturing her own full figure.

Megan was happy to see Kyra was a woman like her. Not as big, but not tiny either. She knew it wasn't entirely fair, but Megan always felt more comfortable with women who carried a little extra weight like she did.

"You're beautiful. And I'm so excited to get to know you better. You can tell me all about this lump of muscle and why in the world you decided to fall for his charm," Megan said, looping her arm through Kyra's.

Kyra laughed and said, "He's definitely charming. I'll give him that."

Justin grumbled behind them as they headed inside. Howler trotted along next to his owner. The boys went to the kitchen while the ladies sat on the couch and talked.

"His teammates are awesome," Kyra said. "You're going to love everyone. They all wanted to come over and meet you, but Slade told them to give you a couple of days to settle in. If you're okay with it, they're all going to come over on Friday."

"All of them?" Megan asked. Fooling her brother was one thing, but deceiving an entire group of SEALs trained to sniff out lies and half-truths was very much another.

Kyra nodded. "Yeah. We all get together all the time. At least once every weekend everyone comes here or we all go to one of the other houses. These guys are all really close."

"That's very cool. I've never liked any of my coworkers enough to want to spend time with them outside of work."

"I thought you were dating someone from work?" Justin asked.

Megan shook her head and forced the emotion back.

"No, that was just casual. It's done now. He wasn't worth my time." *Or my child's.* The thought threatened the tears Megan fought desperately to hold back. "Hey, sorry, can I use your bathroom?"

"Oh, my gosh, of course," Kyra said. "I'm so sorry. I never thought. It's down the hall, first door on the right."

"Thanks."

Megan followed Kyra's directions and locked the door behind herself before the tears made it to her cheeks. She'd cried enough tears for that asshat, but she hadn't cried for her child yet. The tiny, helpless unborn baby just starting its life inside her.

The ex that Megan thought was at least a friend told her the baby couldn't be his because they were not exclusive and he always wore a condom. Megan thought they could have been more than friends who occasionally slept together, but he was screwing other women. She told him he was probably right and ran. Because what else was she going to do? Saddle her child with a useless father for the rest of their life? Saddle herself with a worthless man? Nope. She was going to raise her child on her own. Maybe near Justin and Kyra and Justin's army of friends.

Megan used the bathroom and splashed water on her face. She sucked in a deep breath and shoved down the emotions. She could do this. She had to do this. For her baby.

MASON O'CONNOR stared at the man in the mirror and wondered where his life went. He had hopes and dreams once upon a time. He wanted kids, a full life with his wife. They talked about the house they were going to have one day, the backyard they would have for their family to play in.

Mason glared at his reflection. He was the one who ruined that. He let the outside world get into his head and he pulled the trigger on his own wife. Ending all their dreams in seconds.

It wasn't the first time a nightmare had woken him, but it was the first time in a while. The first year after she died, he barely slept. When he did, he saw her face. Lifeless and cold. It haunted him. But after a year, the dreams began to fade. Mostly thanks to the help of the court mandated psychologist he saw in prison.

Mason shook his head and forced himself away from the memories. He got dressed, swallowed a cup of coffee, and punished himself with a long run. By the time he got back, his muscles were screaming for relief. Instead of a hot shower like he wanted, he settled for a quick, lukewarm one so he would feel it all day. Remind himself that the pain he felt was nothing compared to the pain he'd caused.

He drank another cup of coffee and ate some toast before heading to work. Things had been quiet for the last few days, and if he knew anything about the kind of work they did, quiet only lasted so long.

As soon as he set foot in the office, he knew the quiet was over for a while. The team was running around. They weren't in gear, but they were busy.

"What's going on?" Mason asked Jack as he brushed past.

"We caught a new case. Missing firefighter."

"Why are we being called in on something like that?"

"All hands, dude."

Mason nodded and followed Jack into the conference room. Jack was the jokester of the group, always ready to make everyone laugh, but he wasn't smiling. Shit was serious.

They already had their war board full of data, including a large picture of the man who was missing. Mason didn't recognize him, but he knew the Niagara Fire uniform. The clean cut, smiling man in the photo had no shadows in his eyes, no demons hiding. The guy looked like an ordinary man. Which only made Mason wonder...

"What's the story?" he asked Dex as he put another picture on the board.

Dex was the unofficial second in command. He was crazy smart and unmatched when it came to putting pieces of a puzzle together. And he was a damn good shot when he needed to be.

"His wife thought he was on shift when he didn't come home. Said he usually calls, but it's not unheard of for him to forget since time seems to blend together for these guys. When she didn't hear from him on the second day, she reached out to the station. They said he was supposed to be there three days ago but never showed up. Seventy-two hours missing. Cops tracked his phone, but it's dark. English is going through cameras, and the rest of us are helping dig into his life. Grab a spot and pick an area to search."

Mason nodded and took a seat at one of the computers in the room. He pulled up social media first, fumbling through the program he wasn't familiar with. Mason didn't use any social media. There wasn't a person alive who cared about his day-to-day life, so he kept it to himself. But someone cared about this guy.

Mason kept searching, looking for anything about the firefighter, Wray Allen. He went through photos his wife posted of the two of them, then searched through all the people in those photos to see if there was anything that could tell them where he might be.

By the time he looked up, it was lunch.

"We all need a break," Dunn said. Daniel Dunn was their elected boss. The SEALs, except Mason, built F-BOMB together, but they chose Dunn to run the operation. He was their XO in the Navy and the man the rest of them decided to work under. Dunn and Dex ran a tight ship. They were efficient and effective, and damn good leaders.

When Mason joined the team, he was surprised how easily they welcomed him in. Their first introduction wasn't simple, but once they realized he wasn't stalking Kelsea, things went a little more smoothly. She kept inviting him to gatherings with the group and after a while, they asked him to help out with some of their jobs. Before long, he was offered a salary and an office.

And a new place to call home.

Mason grabbed a sandwich from one of the platters Dunn delivered. He snagged a bag of chips and a bottle of water also. They all ate in relative silence, their minds on the man they were searching for.

After lunch, Dunn stood in front of the board and asked what they were missing.

"I haven't found anything to indicate he's having an affair," English said. As the computer expert of the group, he was the one tasked with finding information that wasn't publicly available, like searching the man's phone records and his inboxes.

"Okay, good. What about family or friends? Anyone with a shady past?"

"No," Dex said. "Not that I've seen. He spends time with the other firefighters. His wife spends time with their wives. His circle is small. Dad was a firefighter. His sister is a firefighter. He has a cousin who's a firefighter. This guy is in deep, and he's squeaky. Not even an unpaid parking ticket."

"What are we missing?" Dunn asked.

They all stared at the board with the man's life on display. Something wasn't there. Something that could tell them what happened to him. People didn't just disappear. There was always a trace. The hard part was finding that trace and seeing it for what it was.

"Let's start at the beginning," Archer said. "He was reported missing on day three, but what happened the last day he was seen. Where was he? What did he do? Who did he see? When were his last social media posts? Let's paint a picture of his life up until he vanished from it."

"He was home over the weekend," Jack said. "Dinner with his family Sunday night. Wife said that's their normal routine. She doesn't remember anything odd happening. They were at his parents' house, came home afterward, watched TV, and went to bed."

"Monday he supposedly went to work, right?" Archer asked.

"Yes," Rocky agreed. "Monday he left, his wife went to work, and since he was working, she didn't think anything of him not being home. He should have been home Tuesday, but she assumed he picked up an extra shift. Wednesday, she called the station. They said they hadn't seen him all week."

"Why didn't they call Monday when he didn't show up?" Dex asked.

They all looked around the room. No one had an answer.

"Dig there," Dunn said. "Who at the station was he friends with? Who should have made that call? Look into the chief and the lieutenant, his bunkmate, best friend, anyone who would have made an excuse or covered this up."

Heads down, they all started digging. Dex got on the phone with the local PD to get statements from the other firefighters. They went through everything.

"Call records. One of the other firefighters called our guy. Thirty-seven seconds. I'm trying right now to find..." English trailed off. He hit a button and leaned back as another voice filled the room.

"Where the hell are you? I covered for you, but you need to call me. I don't know what is going on with you lately, but this shit is not okay. I can't keep doing this. Call me."

The room was silent as they all looked around at each other.

"Well, we have our first lead. Find out what this guy knows. Now."

2

———

MEGAN STOOD AT THE STOVE STIRRING THE RICE AND thinking about her decision to leave home. One day in and she was already bored. Even if she'd told Justin and Kyra she was coming, they still would have had to work. Most people couldn't take three or four weeks off and not lose their jobs.

Technically, Megan was not on vacation. She told her boss she'd call in and keep in touch with her clients. Being the top sales agent for their area, he couldn't say no to her. Which was exactly what she was counting on.

But spending all day without a schedule and without calls to make had her ready to pull her hair out. Megan liked people. She liked to talk to people. Being alone with her thoughts was dangerous because she always ended up making poor decisions. Like the time she decided to give herself bangs. Very bad idea.

Howler let out a yelp and scared Megan. He raced to the door and howled at it. Megan clamped a hand over her ears and called out to him to stop yelling.

Then she heard the keys in the door.

"You are such a crazy dog," Kyra said as soon as the door opened. "We're right here."

She gently moved Howler from in front of the door and made room for Justin to walk in after her. His hand lingered on her hip as he walked by. Justin rubbed Howler's head and sniffed the air.

"Man, it smells better in here than usual. Most of the time, when we get home, it smells like his farts," Justin joked. He walked into the kitchen and grabbed a veggie from the tray Megan took out of the oven a few minutes earlier.

"I noticed," she said with a scowl. "I opened the back door to air the place out. He is a fart machine."

Kyra chuckled. "Just be glad he doesn't sleep in your bed."

"Nope. You two can keep him in yours. Thanks again for letting me stay here. I really should have called," Megan said.

Kyra shook her head and waved a hand. "No, you shouldn't have. You are always welcome here. I'm sorry we didn't have the guest room set up for you."

"It's fine. I don't need much." The guest room doubled as Justin's home gym. Megan didn't mind sleeping in there, but she felt like she was invading their space. She was, but being in a room that wasn't designed for guests made her feel worse. Especially when they didn't know why she was really there.

"I'll move some stuff around so you have more space," Justin said. "I've been meaning to clear that room out, anyway."

Megan smiled at her brother and turned off the heat under the rice. Justin was a monster of a man. He was always big, tall and strong. The only reason people thought they were blood siblings growing up was because they were both big people, but her big wasn't the same as his. She had blonde hair to his dark. She had curves to his muscles. She had green eyes to his dark ones. Megan didn't blend in with her adoptive family at all, but Justin always made her feel like there was no difference between them.

Tears sprang to her eyes. Damn hormones. She focused on the rice instead of on how much it meant to her that her brother was being so sweet. She wasn't surprised by it, but after things with Stuart, Megan was raw and emotional.

"I'm going to get changed," Kyra said. "I'll be back in a few minutes."

Megan nodded as Kyra's soft footsteps and Howler's nails moved away from the kitchen. She was sure Kyra was trying to give Megan and Justin time alone. All she had to do was wait for her brother to say something.

"Is everything okay?" he asked. Right on schedule.

Megan sucked in a deep breath and forced her emotions down. She was getting good at that. "Yeah. I'm just happy for you. After Jessie, I wasn't sure if you'd let someone else in. Kyra is perfect for you. She's amazing. And I'm really happy for you."

"And that's why you're crying?" Justin asked.

Megan sighed and tried to laugh. She turned to face her brother. "It is. I know you hate it when I cry, so I'm trying not to show you."

Justin walked over and pulled Megan into his arms. He held her tight. His big body made her feel like less of a freak. He was big, too. She was normal with her brother around.

"I have missed too much with you. I'm sorry I wasn't there."

"You had a life to live," Megan said, pulling back. Yes, she missed her brother like one would miss a limb, but she wasn't going to make him feel guilty for living his life. He had every right to choose what he wanted to do.

"I also had a sister who needed me."

Megan smiled at him. "I'm still here."

Justin's eyes narrowed. "Do you need me now?"

Megan nodded solemnly. "Yes. I need you to move so I can get a platter and we can eat dinner."

Justin chuckled like Megan hoped he would. He grabbed the platter from the cabinet behind him and handed it to her. "I'll let Kyra know it's safe to come out again."

Megan nodded as Justin went down the hall. She took a deep breath, feeling both painfully guilty and unimaginably relieved that her brother bought her lies. One day, she was going to need to tell him about the baby, but she wasn't ready. One day she would be.

MASON AND DEX parked in front of the firefighter's house first thing the next morning. Mason looked up at it. A bike was on its side on the front lawn. Chairs lined the porch. A welcome mat sat in front of the door. The steel blue color was offset by bright white windows and a cheery yellow door.

"Looks ordinary," Dex said.

Mason nodded and got out of the SUV. He had the same thought. People who ran into trouble usually had a mark that was obvious. So far, they hadn't found anything on the guy. Nothing that would help them learn why he was missing and where he went.

Mason followed Dex to the door and waited for someone to answer. The wife knew they were coming. It only took a few seconds before the door swung open and a tired looking woman tried to force a smile at them.

"Can I help you?"

"I'm Ryker Hamilton, this is Mason O'Connor. Are you Mrs. Allen?"

She nodded and took a step back. "I am. Please, call me Stacey."

"Stacey, nice to meet you. Thank you for agreeing to talk to us."

She nodded again. "Anything to find my husband." She led them to the kitchen and gestured to the well-worn table for four. A high chair was strapped into one of the seats, the others had placemats in front of the chairs. The laminated surface was chipped and peeling away from the metal wrapped edge. Beefy blocks that were obviously add-ins held it up, but it fit in with the rest of the tired looking kitchen.

Dex and Mason sat gingerly on the chairs. Mason wasn't sure it would hold him, but he didn't want to be rude either. Mrs. Allen walked to the stove and lifted a tea kettle.

"Would either of you like something to drink? I have tea, coffee, water—"

"We're fine," Dex said. "Thank you. Are your kids home?"

She shook her head. "My oldest is at school, and the baby is at day care. They're young enough that they don't realize their daddy has been gone longer than would be normal. I don't want them to worry."

"Do you have any idea where he could be, Mrs. Allen?" Dex asked.

She shook her head and huffed a laugh. "If I knew, don't you think I would have found him by now? I've taken off the last two days from work so I could look for him. I've called hospitals and the police station. I've checked with border patrol. I've done everything I can think of to track down my husband, but I can't find him."

"I'm sorry," Mason said. "Do you know of anyone who would want to hurt him?"

She rolled her eyes. "No, I don't. And I don't know of any affairs or any friends who would be harboring him. We have a good life. It's not perfect, but we're happy. He wouldn't just vanish like this. Something happened to him. And everyone is treating me like I'm missing something. Like I'm holding back from telling everyone where he is. I'm the one who called to find out what happened to him. I'm the one who reported him missing."

"We're not accusing you of anything, Mrs. Allen," Dex said.

"Well, it doesn't feel that way." She crossed her arms over her chest and pulled her lip between her teeth. Her entire body trembled. A tear streaked down her cheek and she hurried to wipe it away.

"Mrs. Allen, I understand what you're going through. I know you're scared. When something happens to someone, the spouse is always the first suspect. It might not be fair, but it's the truth. And in cases like this one, when there's no reason for him to disappear, the spouse is looked at even more closely. That doesn't mean we think you had something to do with your husband's disappearance, but we are trying to find him. That's our goal," Mason told her.

"So am I," she said firmly. She glared at him. "I love my husband. He means everything to me. If I had any idea..."

"Mrs. Allen, if you think of anything that could help us, please give me a call," Dex said. He stood, and Mason followed his lead. They let themselves out, leaving her to cry alone in her kitchen.

"Fucking hell, that was rough," Dex said when they were in the SUV.

"Do you believe her?" Mason asked.

Dex nodded. "Yeah. She's shaken up, but she's not acting like a woman who was abused or who is worried about what we'll find. She seems worried about her husband, and that's it."

Mason drew a breath. "That was the feeling I got, too. Now what?"

"Now we go talk to his friend. The guy who covered for him. It didn't sound like the first time, so we're going to find out what he knows," Dex said.

Mason nodded and stared out the window as Dex drove. The two houses were close, likely walking distance. No major roads between them, just a few turns through the neighborhood.

"That's interesting. They live really close," Mason said.

"Yeah, they do," Dex agreed. "I'm not sure it's significant, but we're not counting anything as coincidence here."

Mason followed Dex to another door and waited for another person to grant them entry. He looked a little less happy to see them on his doorstep.

"Mr. Wright, we spoke on the phone. I'm Ryker Hamilton, and this is my teammate, Mason O'Connor," Dex said.

Braden Wright eyed them both, then ran a hand over his dark hair and stepped back. He rubbed the sleep from his eyes and led the way to his kitchen. It was smaller than Mrs. Allen's. Instead of a table littered with placemats and a living room overwhelmed by toys, Mr. Wright's home screamed bachelor with dark leather furniture in the living room and beer bottles and pizza boxes on the kitchen countertops. He didn't offer them a drink or a seat, just leaned against the counter and crossed his arms.

"Do you know where Mr. Allen is?" Dex asked.

Braden looked surprised by the direct question. He pulled back just barely, a small enough move that Mason would have missed it if he wasn't watching the other man. "No. If I did, I would have told the cops who were here and Stacey and our bosses."

"Has he ever disappeared like this before?" Mason asked.

Braden shook his head, but he avoided their gazes. Mason and Dex exchanged one of their own.

"I'd like you to listen to this, Mr. Wright," Dex said. He pulled out his phone and hit play on the recording Braden left on Wray Allen's phone.

As the message played, Braden's shoulders bunched up tighter and tighter around his ears until Mason wasn't even sure he could hear his own voice in the kitchen.

"Can you explain this?" Dex asked.

Braden sighed and shook his head. "Wray is a good guy. One of the best I know. We grew up together, went to college together, played ball together, joined the station together. He's a good guy."

"But?"

"He's a little spacey at times. He's gone out on weekend benders and passed out in his truck. He's taken off for a few days to go fishing and was gone a week. He turns off his phone and disconnects and doesn't realize how much time's gone by."

"If that's true, why doesn't his wife know where he is? Why didn't she say he does this?"

Braden sighed again and looked up at them. "Because she doesn't know."

"How is that possible?" Mason asked.

"We're firefighters. We work weird hours. We're on shift

for a day or two, and sometimes we trade shifts with other firefighters and end up working for a few days. If Stacey can't reach him, she calls me. I cover for him."

"How many times has this happened?" Dex asked.

Braden shrugged. "Not too many. Maybe once a year or so. Maybe more."

"Where does he usually go?" Mason crossed his arms and studied the other man, trying to determine if he was telling the truth or not.

"It depends. Most of the time, I don't ask."

"Your best friend disappears for up to a week, you cover for him with his wife and work, and you don't bother to ask where he is?" Dex clarified.

Braden huffed a breath. "Look, our lives run on trust. If we don't trust each other, we die. It might sound crazy to outsiders, but if Wray was really in trouble, I have to believe he would tell me."

"Except he might be. He's been missing for days and no one knows where he is. You're the only one who knows that he disappears like this and you don't know where he is. How are you so sure everything is fine?"

"Because it always is. He's safe and he'll be back soon. I'm sure of it."

"I'm still stuck on his wife not knowing," Mason said. "He's gone for as long as a week and she doesn't even realize?"

Braden nodded. "She's busy with the kids. And I cover for him. Plus, he works a lot of extra hours, anyway. The guys all know if they have vacation, Wray will usually cover for them, so he ends up working an extra shift or two almost every week."

"That's a lot of extra time," Dex said.

Braden shrugged. "It's good money."

"Do they have money problems?" Mason asked.

"Probably. I mean, they have two kids, so I guess, but we don't talk about stuff like that."

"What do you talk about?" Mason asked.

Braden shrugged. "Women. Work. Sports. I don't know. What do guys talk about?"

"Your message said you were getting sick of covering for him. Does that mean you've been doing it more and more lately?" Dex asked.

Braden nodded reluctantly. "Yeah. I mean, not like a ton, but it's only been a few weeks since the last time he disappeared."

"Where did he go that time?"

Braden glared at Mason.

"When was this?" Dex asked, drawing Braden's attention to him.

Braden stared up at the ceiling. "I don't know. Three weeks ago, maybe four."

"Can you narrow it down? What else was going on around then?"

Braden sighed heavily and looked up at the ceiling. "We worked a double, and we were exhausted. One of the guys on another shift asked Wray if he could cover him for some vacation that weekend. We'd just had a rough two days with that structure fire down on Seventh. When was that?"

"We can look it up," Dex said. "So, it was after that?"

"Yeah. We worked the night of the structure fire and the next night. He came in that weekend to cover and must have left from that shift. He missed our next shift but was back for our weekend."

Dex scribbled the timeline in a notepad while Braden talked. When he finished, Dex looked up. "Thank you. We'll look into this and see what we can find. We appreciate your time today."

Braden nodded and yawned. He followed Mason and Dex to the door and closed it behind them without a word before they made it off his porch.

"He was pleasant," Mason said.

Dex chuckled. "A tired firefighter with a missing best friend isn't going to be in a great mood."

"No, but he could have been helpful. I think he's full of shit."

"Me, too. But he gave us a lead. We know another time Mr. Allen vanished without a trace. Maybe if we can find something about that adventure, we can uncover this one. And then we can convince him to let his wife know when he's skipping town because he's going to lose more than just his job for this if he's not careful."

"Sounds like he should have already. Can you imagine if someone did this in the Teams?"

Dex laughed. "They'd be court-martialed. And so would their buddy."

"Yep. Different world here."

"That's for sure."

3

MASON DECIDED TO HANG AROUND THE OFFICE AFTER THEY got back from talking to Braden Wright and Stacey Allen. He wasn't the programmer that English was, but he knew something was off and wanted to dig.

English ran a program that afternoon to search for Wray Allen after he disappeared the last time. Since the cameras near the fire station were owned by the city, English couldn't see Wray when he left work. He was able to trace his truck, but nothing out of the ordinary happened. He left work, stopped by a grocery store, then went home. Or at least went into his neighborhood. There weren't any cameras in the neighborhood, so whatever happened to him there couldn't be seen.

The whole team was getting frustrated with the lack of progress on the case. The belief was that this was a good man. That he got caught up in something bad, but that he was good. Not being able to find him was weighing on everyone.

By late afternoon, everyone was exhausted from the

search and left to head over to Slade's. Since his sister was in town, they were having one of their regular get-togethers there so everyone could meet her and welcome her to town. Mason considered skipping out, but Slade stopped by his office before he left and specifically asked him to come.

Mason focused on the task at hand instead of wondering why Slade singled him out. He didn't know Slade's sister, and he was sure Slade wouldn't want them involved. The last thing Mason wanted was to test his place in the office.

Instead, he stalled and dug into Braden's past. Braden didn't seem like a bad guy, but Mason didn't like people who lied. He'd seen it go bad too many times to know that lying to protect someone always meant people were doing something they shouldn't be doing. Whatever Wray Allen was involved in was bad news, but Mason had a hunch Braden knew more than he was willing to share.

English already had phone records for Wray, so it was an easy search to find times when he and Braden had been in touch. It seemed they were as close as they sounded, with calls or texts between them multiple times every day. Mason read through all the texts first, but as expected, they were not at all revealing. These two were smart. Nothing was in writing.

Next Mason went through call logs. He couldn't go back and listen to calls they made, but he could see the patterns. The fire department had provided records of when Wray was supposed to be at work and when he actually was at work. Most of the calls that lasted longer than thirty seconds were when Wray was supposed to show up for work and didn't.

And there were a lot more than one in the last three or four weeks like Braden claimed. Mason counted about once a week for the better part of six months.

He wasn't sure exactly what that meant, but it wasn't good. Whatever Wray was involved with pulled him away weekly, not monthly or annually.

Mason tried to track the patterns, but he couldn't find one. Everything was random, as far as he could tell. He hit all seven days of the week, sometimes the first day and sometimes the second of a shift, and the calls were split between Wray calling Braden and the reverse. There was nothing that made sense.

An affair was very plausible, but there was no record of phone calls to unknown numbers. Every call Wray made went to his friend, his wife, his family, or the station. Unless he had a different way to contact someone, he wasn't having an affair.

Mason paced the office and tried to clear his head. His stomach growled, and he realized how late it was. He glared at the screen that gave him no help and knew clearing his head would be the best thing he could do.

Mason closed everything down and locked the office. He went down to his ancient Jeep and headed toward Slade's house.

Mason was barely able to pull off the road and park in front of Slade's. Because he lived in the middle of nowhere, no one cared about the extra vehicles on the side of the road. Mason hoped being the last one there meant he could eat and get out of there without getting trapped by something.

He wasn't the most social of people. The group welcomed him in, but he still felt like he was outside most of the time. He and Kelsea would chat, and that led to Mason and Jaymes becoming friends. Jaymes was Archer's brother, but he didn't serve with the rest of them either, so Jaymes and Mason bonded over the fact that they were outsiders pretending to be on the inside.

Mason went to the door and knocked, then let himself in. He always felt awkward doing that, but Slade insisted on it. He said if the door was unlocked, it was safe to walk right in. But he was careful to warn everyone that if they had to pick the lock or use a key, they were doing so at their own risk because he and Kyra liked to have sex all over the house.

Mason remembered those days.

The noise inside the house was loud enough that even Howler didn't notice Mason let himself in. There were people in the kitchen, and the sliding doors to the back were wide open. Mason closed the door behind himself and looked around for Kelsea and Jaymes. Spotting them in the living room, he headed that way.

Mason glanced around at the others and forgot how to breathe. He swore he knew a minute ago, but as soon as his eyes landed on her, the ability to do so completely left him.

Her head was thrown back in laughter, her thick neck exposed. He never understood the whole vampire thing until that moment. He'd definitely give up everything if it meant he could feast on her neck. Even just a little nibble.

She dropped her head back down and glanced across the room. Her bright green eyes landed on him. The smile lingered on her lips as she catalogued him. Then it widened. She licked her lips, drawing the plump bottom one between her teeth.

She was the stuff dreams were made of. Her curves went on for days. Her full cheeks were round and red, and he imagined her lower cheeks would be the same. Her breasts were large but shadowed beneath the sweater she wore like armor. The only thing about her that wasn't big was her blonde hair, which was cut sharply to her chin.

Mason always loved a big woman. He was bigger than most men he knew, and he liked a woman who matched him. Who could handle a man of his size, both above the belt and below.

"Mason!" Slade called out, finally realizing Mason had walked into the house without waiting for an invitation. He was the last to arrive, and one of the only single ones left in the group, so it was easy to fade into the crowd most of the time.

Mason took a step forward and kept his eyes on the curvy beauty. The way she eyed him every so often made him think she might be up for some after party fun.

Right up until Slade said, "I want to introduce you to my sister. Mason, this is Megan. Megan, this is Mason."

Fuck.

She smiled and extended her hand to his. "It's so nice to meet you," she said in a voice that said he read her right. She was definitely up for an afterparty party for two.

But that was never going to happen. He should have realized the only woman he didn't recognize was Slade's sister, but all thoughts vanished when he saw her. Mason knew better than to get involved with a woman who was connected to his world, especially a woman who might think he was more than a one-night stand. Most women he'd slept with since his wife died didn't even know his name.

Sleeping with his teammate's sister was definitely out of the question. No matter how tempting every curvy inch of her was. She was nothing more than forbidden.

Especially with a name like Megan. His head spun and his heart clenched as hard as his dick. Megan. The name whispered through his mind and tormented him. He couldn't be with a woman who shared the name of the wife he killed.

MEGAN SMILED at Mason and wondered about the ghosts in his eyes. She saw them as clearly as she saw the tension in his bulky muscles and the desire to run like hell out of there.

Once she shook his hand, she released it and released him. She went in search of someone else to talk to. Someone who was actually interested in a conversation. Preferably someone who wouldn't try to read her and see past the lies she was telling herself and everyone else.

Mason stared as she backed away, but once she made it to the women surrounding Lily and her round belly, Megan tore her gaze from Mason's. She thought she heard someone ask him if he was okay, but she ignored it and focused on the woman in the room who seemed happy to have a person growing inside her.

"We should have started months ago. I feel like I'm going to make the wrong decision because we need to just make a decision," Lily said.

"About what?" Megan asked.

"Moving. Archer and I live in an apartment. When he moved in with me, we made it work, but adding a baby is not going to be possible. We need something bigger, and we've been looking, but nothing feels right." Lily scowled.

"You should look near us," Ashleigh said. "There are a few houses available not far."

"Really?"

Ashleigh nodded. "Yeah. We really like the area we're in. It's a good school district, and we like our neighbors."

"I need to look there," Lily said. "Thanks. I never thought to look near where everyone lives. I've just been searching."

"Are you working with an agent?" Megan asked.

Lily shook her head. "Not yet. We talked about it, but Archer is funny about...well, everything."

"Aren't they all," Kyra said wryly. "I love them, but it's like they can't ever see the good in people."

"After everything they've seen, I don't blame them," Pilar said.

Megan wondered what the group had been through. She knew her brother had a bad experience when he was a SEAL, but she didn't know details. She assumed his life now was quieter, even though she was pretty sure he was still involved in things beyond her scope of understanding. Looking around at the women she'd met an hour or two earlier, she realized there was a lot more to all of them than she thought.

Lily was the clear leader of the women, not that she was in charge, but the others followed her lead. It was easy to see why. She was likable and put everyone else at ease. Ashleigh had a few years on them and was like their older sister, even though she never talked down to anyone. Her son was sleeping in Megan's makeshift bedroom at the moment. Pilar and Kelsea were both on the quiet side, but when they said something, the others listened. It was obvious they were well respected and liked. Kyra and Nikki were the newest ones to the group, if Megan had to guess. They were still figuring out where they fit in with the women because both appeared to be closer to the men.

Megan was particularly interested in Kyra since she was

about to become her sister-in-law. Megan herself struggled to fit in with groups of women most of the time, but the group around her was friendly and talkative, and nice. They didn't make comments she couldn't hear, and none of them said anything about her weight. Too many times she'd caught other women staring at her body with disgust or had them question her food choices. These women we just happy to get to know her.

"What do you plan to do while you're here, Megan?" Lily asked, bringing the conversation back to her.

"Oh, just visit, I guess. See the area. Spend time with Slade, although I still struggle to call him that," Megan admitted with a chuckle.

"I call him Justin sometimes," Kyra said. "He's been Slade for so long that I think he needs to remember who he is once in a while."

Megan laughed with the others.

"They all need that reminder," Ashleigh said. "Of course, some of them need to be reminded of their nicknames, not their real names."

A wail pierced the air and everyone turned to stare at the baby monitor sitting in the middle of the room. Megan's entire body tightened at the sound. She wanted to race to it and soothe the baby, but she also wanted to run.

"I got him," someone behind Megan said.

She looked at Ashleigh, who just smiled and reached to turn off the monitor.

"He's so good with Junior," Lily said.

"Archer will be a good dad, too," Ashleigh told her.

"They're all good men," Nikki said. "They've all treated Sly like he's their own."

"They adore him," Kyra said. "And he's such a good kid."

"Thank you."

They talked about kids and families for a few minutes, leaving Megan to wonder. The men passed Ashleigh's son around and entertained him while her husband got a bottle ready for him. Even Sly wanted to be involved in the baby's world and stood over Rocky's shoulder and made faces at him.

"Sly's been asking us if he can have a little brother or sister. He really wants a brother, but he's willing to take a sister, if that's all he can get," Nikki said with a laugh.

"Are you guys thinking about more kids?" Lily asked.

Nikki shrugged. "We've talked about it, but I don't know. We're still getting to know each other. It's only been a few months, and we both feel like we want some time together before we bring in a new baby. At the same time, if we're going to have a baby, maybe it's better if we have one soon so we don't get too comfortable and never want to rock the boat."

"We were the same," Ashleigh said. "Even though I knew who he was years ago, when we found out I was pregnant, we really didn't know each other. We took those nine months to do a crash course on each other. We still struggle at times, but I think that's normal for any relationship."

"We're definitely still getting to know each other," Kyra said. "I love him, but the moods get me. I don't know about the others because they hide them at work, or don't have them, but Slade gets these moods where he kind of shuts down. Has he always been like that?"

Megan nodded. "Yeah. He processes things internally. I'm the loud one most of the time. Jus—Slade tends to think things through and get inside his own head. I talk things out."

"That makes me feel a little better. Sometimes I feel like he's shutting me out," Kyra said with a sad smile.

Megan shook her head. "I think he's just processing. Let him know he can talk things through with you if he does need a sounding board, or that you'll be there if he just needs to think."

"Are you a psychologist?" Kelsea asked.

Megan shook her head. "No, although maybe I should be. I work in sales. I need to understand people to do my job, so I've learned over the years how to read people."

"That's impressive," Kelsea said. "I teach psych at the local college. If you're up for it, I'd love to have you come in and talk to one of my classes. I think it would be valuable for them to see how the things we learn in class can have an impact on real life. Especially my entry level kids."

Megan nodded. "That sounds like a lot of fun."

"I hate to do this, but I think we need to go," Daniel said, joining the group. "He's fussy."

"Another tooth?" Ashleigh asked, getting to her feet.

Daniel nodded. "That's my guess."

She moved closer to her husband and son. Junior whimpered and reached out to her. Daniel handed him over and the baby nuzzled against Ashleigh's neck and grabbed a fistful of her hair.

"Oh, my poor little man. Let's get you home and see if you can get some sleep." Ashleigh yawned.

"Maybe you can sleep if he does," Daniel said.

Ashleigh nodded. "I hope so. Nice to meet you, Megan. Sorry to head out so early."

"Nice to meet you, too. And totally understandable."

Ashleigh and Daniel said good night to the rest of the group. Megan headed to the kitchen to get a glass of water. She really wanted a glass of wine, but water would have to do. Maybe she could pretend.

"Hi," she said, startled by Mason in the kitchen.

"Sorry," he said, making a move to go around her.

"You work with my brother?"

Mason nodded, avoiding her gaze.

"Were you a SEAL with him?"

Mason shook his head. "I was a SEAL, but not with him. I'm older."

"How much older?"

"Too old for you," Mason said gruffly.

"That sounds like a challenge," Megan teased.

Mason finally looked up at her. The pain she thought she saw before was still there, but so was something else. Something deeper and darker. Something that made her pulse race for all the right reasons.

She didn't think she'd ever seen a look like that directed toward her. She'd seen plenty of men look at other women like that, but never her. Mason was the kind of man who could walk into a room, any room, and have women fall all over themselves for his attention. There was no way he was starved for a woman's company.

But the way he was looking at Megan, he was starved for *her* company.

"You're playing with fire."

"Maybe I like to play with fire," Megan said. She had no idea where this woman came from. She was never aggressive with men. She sat back and let them make the first move.

"You're going to get burned."

"Let me come home with you. Let me stay with you for a few days. My brother—"

"No," Mason barked.

"But—"

"No. You don't know me. You don't know anything about me. You don't know how bad an idea that is. No."

He brushed past her and walked out of the kitchen. Megan watched as he walked straight over to Justin and made an excuse, then headed for the door.

He didn't even look back, but something told Megan he was watching her, anyway. And that it wasn't the last she'd see of him.

4

MASON COULD BARELY PULL IN A BREATH. HE SHOULDN'T HAVE gone to that party. He should have just stayed away. Lesson learned.

He barely slept that night, or the rest of the weekend. He ignored calls and texts and tried to fight off the desire he felt for Slade's little sister.

He had to keep calling her that so he didn't do something stupid like take her up on her offer. It would only end badly if he did. Not only would Slade likely kill him, but Mason wasn't sure he could handle a woman like Megan. He wouldn't be able to control himself.

Monday morning came like all the other mornings, with a shot of fresh air and a pot of coffee. Mason punished himself with another extra long run, then a quick, cold shower intended to squash the desire that wouldn't stop racing through his veins. He thought, more than once, about taking himself in his hand to alleviate the need, but thinking about her was a slippery slope, one he didn't need to go on. Focus and determination were the only ways to get past the twisted desire he had for her.

The office was quiet when Mason got there. He let himself in and found English in his office, nose buried in the screen in front of him.

"You need to see this," English said without looking up.

Mason stepped into the office and around the desk. English was a neat person with tidy piles of papers in neat stacks on his desk. The bookshelf behind him had books all lined up. Nothing personal was in the office, but that was normal for all of them. Growing up as SEALs meant personal didn't belong at work. Separate the two in order to get the job done.

English pointed to the screen and Mason zeroed in on what he was trying to show him. "Is that...?"

English nodded. "Yep. A secret account that Wray Allen has. One his wife probably doesn't know about. One that says he is up to a lot more than just fighting fires. If I had to guess, he's deep in debt and looking for a way out."

"This account has twenty grand in it. Why do you think he's in debt?"

"Because these are his family's accounts." English pointed to another screen. "See this?"

Mason nodded.

"This transaction shows him moving money from his family to this account. And see this?" He pointed at the original screen and Mason nodded again. "This account isn't owned by Wray Allen. He's just authorized to make deposits. He hasn't ever pulled money out. The company that owns it has, but not Allen."

"So, this account is owned by a company, and they're requiring Allen to pay them?"

English nodded. "It could be anything, but yeah."

"What is this company?"

"I don't know yet. I just found this. I'm digging into the

company next. We need to know who's behind it so we can find Mr. Allen."

"What can I do?"

English looked up at Mason with a smile and lifted his mug. "You could get me a cup of coffee."

Mason chuckled. He was more than a decade older than English and thought of him as a kid. When he gave Mason looks like that one, with a sheepish smile, he looked even younger. He was still a tough man, but with his blond hair, light blue eyes, and constant smile, anyone who didn't know English would have mistaken him for a beach bum or a trust fund waste of space. He was deceptively smart, which made him a huge asset to the team.

Mason took the mug and filled it, adding a spoonful of sugar because he knew that was how English liked it. When the other man called down the hall to ask for that, Mason was already walking back into his office.

"Yeah, I know."

English looked up at him. "You pay attention to things, don't you?"

Mason shrugged. "We all do. Part of the job."

"Yeah, but it's different for you. You see things the rest of us ignore."

"Maybe it's because I'm old."

English smiled and shook his head. "I think it's because you've seen more pain than the rest of us."

"I've caused more pain," Mason said firmly.

English held his gaze for a long moment, then said, "It's easy to hold on to our own anger and pain. The challenge comes when we try to let go and accept that the world is not all bad."

"What pain are you holding on to?"

English offered a sad smile. "We all have pain."

Before Mason could ask him another question, English thanked him for the coffee and turned back to his computer. Mason left the office and headed to his own, hoping he could do something useful. It had been a week since Wray Allen went missing. That long and Mason knew the odds of finding him alive. He refused to give up, but he was also preparing for the look on his wife's face when she found out her husband wasn't coming home.

The rest of the team showed up slowly over the next hour or so. The office noise grew louder, like a low buzz. They all knew the same thing. It was do or die time for the firefighter.

Dunn called a meeting for everyone to share what they knew. English told them all the same thing he told Mason that morning about the account. Dex and Dunn decided to pay Mrs. Allen another visit to see if she knew about the account or anything about the company English found tied to it.

Shortly after they left, Slade walked into Mason's office and asked, "You busy?"

Mason shook his head. "What's up?"

"I need to get out of here. Clear my head. Want to join me?"

"Hell, yes."

MASON STARED down the barrel of the gun. His finger twitched at the idea of pulling the trigger. He wanted to. Ached to.

He took a deep breath to steady himself and squeezed. He didn't flinch as the bullet sped away from him and hit its mark. The explosion was beautiful. Pink splatter puffed up like smoke before falling to the ground with a splat.

"Nice shot," Slade said with a chuckle. "You showed that watermelon who's boss."

Mason grinned. He loved the feel of a gun in his hand. Of the power that came with the responsibility of being able to pull a trigger and see things destroyed.

He also knew how dangerous they were. Not just from his career as a SEAL, but from the way a gun stole his world once upon a time. A world he never deserved. A world he would forever miss.

Megan.

Mason flipped the safety on and set his gun on the mat in front of him. He knew it was smart to keep up his skills since he'd started working for F-BOMB, but he also knew he had to be careful how much time he spent on the end of a gun. It became an addiction. An escape. The way some people played sports or ran, Mason shot. So much that his gun had become a part of him. An extension. An instinct. An instinct that cost him his wife.

"You're done?" Slade asked.

Mason shrugged. "For now. I'm gonna head out."

"Yeah?"

Mason was ready to make his escape, but something told him the trip to the range was about more than keeping their skills sharp and clearing their heads. "Everything okay?"

"Yeah, of course. I was just hoping to get some advice. But it can wait."

"Advice about what?" Mason asked. He checked his gun to ensure it was empty and put it in his case as required by the range before leaving.

"I, um..." Slade took another shot, then set his gun down. "I want to make sure I'm a good husband."

Mason chuckled at the absurdity of the question. "And you're asking me?"

Slade shrugged. "I know you tried."

Mason drew a deep breath and blew it out slowly. He did try. He also failed. Miserably. Of all the people in their lives to ask about being a good husband, he was the last one Slade should be going to for advice, but for some reason he did.

"Don't worry about it. Forget I asked."

"For starters, know every day could be the last you have together. From the way you and Kyra met, I'm guessing you already know that, but what we do comes with no guarantees. Secondly, make sure she knows how much you love her so that if you don't make it back one day, she won't ever question if you really loved her."

"I tell her all the time."

"Telling her isn't enough. Show her in everything you do. Kiss her when you wake up, touch her whenever she's close, listen to her and talk to her. Do everything you can to make sure Kyra knows she's the most important person in the world to you. You chose each other, and you have to choose each other every single day for the rest of your lives. That's the only way this will work. The only way you can be a good husband."

Slade drew in a breath and nodded thoughtfully. He stared over Mason's shoulder beyond him to the wall.

"Sorry if that wasn't what you needed."

Slade shook his head. "It was exactly what I needed. That's why I asked you."

"I think you're the only one who would ever ask me how to be a good husband. I'm fairly sure the rest of the world looks at me as an example of what not to do."

"I know you loved your wife. What happened was an accident. If you could go back, you would."

Mason absorbed the pain of regret and nodded sharply. "I wish for that every day."

Slade stared at him for a second, then asked, "What do you think of my sister?"

"Excuse me?"

"My sister. I know you're good at reading people. Something feels off with her. She's never visited me before, and now she's here for a few weeks. I've been here for almost three years. Why is she here now?"

"Are you sure it isn't what she said and she wants to get to know Kyra?"

Slade sighed heavily and shrugged. "I don't know. Something isn't right. I saw you two talking in the kitchen the other night. What did she say to you?"

The sultry look on her face flashed through Mason's mind. The moment she realized he was looking at her as a man should look at a woman. The way she looked up at him from beneath her lashes. He envisioned that look with her lips around his cock too many times to count in the days since.

Mason bit down hard on the inside of his cheek to stop the swelling in his pants. The last thing he needed was for Slade to realize his sister was propositioning Mason. Or that Mason almost considered taking her up on it.

"She asked how I knew you. I asked if she was enjoying her visit. That was really it."

Slade ran a hand over his head and stared back at the target. "I was hoping she said something to you. Something that might help me understand what's going on with her."

"Sorry. She spent more time talking to the women than me. Did Kyra say anything?"

Slade shook his head. "No, but she's trying to be friends with Megan. She doesn't want to get in the middle."

"And you think I do?"

Slade's eyes narrowed for a second. "Why would you be in the middle? You don't know my sister."

"Yeah, true, I just meant spying for you. Or whatever."

Slade sighed. "Maybe I should just ask her. I have two women living in my house and I don't know how to talk to either of them most of the time."

Mason chuckled. "Maybe let them talk once in a while."

Slade grinned. "Good idea."

Slade thanked Mason, then went back to focusing on the target fifty feet away. He waved as Mason left, already deep in his own thoughts. Mason preferred it that way. To be mostly invisible.

He locked his gun in his trunk and left the range. Dinner, maybe a beer, and sleep were in his immediate future. After such little sleep all weekend, he was ready for some downtime.

The grocery store was busy. The last thing Mason wanted was to have to work his way around people, but he missed his chance to get there before the crowd. He found a few options for dinners and threw them in his basket, promising himself he'd make a shopping list and eat better one day.

Megan was always good about that. She was the one who made sure he was healthy. She shopped and took care of things at home. Mason had fallen far short of that since he lost her.

"Mason?" someone said from right behind him.

He was in line, almost to the front, but that voice made him want to hurdle the belt and get the hell out of there. He turned and came face to face with her. Face to face with the woman responsible for one of the worst moments of his life.

"Bernadette," he said coldly, trying to choke back the emotion welling up inside him.

God, how similar they looked. Sisters separated by only eleven months. Irish twins, their mom said when he first met the family. They grew up together as best friends, not just sisters. Always there for each other. Going through life together. Graduation, college, marriage, and eventually kids if things had worked out.

They hadn't.

"What... why are you here?" Her chest heaved with the question. She stared at him, her eyes wide, tears forming at the edges.

God, she looked so much like Megan. So similar that he wanted to pull her into his arms and pretend she was. Just for a minute.

"Do you live here?" Bernadette asked, her voice rising. She was starting to draw the attention of the other people nearby.

"Are you ready, sir?" the cashier asked.

Mason turned and looked at him, feeling like he wasn't really there. He put his things on the belt and followed them toward the guy who couldn't have been older than twenty. What Mason would give to go back to that age. To the age when he met Megan. When he fell for her on sight. Maybe he could warn her. Warn them. Change things.

"How long have you been out of jail?" Bernadette asked. Her voice shook with the question.

The guy bagging the groceries faltered, looking between them. Fear swept into his gaze. His knuckled turned white with the grip he had on Mason's frozen dinner.

Mason wanted to tell him she was crazy. Reassure him in some way. But there was nothing he could say.

"A few years," Mason finally answered Bernadette.

"Years? You've been out for years? Why the hell do you get to walk around free when my sister is in the ground? You killed her, Mason. You killed my sister. You don't deserve to be a free man."

Mason tossed cash at the guy and grabbed his bags. He started to walk away when a manager stepped in front of him.

"Is there a problem here?"

Mason looked at the twerp. He couldn't actually do anything to stop Mason, but he was the person of authority, and Mason respected authority. From day one, he knew his father was in charge, then his CO, his wife, and now his boss. Mason was smart enough to know when a situation spiked, it was best to just get the hell out.

"No, sir. I'm just paying for my groceries."

"He killed my sister," Bernadette growled. Or maybe howled. It was somewhere between the two with a crack in her voice that split open all the raw parts of Mason.

"Um..." The manager fumbled to come up with something coherent. He clearly didn't expect that answer.

"I've served my time," Mason said firmly, locking eyes with the manager so he knew Mason wasn't a threat.

"Sir, I have your change," the kid at the register said. He held it out to Mason, his hand shaking.

Mason took a deep breath and opened his hand for the change and the receipt. The kid dropped both into Mason's palm. He closed it long enough to dump the contents in his grocery bag, then turned back to the manager.

"I just want to leave," Mason told the manager.

He looked between Mason and Bernadette and finally

nodded and stepped to the side. Mason walked away as Bernadette shouted after him that he was a killer and he still needed to pay for what he did to her sister.

If only she knew he paid for it every time he closed his eyes and saw the life drain from hers.

5

Mason stared up at the ceiling of his crappy studio apartment. Every time he tried to tell himself he should move some place new, he remembered the look in Megan's eyes when she realized she was going to die. And that he was the one who took her life. He didn't deserve more than the shithole he lived in, and he never would.

If he ever thought about moving again, all he needed to do was remember seeing Bernadette and those thoughts would go away.

He didn't blame her for her anger. She had every right to feel it. He bounced between anger and shame most days. But the last couple of years working with F-BOMB started to give him a chance to feel useful again. Like he was making a difference in the world.

But Bernadette with her auburn hair and her dark brown eyes... she and Megan could have been twins. Bernadette was always thin to Megan's curvy, but otherwise, they shared a striking number of traits. Right down to the way they laughed. They would finish each other's sentences and could have conversations without ever speaking. Mason never wanted to come between them and welcomed Bernadette into their lives. He considered her a sister, until she showed up at Megan's funeral with the police and insisted they arrest Mason for Megan's death.

It didn't matter that Mason had been questioned and released, they listened to her. And when they asked Mason for specific details, he didn't fight the charges brought against him. He wanted to be punished for what happened to Megan. It didn't matter that it was an accident. He didn't deserve to live a free life if she couldn't also.

It took years of court mandated therapy before Mason could begin to accept it was an accident and that shit happens. But one conversation with Bernadette and all those years were gone. He would have gone to jail all over again if she called the cops right then. Because in that moment, all that guilt rushed right back to the surface.

The silence and the remorse pressed in on him. He stared at the bottle of bourbon on his coffee table. Glared at it. He wanted nothing more than to rip the seal and drain the brand new bottle, but he just glared at it. It had been years since Mason had a drink like that. A beer with the guys, a drink on the rocks once in a while, but drinking alone was out of the question. When he drank alone, the pain rushed in.

He swallowed roughly, feeling like he had stones in his throat instead of saliva. He leaned forward and grabbed the bottle. He slid it out of the paper bag they gave him at the store and stared at it. It seemed innocent enough. Something simple. A bottle of liquor was no big deal.

He tore the seal and twisted off the cap. He inhaled deeply. The pungent bite of the alcohol filled his nose and the room. He brought the bottle up, but before he could press it to his lips, there was a knock at the door.

He stared at it, half expecting the knock to be followed by a shout that it was the police. There to arrest him again. He waited. The door didn't swing open on its own. No shouts came from the other side.

Mason thought maybe whoever was there left, but another knock sounded. Louder this time. More insistent.

Mason jammed the cap back on the bottle and set it on the table. He stomped to the door as the person knocked a third time. He yanked it open as he shouted, "Jesus, what the hell?"

"Hello to you, too," Megan said with a smile. No. Slade's little sister. Megan was Mason's wife. He couldn't confuse the two of them. Not when his mind was already messed up.

"What are you doing here?"

She shrugged and brushed past him, letting herself into his tiny, crappy apartment. "I came to see you."

"This is not a good idea," Mason growled. He stayed at the door, holding it open so she could leave. She needed to leave. He couldn't have her there. If she stayed... No. Her staying wasn't an option.

She smiled at him. "What isn't a good idea?" She looked innocent. Like she really had no idea what kind of danger she was playing with. She probably didn't know anything about his past, but that didn't mean she should show up at a stranger's door and let herself in.

"How did you find out where I live?"

She shrugged. "I have my ways."

"You need to go."

"Why?" She walked around like she owned the place. Like she belonged there. She sat on the couch and raised an eyebrow at the bottle of bourbon on the table. "Not my favorite. Just water for me."

"I don't remember offering you a drink."

She stared at him, one brow raised, until Mason sighed and slammed the door. "One fucking drink." He stomped to the kitchen, a kitchen that was really cabinets and appliances in the corner of the open room, and yanked the cabinet door open. He snatched a cup from inside, then slammed the door. He filled the cup from the faucet and carried it over to her, setting it on the table. He stepped back and crossed his arms over his chest, waiting.

She looked up at him and smiled. That fucking smile. She was far too young for him, and when she smiled, she looked way too sweet and innocent. The three together were a dangerous combination.

"Thank you."

He grunted in response and couldn't stop himself from staring as she lifted the cup to her lips. She licked them before opening her mouth. Her tongue darted out and caught the underside of the cup, and his cock hardened. He was jealous of a fucking cup. And losing his damn mind.

He stared at her while she drank the water, slowly. Her throat bobbed with each swallow. Her eyes lifted to his over the upper rim. His cock pressed hard against his zipper. He wanted to knock the cup away and put something else in her mouth.

Fucking hell.

"Aren't you going to sit?" she asked, patting the seat next to her.

"No. Because you're about to leave."

"Actually, no, I'm not. I'm staying here tonight."

"Like hell you are."

"Are you married?"

"No."

"Engaged? Involved?"

"No."

"Gay?"

"No."

"So it's just me." She nodded and drew a breath. She stood and smoothed a hand over her shirt. "I guess I misunderstood things the other night."

She moved toward the door, but he couldn't let her walk away like that. He knew he should. That if she was hurt, she wouldn't come back. But he couldn't let her think he didn't want her because she wasn't enough for him.

"There isn't a damn thing wrong with you," Mason growled. Her back was to him, her hand on the knob. She didn't turn, but he could tell she was absorbing his words. "You're... shit, you're fucking gorgeous. You don't have any idea what you do to me. But I'm wrong for you. You and me can't happen."

"Why not?" She turned to face him, her arms crossed under her plump breasts. They lifted, begging Mason to bury his face between them.

"Fucking hell, Megan. I'm a hundred years older than you are, for one. For two, your brother will kill me. And for three—"

"My brother knows I'm here. He doesn't care."

Mason stared at her for a long minute. "There's no way he knows."

She shrugged. "He does, but even if he didn't, I'm an adult. I'm thirty years old. I'm not a child."

"You're still too young for me."

"Just tell me I'm not pretty and I'll go. I don't need you to placate me with lies because you don't find me attractive."

Mason stormed across the room and pressed himself against her. Her back hit the door. He ground himself against her core, making sure she felt just how much he wanted her.

"I'm not lying. You're making me so crazy I don't think I can keep my hands off you for much longer. But this is a bad idea."

She looked up at him, her eyes wide and her mouth a perfect circle of shock. She sucked in a ragged breath, lifting her breasts and rubbing them against his chest. She dropped her purse to the floor and leaped at him, wrapping her arms around his neck the same moment she pulled him down to her.

Mason tried to resist, but she caught him off guard, and the moment their lips touched, he knew he was fucked. In every way possible.

He just wasn't sure if that was a good thing or a bad thing.

MEGAN KNEW the moment she saw him that he was dangerous. That he was the kind of man who could rip someone to shreds if he decided it was warranted. She knew he was wrong for her on every level. But she needed wrong. She needed a man who wasn't going to make her fall in love. A man who wasn't going to fill her head with empty promises and whispered niceties. She needed sex. Good, hard, dirty sex that would remind her she was a woman.

Mason's hands tightened on her sides, pinching, stilling her. She was sure he was going to set her to the side and walk away, but then his hands slid around her back and he pressed himself to her again and she nearly cried with relief.

Showing up there was a risk. One she wasn't sure was a good idea or a bad one. Justin would kill her if he knew where she was, but Megan didn't answer to her brother. He would never know Megan slept with his friend.

Mason thrust his tongue into her mouth and pushed away all thoughts of everything except the two of them. He leaned his weight on her, letting her feel the hard line of his erection beneath his jeans. Megan wanted that. She wanted him. She wanted to be more than a human incubator.

Mason took a step back and stared at her. Megan wanted to leap at him again, but the look in his eyes was no longer angry. There was something else there. Something she didn't understand. Something that looked like regret or pain or...

"You're beautiful," he whispered, his voice reverent and rough, like he couldn't stop himself from saying the words, but he didn't want to.

"Take off your shirt," Megan said in response. She'd been dying to see him without a shirt on since he walked into the room at Justin's. She could tell he was strong, but she wanted to see his muscles.

The man did not disappoint. He did as she asked and yanked his shirt over his head. He tossed it to the side and stood still in front of her, letting her look at him.

Megan took a tentative step forward and looked up at him, silently asking permission.

"If you're spending the night, you're going to need to touch me, eventually. Unless that was a friendly kiss." His voice was a blend of frustrated and patient, and the jagged edge of it danced over Megan's nerves like a delicate touch. She trembled and reached out to him, putting her hand on his chest. He sucked in a breath.

Megan looked up at him and met his gaze. He stared down at her from a good six inches. He didn't pull back or close his eyes, he just watched, which gave Megan the courage to keep going.

She put her other hands on him and slid them around

his exposed upper body. She traced the muscles with her fingers, then with her tongue, loving that Mason wasn't trying to guide her. He was simply letting her explore him. Letting her take what she wanted from him.

"Take off your shirt," Mason said. He growled as Megan nipped at one of his nipples.

She lifted the hem of her shirt and pulled back. "Can we turn off the lights?"

"No," Mason growled, reaching for her.

Megan hesitated, considering pulling her shirt back down and just leaving. She didn't want to, but she also didn't want the beautiful specimen of a man to see all her flabby parts. She had far too many of them, and while she wasn't showing yet, she didn't want him to think she could be pregnant. She'd been accused of it plenty over the years. The curse of being overweight with a big belly.

"I want to see you. I need to see you."

Megan was sure he'd take one look at her and tell her to cover up. She had to know. She had to know if he was pretending when he said he wanted her or if he meant it. The blow would be enough to send her back home, enough to make the decision for her about staying or leaving, but she couldn't stay and not know.

She lifted her shirt again, slowly, waiting for him to tell her to stop. She watched his face. He sucked in a breath when her stomach was exposed. He blew it out in a growl when her black lace bra came into view. And when she pulled her shirt over her head and moved to drop it to the ground, he cupped her breasts and buried his head in them.

"Oh, fuck," he whispered against her skin. "So soft." He licked the skin between her breasts and kissed his way to one nipple. He sucked hard, drawing the tight bud into his mouth through the fabric. Her breasts had been sensitive for weeks, and the rough treatment made her cry out.

"Oh, God."

He growled in response and moved to the other one. She couldn't stop herself from latching onto his head and holding him there. Her nipples had never been so sensitive. She couldn't let him stop.

His hands went around her back, and the pressure of her bra released. He tugged it from her arms and leaned back just enough to remove the barrier between them. His mouth went right back to work, sucking on her nipple again, and she threw her head back in ecstasy.

"Oh, yes," she moaned.

"Love this," he groaned. "More."

She couldn't stop if she tried. It had been months since she'd touched a man, and she was losing all hope that her body would feel normal again. If this was what sex was like when she was pregnant, she might get pregnant over and over again so she could feel this good. And they hadn't even made it to the good stuff.

Mason squeezed her breasts together and sucked both nipples into his mouth. Megan cried out, her body tightening with a mini-orgasm teaser. She whimpered, needing more. And Mason clearly got the message.

He pulled back and stood upright before guiding her to the bed in the corner of the room. The entire place screamed bachelor pad, but Megan didn't care how the man lived. She only cared how he fucked. And she was about to find out.

"Take off your pants," Mason growled. He reached for his button and zipper and shoved his pants down roughly. His cock sprang up, long and thick. It was surrounded by tight curls and tighter muscles.

Megan's mouth watered at the sight of him. She always enjoyed giving blow jobs, and seeing Mason's cock made him irresistible. She dropped to her knees in front of him and licked the tip. He groaned.

"Fucking hell." He stared down at her as she parted her lips and sucked him inside. He thrust into her mouth, hitting the back of her throat before he was all the way inside. She tried to relax her muscles and take more of him in, but he was too big. It didn't seem to matter to him, though.

Megan cupped his balls and worked her head back and forth. Mason threaded his hands into her hair and guided her to the rhythm he wanted. He grunted and swelled, then yanked her back.

Every muscle in his body tightened, and he groaned. "Fuck."

"What happened?"

"Take off your clothes. Now."

Megan had never seen a man like Mason. A man who was so close to the edge that he could barely breathe. He moved to the nightstand next to his bed and yanked the drawer open. He tore a condom open and rolled it on, flinching as he did it.

"I need you naked," he growled over his shoulder when he saw she hadn't moved yet.

Megan jumped into action and stripped off her clothes. Her thighs were wet where they came together, her entire body ready for Mason. Sucking on him was the best fore-play she'd ever had.

Mason moved toward her, stalking her around the edge of his bed. She didn't run from him or play games. She wanted him as much as he clearly wanted her. He didn't slow down as he approached and slammed into her body all at once, his arms locking around her back the same moment his lips claimed hers in a kiss that sent her mind spiraling and her body into overdrive.

They panted as they came apart, and Mason spun her away from him. He kissed his way down her spine and licked his way back up. He pressed gently between her shoulder blades until she bent over the edge of the bed. His thighs rubbed the backs of hers and his cock lined up perfectly with her entrance. He pressed her lower back to tip her hips up, then groaned with her as he eased inside.

"Fuck yes," he said, stilling once he filled her.

"No kidding," Megan replied.

He slid out, then slammed into her, the force of his stroke pressing her face into the mattress. She moaned in response.

"Need you," he grunted. "So good."

He held onto her hips and pumped into her. Megan pressed back against him, meeting every stroke with her own. She'd never been with a man like him. A man who made her feel like she was beautiful. Most of the men she was with made her feel like she was good enough, but Mason... Mason made it seem like the whole thing was his idea. Like he couldn't get enough of her.

He grunted as he got closer. It didn't take him long. Megan squeezed her channel around him, and he sped up, fucking her harder, faster. He slammed into her, stilling deep inside and swelling. She gripped him again and felt his cock release into her.

"Fuck," he grunted, the word ripped from him. A shout in her ear that nearly sent her over the edge. And the only disappointment in the whole thing. She didn't get to come.

He laid on her back, struggling to catch his breath, while

Megan wondered how she could have some privacy for her own orgasm. She wasn't going to touch herself right then and there, even though she knew it wouldn't take long. And going back to her brother's house to do it was all kinds of weird. But she needed to come. She was tender and ready, and she'd be crabby if she didn't alleviate the building pressure.

Mason shifted slightly and kissed her back. He lifted himself off her back, but he didn't move away. He stroked a few times inside her, then said, "I should have taken care of you first."

"It's fine," Megan lied.

"It's never fine," Mason growled. His hands slid around her body, one going to her sensitive breasts and the other between her thighs. "Can I touch you while I'm still inside you?"

Megan's answer was a moan.

He brushed a thumb over her nipple and cradled her clit between two fingers, and Megan cried out again.

"Squeeze my cock, beautiful. Let me have it," he whispered. "Don't hold back."

Megan was surprised to learn she was a fan of dirty talk. She tilted her head to the side so his lips were against the shell of her ear. "Talk to me."

"You want to hear how good you feel? How I want to fuck you again? How I could fuck you again right now. Especially if you keep squeezing my dick like you are. You're so fucking wet for me. And these nipples... I can't get enough of them. The sweet taste of them. Are you going to let me suck on all of you?"

"Yes," Megan moaned.

"It's a good fucking thing we have all night."

"Yes," Megan screamed, her orgasm finally breaking

free. He didn't let up as she came hard, her entire body shaking with the intensity.

"Fucking hell. That was amazing." He finally pulled out and flipped her onto her back. Mason spread her thighs wide and moved to enter her again, then froze.

Megan looked at him, wondering what was wrong. Something was definitely wrong.

"Please tell me you weren't a virgin," Mason said quietly.

"What? No. Why would you ask me that?"

"Because you're bleeding. Please, God—"

Megan shook her head and moved to get up. "I'm not a virgin. But I am pregnant."

6

———

MASON KEPT ONE EYE ON MEGAN THE ENTIRE TIME HE DROVE to the hospital. She insisted they didn't need to go, but he wasn't taking any chances. He'd already fucked up enough. He wasn't going to brush this off and have her lose her child, too.

"It's not your fault," Megan said quietly.

Mason grunted. Everything was his fault.

He stopped in front of the emergency room door and slammed the Jeep into park. He went around and met Megan as she was climbing out. He helped her get inside, leaving his vehicle in the driveway and not caring if they towed it away. All that mattered was getting her help.

"She's pregnant and bleeding," Mason barked at the woman behind the desk.

That got her moving. She jumped up and signaled for someone. A man hurried over with a wheelchair. Megan sat in it and they disappeared.

"Do you need to move your vehicle?" the woman asked.

"Yeah, but—"

"She'll be fine. They'll take care of her. I'm assuming you're the father?"

It was a question, not a statement. Did he have a right to be there? Was he going to be allowed back to see her? Did he matter?

He knew the correct answer was no, but he opened his mouth and said, "Yes," anyway.

"Okay, Daddy, go move your vehicle and come right back in. Mom has insurance cards?"

Mason nodded absently and turned toward the door. He got her there. He was getting her help. She survived long enough for that. He hoped her baby would, too.

MEGAN SMILED at the technician as she squirted gel on her belly and grabbed the wand. Her doctor said an ultrasound too early wouldn't show anything, so she hadn't had one yet.

"How far along are you?"

"Not far," Megan said. "Only about nine weeks."

"Okay. We should be able to hear a heartbeat, but sometimes they aren't in a good position. Have you had an ultrasound yet?"

Megan shook her head and stared at the screen. She couldn't make out anything other than black and white splotches that didn't amount to anything for her.

"It can be a little scary because you don't really see anything, but it's okay. Is this your first?"

Megan nodded. "Yeah. I..." She sucked in a ragged breath. Being pregnant was not something she asked for. It wasn't a plan. Until that moment, laying on the bed in the ER and praying the technician found a heartbeat, Megan wasn't even sure she wanted the baby. Now, she couldn't imagine her life without the tiny person growing inside her.

The technician hit a few buttons, then a whooshing sound filled the small space. "There's the heartbeat."

"Oh, my God," Megan breathed. Tears ran down her cheeks and relief flooded her.

"I recognize that sound," the nurse said, coming back into the room.

"Yep. Everything looks good to me. I'll take a few pictures and double check everything, but I think you're going to be okay," the technician said.

"Thank you," Megan cried. She wanted to reach over and hug the other woman, but she was still examining her.

The nurse walked around the hospital bed and grabbed her hand. "You're going to be fine."

"Thank you. I never thought... I guess I should have."

"It happens. We get carried away and forget. Most of the time it should be fine, but there are things your doctor can do if this continues."

Megan took a deep breath, her first since Mason froze. "I don't think it'll come to that, but it's good to know." Mason wasn't likely to go anywhere near her ever again.

"I think we're all set," the technician said. "This all looks great to me. I don't see anything that's concerning. Do you have any questions for me?"

Megan shook her head. "I don't think so. Thank you."

"Of course. Let me know if there's anything else you need."

A knock on the door turned all their attention to the woman who was at the front desk when Megan arrived. "Daddy is out there pacing. I told him I'd come see how things are going. Can I give him an update?"

"I didn't know he was here," the technician said. "He's welcome to come back. I can update him."

Megan opened her mouth to say something, but her voice stuck in her throat. He waited. And he was nervous. A tear ran down her cheek. The nurse turned to her and offered her an understanding smile.

"It's a relief, isn't it?"

Megan nodded even though she knew the nurse thought she was crying over the baby instead of Mason. She half thought she was going to need to order a ride.

"She's right here," the woman from the desk said.

"Megan. Are you okay? Oh, God, I'm so sorry," Mason said as he raced to her side. He cupped her cheeks and leaned down so his face was right over hers, his forehead against hers.

"Mason?" the nurse said with venom in her voice.

He froze again, like when he saw the blood. He closed his eyes and pulled back from Megan to look up at the nurse.

"You're the father? This is your baby? How...?"

"Hello, Bernadette."

"I... Don't come back here. Ever."

The nurse stormed out of the room, pushing past the technician and the woman from the desk. They looked between Bernadette and Mason, then to Megan sadly.

"What was that all about?" Megan asked.

"Nothing. Are you okay? Is everything...?"

"Fine," Megan said, forcing a smile for him. She wanted to press for more information, but she had no right. He wasn't the father like the others assumed. He was a one-night stand. A man who would be gone now that he knew she was pregnant. Just like the father of her baby.

"I, um..." the technician stammered.

"Yeah, we're going," Mason said gruffly. "Do you have all your stuff?"

Megan nodded and let Mason help her off the bed. He wrapped an arm around her, protecting her from the staff that was so kind and friendly only moments ago. He led her to the door and walked her outside, his arm around her the entire way. He opened her door and closed it behind her when she buckled her seatbelt.

He jogged around the front of his SUV and got in next to her. He started up the vehicle and pulled out of the lot without a word.

"What was all that about?" Megan finally asked.

"Nothing," Mason answered. His voice said not to ask again.

Megan stared out the window, wondering where Mason would stop. Most likely, he'd drop her off at her brother's house. She was surprised when he pulled over into a shopping center.

"Are you hungry?" he asked.

Megan nodded slowly, not looking at him.

"There are a bunch of options here. Anything look good?"

Megan looked out and spotted the pizza place. "Pizza sounds good."

"What do you like on it?"

"Anything. I'm easy."

"Are you sure?"

Megan nodded.

"Do you want to go in with me?"

Megan finally looked at him. He was trying. He was just as out of his depths as she was, but he was trying. She nodded, and instead of looking frustrated, he looked relieved.

He waited for her at the front of his SUV and reached for her hand as they walked to the door. Megan wasn't sure what to make of that, but she didn't pull away.

The smell of cheese and baked bread made her stomach growl. She wasn't that hungry until she walked in, then she wanted one of each. Each what didn't matter, just one of each.

They waited in the short line until it was their turn. Mason ordered extra cheese, sausage, and sweet peppers on their pizza. He added garlic knots, a cookie pizza, and a two-liter of pop.

"Is that okay?" he asked her.

Megan nodded, her mouth salivating at the sound of all of it.

Mason paid, and they stepped to the side to wait for their food to finish cooking. Others walked in and picked up their meals, every order passing over the counter making Megan more hungry.

"Well, hell. I never thought I'd see you again," a man said, walking over to them.

Mason stiffened and took a slight step away from Megan. "Same."

The man grinned and reached for Mason's hand. "Good to see you again. What have you been up to?"

"Working. You?"

"Same," the man said, matching Mason's tone. "Who's this?"

Mason didn't even glance at her. "No one you need to know."

The other man raised an eyebrow but didn't press. His gaze slid down Megan's frame and back up before he met her eyes with a smirk. "Be careful with this one," he said to Megan.

Megan forced a smile at the man. He definitely gave her a bad vibe. She couldn't put her finger on it, but there was something dangerous about him. Something that screamed in her head to steer clear.

"Mason!" the man behind the counter called out.

Mason stepped forward and grabbed the boxes, then wrapped an arm around Megan and pushed her toward the door.

"Nice to see you again, Mason," the other man said with a chuckle.

Mason ignored him and ushered Megan into his SUV. He opened her door and stared back at the pizza place while she got in, then he set the pizza in behind her seat and hurried around to the driver's side. With his gaze still on the storefront, they took off.

"What was that?"

"Nothing," Mason growled. It seemed to be his word of the night.

Megan sat quietly and debated what she should do. Mason was kind to her when no one was around. He was amazing in bed. He was exactly what she was looking for. She didn't want a relationship, and even though it comforted her when he held her hand and acted like he cared, that wasn't what she was after. It was nice to not be alone, but she wasn't looking for a father for her baby. She was looking for a night of good sex. And she got it.

Mason himself said she wasn't important. He ushered her around like she was incapable of taking care of herself. But she was very capable. She was going to prove that. To herself and everyone else.

Mason drove home in silence. He couldn't remember the last time he felt the way he did. Probably when his Megan was still alive. He screwed up plenty with her, but with her, he always knew how to fix it. With Slade's sister, he was lost.

She followed him up to his apartment and inside. But after that, she looked a little lost. Exactly how he felt.

"I should just go," Megan said after a minute.

"Why?"

She looked carefully at him. "I'm not here for some grand romantic gesture. I had no intention of telling you or anyone else that I'm pregnant. I don't want anything more from you than what we did earlier. I should go."

"No, wait," Mason barked. He did that a lot with her. Snapping orders and taking his frustration out on her.

"I'm not a dog. I'm not someone you can yell at and expect me to listen to you. I ambushed you and threw myself at you. You didn't ask for this, and I don't want you to feel like you have to take care of me because you know my deep, dark secret."

"Slade doesn't know?"

She hesitated, then shook her head.

"Why not?"

She sighed heavily and laughed. "Because he's my big brother. Because he'd lose his shit. Because I don't want to tell him."

"Why did you tell me?"

That earned him a glare and a duh look.

"You wouldn't have told me if you hadn't started bleeding."

"I would have been long gone by now if that hadn't happened."

"You said you were staying the night."

She snorted. "I haven't stayed the night with a man... in a long time. I don't intend to do so with you."

"What's so wrong with me?" Mason asked, puffing out his chest.

She rolled her eyes. "For one, I had to chase you down. Two, you told multiple people tonight that I'm not important. And three, I'm sorry, but I only wanted sex. I'm not looking for more than that."

Mason had to admit it was a little bit of a blow to hear she wasn't really interested in him. No, he didn't want to want her, but he did. She made it sound like he was convenient more than anything else. And the rest...

"The people we talked to tonight are not important, and they don't need to know anything about you or how we know each other. I... I have a past. One you clearly don't know about. I don't want you to get hurt because of me."

"I can take care of myself."

"I never said you couldn't, but your brother will kill me—"

"I do not answer to my brother."

"Maybe not, but I do. He's one of my teammates, and technically, one of my bosses. I am not looking to cross any lines."

Megan glanced toward the bed and raised a brow. "I think it might be too late for that."

"He's never going to know about that," Mason growled.

"Agreed," Megan said. "Because this is never going to happen again."

"Then how about we start over as friends? Eat this pizza and watch a movie or something."

"Seriously?"

Mason shrugged. "Sure, why not. I get the feeling you could use someone to talk to. And I—"

"And you are trying not to drink alone."

Mason smiled at her intuition. "Something like that."

Megan drew a deep breath and shrugged. "Okay, fine. Friends."

"Friends," Mason said, wondering how in the hell he was going to pull this one off. He knew trying to be friends with her was going to blow up in his face. He already couldn't wait to be inside her again, but he couldn't. He couldn't risk hurting her or her baby. So they'd be friends. Or something.

Megan flipped open the pizza box while Mason found them some cups and filled them. He turned on the TV and searched for a movie they could both enjoy, finally settling on an action movie.

Everything was going well until they finished eating and leaned back on the couch. It was a small couch, something Mason found on the curb one night. Free was his price range, and since he never had people over, he didn't worry about the fact that it was closer to a loveseat than an actual couch. But he and Megan were big people, and when they leaned back, their entire sides touched.

"Sorry," Megan said, moving closer to the edge.

Mason followed suit, but the couch was too small for either of them to really go anywhere. Mason drew in a breath and her scent filled him. He hardened.

"You need a bigger couch," Megan said with a laugh.

"Just relax," Mason growled. "Stop moving."

"What the hell is wrong with you now?"

Mason grimaced and stilled his breathing. "Nothing."

"Something's wrong. You look all pissed off again. We were enjoying pizza. What happened?"

Mason turned and looked at her. Her eyes were

narrowed and angry. When she saw the look on his face, they softened, then widened with realization.

"Are you...?"

"I'm trying to be friends."

She glanced down and sucked in a breath when her gaze landed on his erection, pressing against his zipper.

"Just ignore it. It'll go away."

"I know how to make it go away," she said.

Mason swore and pushed off the couch. He stomped across the room and stopped in front of the kitchen counter. He grabbed the edge so he didn't turn around and reach for her.

"Maybe we should amend our earlier agreement," she said, her voice far away. "Pregnant women supposedly get really horny. I... the father isn't in the picture. He hasn't been. We weren't really together. I'm only here for a few weeks. Maybe we could be friends who occasionally have sex. Or something."

"I... I can't. You're Slade's little sister. You're not someone I should have ever laid a hand on. And—"

"I'm not a virgin. I'm not a child. I'm not fragile. I'm a woman. And I came here tonight because my brother trusts you. If you're worried about me getting attached, that won't happen. I have a child to think about, and I'm not bringing anyone into their life. I'm going to raise this baby on my own."

Mason turned and looked at her. He admired her determination and her spirit. She was strong and confident, and she knew what she wanted. He was so worried about tainting who she was because of their age difference and the differences in their lives, but she was right. She wasn't fragile. She was tough, and she could probably kick his ass if she wanted to.

"Sit down and finish the movie. Then I'll go," Megan said.

She leaned back against the couch and focused on the TV. She wasn't playing with him. She wasn't trying to convince him. She was being herself. A woman who knew what she wanted but wasn't afraid to walk away.

"Okay," he said, answering the question she posed earlier, not agreeing to what she just said.

She still didn't look at him. Just stared at the TV.

"I said okay," Mason repeated.

"Yeah, I heard you. But you're not sitting down."

"Because I wasn't agreeing to that."

Her gaze snapped to his. A slow, sexy smile curled her lips.

"You're staying here tonight," Mason said.

Megan grinned wider. "Good. Because I wasn't going back to my brother's house, anyway."

Mason laughed and finally sat back down. The movie played, but it was long forgotten.

7

The last thing I needed was a mess on my hands. I'd worked too long and too hard to have anyone fuck it up. Mason fucking O'Connor. He was a thorn in my side. I knew eventually there would be an issue, but the last thing I expected was for it to come from him.

There was always something about him that I didn't trust. I could never put my finger on it, not until the truth about him came out. He wasn't the man he appeared to be. People rarely were.

I had learned a few things since we last saw each other. A few things about the way people work and about how to get things done. It didn't take long to find out everything about him. Where he worked, what he did for a living, and where he lived.

"Fuck," I shouted into the silent room.

"Everything okay?" Eli asked.

I glared at him, trusting that the look on my face was enough for him to understand that no, everything was not fucking okay.

"What's going on?"

"We need to cut him loose."

"What? Why?"

"Because people are looking for him. Because people are asking questions. Because I fucking said so."

Eli was clearly surprised by the request. It wasn't one I made often. Usually, the people we picked up didn't get off as easily, but if Mason was looking into his disappearance, the firefighter needed to go.

"What do you want me to do with him?"

"Drop him off on his doorstep."

"Alive?"

"Yes, alive. The hell that will rain down on us will be much worse if he's dead. And don't let him back in the fucking door. Ever."

"Got it."

Eli turned and walked away. He was going to do what I said because he was a smart man. Not smart enough to not be greedy, but smart enough to know if he defied me, no one would find his body.

I knew people were asking questions, but I didn't know Mason was one of them. If I'd known... nope. That didn't matter. I knew Mason. I knew how he operated. And I knew he'd do anything with the right motivation. And *she* was definitely the right motivation.

MASON MADE it into work before everyone else. He left Megan sleeping in his bed, again. The first morning they woke up together, naked and reaching for each other, Megan declared she was going to stay with him for the rest of her trip. Mason didn't like the idea, but she had ways of convincing him to do whatever she wanted.

After three nights together, Mason accepted she was right and that staying with him was a great idea. She bounced back and forth between being so exhausted she slept all day and so horny she kept him up all night. Not that he was complaining.

He was still surprised Slade hadn't said anything to him. Megan said Slade knew where she was staying, but Slade hadn't mentioned anything at all. Was he waiting for Mason to say something? It didn't matter. He wasn't bringing that up. If Slade was okay with it, Mason wasn't going to poke the bear.

Mason made coffee and carried a cup to his desk to check his emails and see if there was anything going on that day. They were still looking for the missing firefighter. It had been ten days since he disappeared, and there was still nothing on him besides the secret bank account.

One by one, the rest of the team filtered into the building. They all did the same thing as Mason and kept to themselves to start the day. They were working on multiple cases that week, which meant things were busy. Busier than usual, but word was getting out that F-BOMB were the ones to call if someone needed help.

"Meeting. Now!" Dunn shouted down the hallway.

Mason jumped up and hurried to the conference room with the others. Dunn never called a meeting immediately unless something big happened.

"Our firefighter is back," Dunn said with zero preamble. "We need him questioned."

"He's back? Just like that?" English asked.

Dunn nodded. "His wife told the police that he returned. Captain Patrick sent someone over there. The guy's in rough shape. He claimed he was in an accident and that he hit his head and didn't know where he was for a few days. Now, he's back and recovering."

"Do we believe him?" Dex asked.

"Not even a little," Dunn said. "I want you two to go see him. Get a read on him. Find out what the hell happened."

"Why?" Mason asked.

All eyes swung to him.

"Sorry, but just wondering why. If this guy doesn't want to tell us what happened, why are we wasting manpower on it?"

"Because something happened. And just because he's back doesn't mean everything is fine. If he was taken once, he could be taken again. And if he's involved in something, we need to find out what before someone else disappears for good. We still don't know what the deal with that bank account was since the wife wasn't home. We need answers," Dunn said.

Mason nodded, but he still didn't like it. The whole situation pissed him off. They were busting their asses to keep up with everything they had going on, and this guy vanishes on his wife and kids for more than a week, then returns and won't talk. Why bother with him?

But Mason was a good soldier so he followed orders and went with Dex to Wray Allen's house.

"Let me do the talking," Dex warned him as they pulled up in front of the house.

Mason nodded. He looked around as he got out of the SUV. The grass was flattened near the road, and if he wasn't mistaken, there was blood on the sidewalk. "Look at this."

Dex followed him, and they traded a look. "He was dropped off."

"That's what it looks like. Literally," Mason agreed.

"Still think we don't need to know what happened?"

"I just don't know why we're wasting our efforts on a closed case."

"Because it isn't closed. Attempted murder just means they didn't finish the job, it doesn't mean they shouldn't be punished. Releasing the guy you kidnapped doesn't mean you shouldn't pay for taking him in the first place."

Mason drew in a breath and nodded. He knew Dex was right, but there was a big part of him that knew the trip was going to be a wasted one.

They knocked on the door and waited. Voices inside told them someone was home.

"Hello," Mrs. Allen said as she opened the door. "I'm sorry, but my husband is home. I thought the police would let you guys know."

She held a squirming baby in her arms. Drool rolled down his chin onto the bib he wore that declared he was *Awesome Like Daddy*. Mason stared at the baby and wondered if he'd ever meet Megan's child. The thought of not meeting him or her bothered him more than it should have.

"...some questions," Dex was saying. He nudged Mason, and Mason nodded in agreement, although he had no idea what he was agreeing to.

"He's sleeping," Mrs. Allen said. "He's very tired."

"Mrs. Allen, we're trying to help. I understand you want your life to return to normal, but we want to make sure it can stay that way," Dex said firmly.

Mrs. Allen took a breath and nodded. She stepped back and let them into the house. She headed down the hallway to the kitchen like last time. There was another child at the table with a hunched over Wray Allen.

"Who was at the door?" he asked, his voice rough with sleep or frustration, or maybe something else.

"These men want to talk to you," she said softly.

Wray Allen jumped and spun on them. "Who are you?"

"We work for an organization called F-BOMB, Mr. Allen. We were brought in to help find you, and we have a few questions," Dex said.

"I already spoke to the police."

"And now you need to speak to us," Mason said.

Wray glared at them. Neither Dex nor Mason were willing to back down. Especially not after seeing the firefighter. The bruises on his face were consistent with punches, not an air bag. An air bag might have broken his nose and left him with bruising around his eyes, but he had neither. His injuries were focused on his cheeks. One had a large bruise that was already purple. The other cheek had red marks to indicate it was a newer injury. The way he held his left arm made it look like his collarbone might also be broken. And possibly a rib or two.

He was not a man who'd walked away from a car accident. He was a man who'd been used as a punching bag.

"Fine," Wray finally said. "What do you want to know?"

"What injuries do you have?" Dex asked.

Wray shook his head and winced. "I hit my head in the car accident. I don't really remember much."

"What hurts?" Mason asked.

"Everything," Wray said with a chuckle.

"Have you been to a doctor?"

"No." His tone said he didn't intend to either.

"How do you know?" Dex asked.

"Excuse me?"

Dex shrugged and moved closer. "If you don't remember anything, how do you know you didn't see a doctor?"

"I don't remember going to one. Weren't you supposed to help me? Why are you acting like I did this to myself?"

Dex looked at the child sitting in front of them and back to Mrs. Allen with the other kid on her hip. A glance at Mason said he wanted to push harder. Mason nodded. "Maybe we should speak in private, Mr. Allen."

"Why? I have nothing to hide."

"Really? What about your secret bank account?" Dex growled.

Wray Allen's eyes went wide. He cast a glance toward his wife. She tilted her head to the side. "Wray?"

"It's fine, honey. You get the kids ready. I'll go with you to drop them off. I'll see these men out."

Wray stopped in front of Dex and Mason and lifted his brows, waiting for them to turn and head back to the door. The three of them stared at each other for a long moment before Dex finally folded and walked. Mason followed behind him with Wray on his heels.

On the front lawn, Wray hissed, "Who the hell are you?"

"We told you who we are, Mr. Allen. Our organization finds people. Especially people who don't want to be found or who aren't meant to be found. What can you tell us about the bank account?"

"It's not mine," he huffed.

"Funny because it has your name on it."

"And I have no idea what you're talking about." He crossed his arms and leaned back on his heels. He was lying, but proving what someone knew was not an easy task.

"Who whooped your ass?" Dex asked, his tone matching Wray's aggravated one. He was goading the other man, questioning his ability to defend himself.

"I was in a car accident," Wray growled.

"Nice story. Bullshit, but whatever." Dex stepped closer to Wray.

"I could whoop your ass right now," Wray said.

Dex grinned. "You'd be on the ground crying if you tried. Between your broken collarbone, cracked ribs, and the bruises on your face, you wouldn't last thirty damn seconds."

Wray scowled at Dex but didn't argue.

"Where's your car?" Mason asked.

"What?" Wray's attention shifted.

"Your car. You said you were in an accident. Where's your car?"

"Totaled. They couldn't fix it."

"Where was the accident?"

"North. By the lake."

"So, Olcott? Lockport?"

"Um, yeah, somewhere like that."

"What were you doing up there?"

"Visiting a friend."

"Is he the one who kicked your ass?"

"I said it was an accident."

"Oh, yeah. That's right," Mason said. He continued to glare at Wray. All three of them knew his story was a lie, but without the truth, they couldn't find the people responsible for Wray's disappearance.

"Well, if you think of anything else about your... accident, your wife has our number. Feel free to call us anytime. You know, in case your friend or one of his friends decides to visit you here or something else happens," Dex said.

For the first time, Wray's composure slipped. Fear snuck into his eyes, and his posture changed. For whatever reason, he never thought about his captors paying him a visit at home. It was clear they knew where he lived. It was only a matter of time.

"Have a good day," Wray snarled. He walked back to his house, glancing over his shoulder the entire time. When he closed the front door, the lock clicked into place immediately.

"Do you believe him?" Dex asked.

"Not a word. He's scared now."

"Yes, he is. Hopefully that means he'll talk."

Mason nodded. "We can only hope."

THEY RELAYED their conversation with Wray Allen to the rest of the team when they got back to the office. None of them believed his story about a car accident. Dex managed to get a few pictures of Wray to show everyone his injuries and they all agree he looked more like the wrong end of a punching bag than a car accident victim.

English was looking for anything on traffic cameras that would help them find whatever vehicle dropped off Wray in front of his house, but nothing stood out. There were vehicles that entered and left the neighborhood, but none that seemed out of the ordinary. It would be nice if the bad guys put signs on their vehicles to let everyone know they were the ones who did something bad.

"How long are we going to chase this?" Jack asked.

"Chase what?" Dunn asked.

"Chase Allen? He won't talk. He's not willing to tell us what happened. He's still in trouble, but we have no leads. We don't even know why he was taken. We're nowhere, except now we have a witness who won't tell us anything," Jack said.

"We follow what we do have," Dunn said. "We track the money, we follow his movements, we dig deeper. If he's covering for someone, he's either afraid of what they'll do or he's involved. From the pictures, I'm guessing he's not a part of it, but he knows his fair share."

"This looks like punishment," Mason said.

"Punishment? Of course it looks like punishment," Archer said. "What else would it be?"

"There's a difference between torture and punishment for not holding up your end. Torture is meant to inflict pain to break the other person. It's getting something out of them. It's designed to make them beg for you to stop. Wray looked like he might have cracked ribs and a broken collarbone, but I didn't see any cuts. His hands were fine. He was walking. They want something from him, and they needed to leave him whole enough to get it. This was a warning. They're going to collect," Mason said.

"And when they do, he won't come back," Dex said.

Mason nodded. "That's what I think, too."

"Fuck," Dunn breathed. "We need to find out what happened. If they're coming back for him, there's no way to know if they'll get the wife and kids, too. We really have no idea who's behind this?"

English shook his head. "The trail is cold. The account is run through international banks and shell corps that are based in countries that don't care if things are legal."

"Have you looked for other accounts these companies have open? Other people they might have accounts tied to?" Rocky asked.

English shook his head slowly. "No, I didn't. Let me see what I can find." He stood and left the meeting.

"Good call," Dunn said. "Okay, we keep looking. I get it. I don't like this one either, but something is going on. And if it's big, we need to figure it out before more people vanish. Because not all of them will come back. Mason and Dex, you two stay on this one. Everyone else, keep working on the cases you have. We're not going to use all our manpower on one case. Especially a case that feels chilly."

Everyone nodded and went back to their offices. Mason sat at his desk and scrolled through his phone. He missed a text from Megan earlier and smiled when he saw it.

Megan: Feeling good today. Going sightseeing.

Mason: Have fun. Make sure you go to Goat Island. Lots of walking trails and great views.

He set his phone down and stared at his computer. He knew he should try to find out something new about Wray Allen, but his fingers typed in another name instead.

He'd been resisting the urge to dig into Bernadette since he ran into her at the grocery store and hospital. He had no idea she was a nurse, or that she worked there. He hadn't kept up with her for obvious reasons.

Mason pulled up Bernadette's social media and scrolled through. Most of it was pictures of a dog she had. There were a few shots of her and her husband, Adam. Mason liked him. They were good together. Then he got to one that made him freeze.

Megan's face smiled back at him from the screen. A tribute. Posted a few months ago on the anniversary of her death. Mason learned over the years to pretend the day wasn't important because it hurt too much, but Bernadette honored the woman they both loved with a public post that stole Mason's breath.

My sister was a shining light in the world. She was beautiful, but not just on the outside. She wanted to make the world a better place. She wanted everyone to be loved. She believed in the beauty of people.

But she was taken from this world. She was taken from us all.

Megan was an amazing woman, but she was killed by someone who said he loved her.

Love should be cherished. It should be celebrated. So today, I celebrate the love I have for my sister. She's gone, but she'll never be forgotten and she'll never be replaced. She's still a shining light in my life, one I know will never fade because I will always love and miss her.

I love you, Megan. Now and forever.

Mason read the words again and tried to breathe. He did love Megan. She was everything to him. Losing her was the biggest regret of his life. He would never forget her, but replaced...

His phone buzzed with a text. Megan. The other Megan. Slade's sister, Megan. The woman who was replacing his wife.

No, not replacing. Their arrangement was about sex, not love. Not commitment. Just sex. But when he said her name, this Megan's face was the one that came to mind, not his wife's face. That one was fading.

He was replacing her.

And he was an asshole for it.

8

MEGAN LEANED AGAINST THE RAILING AND STARED INTO THE rushing water next to her. The spray floated up and dampened her face. The power of Niagara Falls was something she saw on TV, but until she was standing next to it, watching the water run, she didn't really get it.

Goat Island was beautiful, and not something she would have thought to go to on her own. She was grateful Mason recommended it to her. The fresh air and the stunning views made her feel at peace. That was something she hadn't felt since two lines appeared on that stick.

She put her hand over her stomach and wondered what her life would be like in a few months. The longer she stayed in Niagara Falls, the more she liked it, but she knew her mind was muddled by her time with Mason. He was a good man, and he was phenomenal in bed, but Megan wasn't looking for someone to share her life with. The only reason she'd stayed with him was because she wasn't being watched when she was there. At Justin and Kyra's, she felt like they were waiting for something to happen.

That wasn't why she came to New York. She wanted to

stand on her own. Yes, she hoped she'd connect with her brother and his friends, but she wanted distance from the baby's father and clarity for herself. So far, the only clarity she'd gotten was she was seriously lacking in the amazing sex experience department.

She smiled to herself. She couldn't say that anymore.

Megan felt like she was on vacation. Like she'd met a guy on a trip and was living in an alternate reality. But this could be her life. Well, the location could be. She wasn't interested in anything permanent with Mason. He was great, but she had to put her child first.

"Excuse me," a woman to Megan's right said. "Would you mind taking a picture of us?"

"Of course. What would you like in the background?"

"If you can get any of the Falls, that would be great."

Megan nodded and took a few steps back so she could see more of the setting. The young couple smiled at each other and shared a kiss. Megan took a quick picture, then a few more when they were looking at her again.

"Let me know if you'd like more," Megan said as she handed back the phone.

The couple looked at them together and grinned. "These are perfect. Thank you so much."

"You're welcome. Have a great day."

"You, too!"

Megan smiled as they walked a little farther away and leaned over the railing. She was never like that with the father, with Stuart. He was nice, but he never looked at her like she was the most important person in his world. She should have seen it, but Megan was more interested in being in his world than risking being cast out. They were friends for years, and when they first slept together, she thought it was a natural transition. Stuart clearly did not.

They got together off and on for the better part of a year. Megan wasn't in love with him, but she liked him. He was a good man, or so she thought. When she found out she was pregnant, she assumed he would at least offer to support her.

His accusations of her sleeping with other men stung, but the realization that Stuart was never going to see her as more than someone to sleep with when he was drunk hurt worse. Megan bought her ticket to Niagara Falls the next day and hadn't seen Stuart, or heard from him, since.

It was better that way. Even if she went back to Kentucky, she wasn't going to get together with him again. She learned her lesson. And she knew having a child would mean putting their needs ahead of her own constantly. Which meant after things ended with Mason, she was done with men for a while.

What a way to go out.

Megan walked around the island and enjoyed the fresh air. When her stomach rumbled, she decided to head into the city and try to find some lunch. Maybe she could check out the F-BOMB office.

She dug out her phone and debated on calling her brother or Mason. If she called Mason, Justin would know something was going on. She wasn't ready for her bubble to pop, so she sent Justin a quick text asking if he was free for lunch and if she could check out the office.

Justin: We're ordering in. Plenty of food. Come by and we'll show you around.

Megan replied that she'd be there soon and ordered a ride from Goat Island. She was dropped off in the garage under the building where Justin told her to go and sent him a text that she was there. He replied that someone would be down to get her soon.

Megan looked around the lot and waited for someone to meet her. She knew what they did was dangerous so it made sense she couldn't just go up on her own. She reached up to run a hand through her hair and realized it was full of knots. She dug for her brush as the elevator opened and Kyra walked out.

"Kyra," Megan said, smiling and waving.

"Hey. Slade said you were here. I would have been down here waiting for you if I'd known you were coming." Kyra held the elevator open while Megan walked over.

"It's fine. It was kind of a last minute thing. I was sightseeing a little and decided to see if Justin was free for lunch."

Kyra pushed a button, and the doors slid closed in front of them. "Is your friend working today?"

Megan nodded and brushed her hair to avoid looking at her future sister-in-law. She wasn't sure Kyra had the same talent for spotting lies that Justin had, but Megan wasn't taking any chances. "Yeah. I'm on my own during the day."

"That stinks. I can take a day off and we can go do something one of these days. I feel so bad we didn't plan for that," Kyra said.

Megan chuckled. "I should have known better than to do a surprise trip. The work you guys do…"

"It's rewarding," Kyra said. "I was so unhappy before, but this job and the work they do make me feel like we're really making a difference in the world."

"You are. I just sell office supplies to businesses. I don't feel like I'm doing much to make the world a better place."

Kyra shook her head. "We all have a purpose. And selling office supplies to businesses is helping those businesses to do their work. You're making people's lives easier and allowing them to do their jobs."

"You're kind for saying that."

Kyra laughed. "I run this office. Let me tell you, if our suppliers weren't on top of things, it would make my life hell. These men never think about the things they need, they just expect everything to be there when they go look. It's huge for me to have the option of setting up regular orders and things just arriving on time, and to know I can call and add things easily. You're helping. Trust me."

Megan smiled. "Thank you." She never thought of the work she did as particularly inspiring or life changing, but she also rarely talked to the people who actually used her products. She dealt with management and the decision makers. If she stayed in her current job, she wanted to make more of an effort to meet the end users.

The elevator doors whooshed open and Kyra stepped into a plain lobby. Megan followed her to a secure door that required Kyra's keycard to open. Inside, the semblance of calm from the bland lobby vanished.

"Whoa," Megan said.

Kyra nodded. "It's like this a lot. We're working on a few different cases right now and things get busy. That's why I brought in lunch. They wouldn't slow down to eat if I didn't force them."

Megan moved against the wall as Jack raced by her. He smiled and said hello, but he didn't stop to talk or flirt. A few of the other guys moved across the hallway, going from one office to another, but Kyra led Megan through the chaos to the break room at the back of the hallway.

"We can hang out in here for a minute. There are drinks in the fridge and snacks. Help yourself. Lunch should be here in about ten minutes," Kyra said. She went to the fridge and grabbed a bottle of water. She offered one to Megan, who nodded.

"There you are. Found the place okay?" Justin asked, joining them. He kissed Kyra, then walked over and hugged Megan.

"Yeah, no problems. I'm learning my way around," Megan said.

"Is your friend showing you the city?" Justin asked.

"She said her friend is working," Kyra said. "I was thinking of taking a few days off so we could spend some time together." Her pointed look said she wanted Justin to do the same.

"Yeah, that's a great idea. I... should... too?"

Megan chuckled. "You guys don't have to. Really. I'm finding my way around and enjoying some downtime."

"Uh, hey," Mason said. He stopped at the door and looked at the three of them.

Shit. Megan didn't think to warn him. She froze for a second, wondering what he was going to do. Normally, when he got home from work, she greeted him with sex before dinner. She obviously wasn't going to do that at their offices, but they hadn't been in public together since their trip to the hospital.

"Hey, Mason. Megan decided to come have lunch with us. You only had a minute to talk the other week, but I'm guessing you remember her," Justin said.

Mason nodded slowly and glanced at Megan. Her wide eyes must have translated her intended message because he smiled and said, "Nice to see you again."

"You, too," Megan said with a smile.

"Megan has been sightseeing alone. She's staying with a friend instead of us and she told Kyra her friend is working, so she's on her own. You've lived here longer than we have. Anywhere she should check out?" Justin asked.

"My favorite place around is Goat Island," Mason said.

"It was beautiful," Megan said without thinking.

"You already went there?" Justin asked. "Oh, your friend must have mentioned it. Where else have you been?"

Mason watched her as she spoke with her brother. Megan knew she should have told him the truth, but she knew if Mason found out Justin didn't really know where she was, he would insist on taking her back. She wasn't interested in that.

"Lunch is here. Why don't you come with me to get it?" Kyra said to Justin.

He grinned at her and slid an arm around her waist, holding her close as they walked out of the break room together, forgetting the rest of the world existed.

"You lied to me," Mason said once they were alone.

Megan straightened her spine and held his gaze. "Yes."

His brows tugged together. "No explanation?"

Megan shrugged. "Why? I lied because I wanted to be with you. I knew you'd say no—"

"I did."

"And that if you knew my brother didn't approve, you would send me back."

"I would have."

"I didn't want that, so I lied. I told him I was going to stay with a friend, and I told you he knew I was staying with you. I only intended to be with you that first night, but..."

"You can't lie to me," Mason growled.

"We're not together. We're not building a life. It's sex."

"We're friends," Mason said, sounding hurt.

Megan drew a breath and nodded. "You're right. We are. And I'm sorry."

"You have to tell Slade where you're staying."

Megan shook her head. "I don't think that's a good idea."

"He needs to know."

"I'll tell him, eventually."

Mason raised an eyebrow.

Megan grinned. "Are you going to tell him?"

Mason sighed heavily.

"I promise I'll tell him. I just have to figure out when. Okay?"

"Do I have a choice?"

"You can tell me to leave."

Mason held her gaze for a long moment, then finally shook his head. "I don't want you to leave."

"Good."

"But this isn't over."

Megan grinned. "I know."

"Lunch is here," Justin called down the hallway.

"I'll meet you down there. You'll see the vultures."

"Are we okay?" Megan asked.

Mason nodded. "Yeah. You go ahead."

Megan knew something was off, but she wasn't going to push. She meant what she said. They weren't building a future which meant she had no right to ask if he was okay. He was giving her space to figure her stuff out, and she would give him the same. Or at least try.

MEGAN WALKED down the hallway without looking back. Mason hated himself for wishing she did. He hated himself for wishing she was honest with Slade about where she was sleeping at night. And all that meant he hated himself for doing exactly what he vowed never to do. For replacing his wife.

The words from Bernadette's page were still echoing in his head when he finally walked into the conference room and got lunch. He took a seat in the corner, away from Megan and Slade, and the guilt that threatened to choke him.

Lying never got him anywhere. Mason wasn't a fan of it, in work or in his life. He wanted to tell everyone in the room that Megan had been staying with him, but she had to do it her way. He just hoped her way didn't result in him losing his job and the people he considered friends.

Megan laughed at something Slade said, and the sound made Mason smile. She was healing parts of him he didn't realize were still broken. Being with her was more than just sex for him. She was an amazing woman, and she was going to be an amazing mother.

Mason always wanted a family. He and Megan were talking about it before she died. She wanted at least three kids. He thought she was crazy, but he would have done anything to make her happy.

He stared across the room at the other Megan and realized he felt the same way about her. Not that he was in love with her or wanted to build a life with her and raise her child, but he wanted to see her happy. He wanted her to have everything she wished for in life.

She laughed at Slade and looked up and caught him staring at her. She tilted her head to the side in question, but Mason just smiled and shook his head.

As the team finished lunch, they all went back to their work. Slade showed Megan around the office, telling her as much as he could about the work they did. Mason listened to his voice as they walked around and tried to focus on the tasks in front of him.

Until Megan said, "It's good to have people you can count on who will do anything for you. People who will put your needs ahead of their own. I think we all need a friend like that."

The wheels started turning in Mason's head. "Say that again," he shouted as he got up from his chair and went into the hallway.

"Say what?"

"You said it's good to have people who will put your needs ahead of their own. Like someone who will lie for you or who will drag you out of the ditch you're in when your absence is noticed," Mason said. He rubbed his jaw.

"What are you thinking?" Slade asked.

"Dex and I showed up at Braden Wright's house. A few days later, Wray Allen comes home."

"Yeah? So?"

"What if he knew where Allen was the whole time, but he knew his wife would be pissed? What if he went and found him?"

Slade shook his head slowly. "He's the one who called and said he wasn't covering for him. Why wouldn't he just go get the guy in the first place?"

Mason stared up at the ceiling and thought about it. "I don't know. But something about him isn't right. He knows more than he's sharing."

"They both do," Dex said from behind Mason. "I've been wondering something similar about Wright. He was shifty when we talked to him. He acted like he was trying to protect his friend. Can we lean on him again?"

"We need more before we go back over there."

"Like probable cause?" English said from inside his office.

Mason stopped in front of his door. "Do you have something?"

English shrugged. "I think I might. And I think it might

make him talk. I just found another account owned by the same company, but with Braden Wright's name on it."

"So, he is involved. And he's in just as deep as Allen," Dex said.

English shook his head. "I don't think so. His account has twice the money in it. I think he's in even deeper."

"Which means we owe Mr. Wright another visit," Dex said.

Mason nodded. "It sounds like we do."

9

———

Dex and Mason parked outside the fire station where Braden Wright and Wray Allen worked. Wray was still off, but Braden was supposed to be on shift. The crew was wandering around, inside and outside, checking equipment and cleaning.

With a silent nod, both men got out of their SUV and headed toward the first guy they saw. Having worked in a team environment, they understood how the firefighters were likely to protect each other.

"How ya doing?" Dex asked as they approached. "We're looking for Braden Wright."

The man looked up and catalogued the two of them, including the logos on their shirts. "And you are?"

"I'm Ryker Hamilton and this is Mason O'Connor. We work for F-BOMB. We've been helping the police with Wray Allen's disappearance," Dex explained.

"Allen's back. He was in a car accident."

Mason glanced at Dex. Dex rocked back on his heels and nodded. "We heard. But we still have some questions. Is Mr. Wright here?"

The guy finally nodded and called to someone inside, "Find Braden. He has visitors."

Dex thanked the man and headed toward the next person.

"Braden's in the weight room," a woman not far from the door said. "Straight up the stairs and to the back."

"Thanks," Dex said as they walked past.

There was no doubt in Mason's mind that Braden already knew they were there. Hopefully, he didn't skip out the back, but if he did, he would have even more questions to answer.

The weight room was exactly where the woman told them it would be. Braden Wright was the only one in there. He was staring at the door and drinking a bottle of water when they walked in.

"Gentlemen," he said. He looked even less thrilled to see them than he had before.

"Mr. Wright. We have a few more questions," Dex said.

Mason stood at the door and crossed his arms, making sure Braden knew he wasn't getting out if he tried. Braden raised a brow at him and turned his focus back to Dex.

"I'm not sure I'll be able to help you, but I see I don't have a choice."

Dex dove right in. "We know you're involved with the same thing Mr. Allen is. We found your secret account, too."

"What secret account?" Braden asked.

"The one you're allowed to deposit money into but not pull money out of. The one owned by Marzette Corporation. The one we believe is set up for you by whoever it is you two owe money to."

"What the fuck are you talking about?" Braden asked. "I've never heard of Marzette Corporation and I don't know anything about an account I have to put money into. I have one bank account. I have savings and I have checking and I have my pension. I don't have secret accounts. Who the hell would I be hiding it from? And why?"

"You don't know anything about the account?" Dex clarified, sounding like he thought the man was full of shit. Mason wasn't entirely sure.

"No. I have no idea."

Dex took a step closer. "Whoever took Mr. Allen did so knowing what they could do to him. Whoever took him dropped him off on his front lawn. They know where he lives. You might not have people you're trying to protect, but he has a wife and two kids. He has people who rely on him to come home, who could be in danger if you don't tell us what's going on."

Braden glared at Dex and got in his face. "Just because I don't have a wife and kids doesn't mean I don't give a shit about anyone else. Stacey is like another sister to me. I'd do anything for them. And if I knew what the hell you were trying to get at, I'd tell you, but I don't know. Whatever Wray's involved with is not something I have a hand in. So, you can get the fuck out of here. Next time you show up at this station without an invitation, I'll have you arrested for trespassing and harassment."

Dex didn't budge for a full minute. When he finally did, he nodded and thanked Braden for his time, then turned and nodded for Mason to lead the way out of the fire station.

Neither of them said a word until they got back to the SUV and were on the way to F-BOMB offices.

"I hate to say it, but I believe him," Mason said.

Dex nodded. "I do, too. He doesn't know a thing. But he's scared. He knows whatever it is, it isn't over and that he has to protect Allen's family. He'll call."

"I just hope this works," Mason said.

Dex chuckled. "Yeah, me too."

WHEN MEGAN LEFT the F-BOMB offices, she went straight back to Mason's apartment. The morning left her feeling worn out, and she needed a nap.

Justin asked if she was sleeping since she said she was tired, and Megan laughed it off as though the question was ridiculous. He didn't push, but she could tell he wanted to.

Mason's scent wrapped around her when she laid down on the bed. Her thighs tingled with need, but she pushed the feeling aside knowing it would be much better if she waited until he was home to do naughty things with her.

Sleep evaded her for long enough that Megan turned on her laptop and grabbed her phone. She called her boss to check in on things while her computer was loading.

"Megan. How are you?" Douglas said in greeting.

Megan smiled. She liked Douglas, but she didn't love working for him. He was a nice guy, but he was an ineffectual manager, and sometimes a little underhanded in how he did things. "Hi, Douglas. I'm doing well. How are things at work?"

"Everyone is asking when you'll be back, but I told them you're taking a much needed break. These vultures are trying to convince me to let them work from elsewhere, but I know you'll get your work done and they won't, so I keep making excuses for why I'm letting you."

Megan laughed with him and rolled her eyes. If she decided to go back, it would be one more thing she would have to deal with. Her coworkers already didn't like her. The women looked down on her because of her size, and the men dismissed her for the same reason. None of them thought a woman who couldn't squeeze into a pants suit and stilettos was worth shit on sales calls.

She proved them wrong by being one of the top salespeople month after month, which then pissed them off for a completely different reason.

"I appreciate you letting me take the time to visit my brother. It's been a good visit. And I'm keeping in touch with my clients, of course." Megan paused when she saw a new meeting on her schedule for the next day. "I see I have a call tomorrow with Mr. Richardson. Have you heard anything from him lately?"

Mr. Richardson was an old client of Megan's. He owned a large metalwork facility in southern Ohio. He used to be her biggest client, but he canceled the contract with her a year earlier. She hadn't heard from him since.

"Oh, Mr. Richardson. Well, I heard he might not be happy with the service he's getting. The new company he started working with wasn't able to deliver items to him consistently, and he might be looking to come back."

"Were you going to prep me for this?" Megan asked. She sat up and searched around for a pen to take notes.

"You don't need preparation. You know what you're doing," Douglas said with a chuckle.

Megan groaned inwardly. What should have seemed like a vote of confidence annoyed the shit out of her. Douglas was always unprepared himself, so he didn't bother to give others an option to be prepared. Megan preferred to research potential clients before a meeting with them, and with a client like Mr. Richardson, the last thing she could afford to be was unprepared.

"I do, but I still want to have some information ready. Like what he was using when he left us, where he went if I can find that, and what we could do differently to draw him back. He was a huge client. This meeting shouldn't have been scheduled for me without giving me advanced warning."

"Well, I am your boss, so I think I have the option to schedule whatever meetings I see fit to schedule. Plus, his assistant asked specifically for you. I tried to tell her I could handle it, but she insisted. I didn't really have much of a choice."

The bitterness in his voice told Megan all she needed to know. Douglas intentionally left her in the dark, hoping she would fuck up the meeting so he could swoop in and save the day. He was trying to sabotage her. With a massive client.

"You're right, Douglas. I apologize for questioning you. I need to go. It was good talking to you."

"You, too, Megan. Have a good day!"

Megan hung up and rolled her eyes again at the cheeriness in his voice. How the man could be so happy one second and so bitter and hateful the next was beyond her.

If she wasn't pregnant and in need of health insurance, she would consider a new job if she returned to Kentucky. Hell, maybe she'd consider it, anyway. If she went back, she wasn't going to be able to keep up with the travel and the long hours once the baby arrived. Her coworkers with families all had a significant other who was the primary caregiver to their children. Megan would be on her own, and unless she wanted her parents raising her child, she needed options.

Megan pulled up the history she had on Mr. Richardson and his company. She refreshed her memory on his personal life so she could ask about his family, then she ran through a year's worth of orders and did a comparison to current costs so she could discuss the difference.

When she had those figures pulled together, she ran

through each item and substituted some new options that her current clients said were better. She broke down what would be a monthly budget for everything and saved the file.

As soon as she hit save, Megan felt like she hit a wall. The exhaustion that sent her to bed earlier overwhelmed her. Instead of fighting it, she pushed the computer to the side and laid down. She closed her eyes and was out before her head even hit the pillow.

Five minutes later, she groaned and swatted. She heard a soft chuckle. Something brushed against her cheek. She swatted again. "Why? I just fell asleep!"

"You've been out for hours," Mason said.

"Hours? That's not..." Megan pried her eyes open and realized he was right. It was no longer light outside, the apartment smelled wonderful, and her bladder was definitely full.

Megan groaned again and pushed herself up. Mason helped her stand, then she rushed to the bathroom. After she washed her hands and met him in the living room, she realized she was starving.

"Did you have a good nap?" Mason asked.

Megan nodded. "I guess the day wore me out. I had work to do this afternoon and when I was done, I couldn't keep my eyes open."

"I know," Mason said with a laugh. "When I got home, I tried to wake you up, but you didn't budge. I watched you until I knew you were still breathing. Scared the hell out of me."

"Sorry. I'm still getting used to how much energy I have with this one sucking it all out of me. I meant to have dinner ready when you got here."

"You don't have to cook for me," Mason said at least the tenth time.

Megan shrugged. She was already living in his apartment, eating his food, and forcing him to lie to her brother about where she was. The least she could do was cook dinner.

"Sit down and eat. We'll watch a movie and talk about how we're going to tell your brother you're staying here."

Megan glared at him. "Not fair."

Mason gave it right back to her. "Neither is forcing me to lie to the man. He's my boss. And you're his baby sister."

"I'm not a baby."

"No, you're not, but he also doesn't want to think about the things we've been doing since you've been here."

"Speaking of which…" Megan said.

"No," Mason argued. "You're not going to distract me with sex right now. Eat. If you're this exhausted, you need food. And you need more sleep."

"Sleep is overrated," Megan said as she yawned.

Mason chuckled. "Want to try that again."

Megan glared at him but did as he asked and sat down to eat her dinner.

WHEN THEY WERE DONE with dinner and Megan agreed she would tell her brother where she was staying, Mason asked about the rest of her day.

"Goat Island was beautiful," she gushed. "I'm so happy you told me to go there. The views were stunning."

Mason nodded. "I always liked it there. It's still busy, but it's almost quieter than the rest of the Falls. Most people go there for the tours, but to walk around, it's my favorite place."

"I never would have known to go there. I hope to go back while I'm in town. Justin and Kyra were talking about taking some time off to spend with me while I'm here. We're going to have to think of other things to do," Megan said.

Mason pursed his lips. "You're going to need to tell them you're staying here first."

"I told you I will."

"You also told me you already did."

"Yeah, yeah. It'll be fine. Justin never stays mad for long. And they're about to be married. The last thing I needed when I'm pregnant and turned on all the time is to listen to my brother having sex."

"First, I didn't need that image. Second, all the time?"

Megan rolled her eyes and nodded. "Pretty much, yeah."

"Like right now?"

"Pretty much, yeah," Megan said.

"How turned on?"

Megan shrugged and bit her lip. For all her boldness showing up at his door a few days ago, talking about her desires was different. Telling him she was turned on laying on his bed was different.

"Megan," he groaned.

"A lot, okay? All the time. Especially when you're being sweet to me."

"What about when I'm not being sweet to you?" he asked, his voice low and rough.

Megan sucked in a ragged breath. "Yeah, then, too."

"Take off your clothes."

"Um..."

"Now, Megan. Strip. Get on the bed."

"But... are you sure?"

Mason stood and removed all of his clothes. His cock stood straight up, a drop glistening on the tip. "Yeah, I'm sure."

Megan's entire body trembled at the sight of him. He'd been gentle since their first night, and she could tell he'd been holding back with her. The fire in his eyes said she might get some of the man she went searching for when she showed up on his doorstep. The man who made her wet without even touching her.

Mason moved to the bed and smoothed out the covers. He set her laptop and notebook on the coffee table and grabbed a condom from his nightstand. Megan watched him the entire time, letting the anticipation build inside her.

When she finally stood, Mason turned to watch her. She took off her shirt with his eyes on her breasts. She unhooked her bra with his hand on his jaw. She dropped her jeans and panties with his hand wrapped around his cock.

"Fucking hell, you're beautiful," he said.

"You don't have to say things like that."

"I don't say things for the hell of it. I say things because I mean them. So when I say you're beautiful, it's because you're fucking beautiful, okay?"

Megan licked her lips and nodded. She didn't know him well, but she could tell he meant that. And the way his cock swelled in his hand as she moved closer said he wanted her as much as she wanted him.

"Lay on the bed," Mason said when she stood in front of him. "Spread your thighs wide."

Megan's body tightened at the command, and she did as she was told. She watched him as he let his eyes caress her entire body. Her nipples hardened and stood on end as her core softened and made space for him. She was ready.

Then he lowered himself to the floor and pressed her thighs wide with his large hands. The gentle touch and the forceful motion made her jump. "Wide, Megan. I'm a big man, and I need space to work."

"I'm not one of those women with a natural thigh gap," Megan said.

"No, you're not," Mason said, sounding more pleased about that than disappointed. "Your thighs are thick and luscious and perfect. I'm going to bite them and then I'm going to suck on you until you can't take any more."

"Please," Megan begged. She couldn't take any more talking. She needed him to do it. Because if he didn't make a move soon, she was going to combust right there on his bed.

"I can't wait to taste you. Are you ready?"

"Yes," Megan cried.

Mason groaned as he swiped his tongue through her wet folds. Megan's hips lifted, her body already primed and ready for him. One brush over her clit and she was trembling.

"Have you been thinking about me today?"

"Yes," she confessed.

Mason licked her again and her eyes slammed shut. "Are you going to come for me tonight?"

"Please."

He licked her again, and she moaned loudly.

"How many times are you going to come for me tonight?"

"I... I don't know."

"That's okay. We'll start with one right now." As he finished his sentence, he sucked hard on her clit and Megan splintered. Her already sensitive body burst and she screamed his name, letting out all the pent up desire and desperation she'd been holding onto all day. And she was so right. It was so much better when he was there to do all the dirty things to her.

Mason pressed a finger inside her and teased her tender flesh. She whimpered and moaned, on the edge again but unable to get there without his help.

"More?" he asked, the word a whisper against her thigh.

"Yes," Megan cried. "Please."

Mason nipped her thigh, then sucked a large chunk of it into his mouth and pressed his tongue to her skin. She whined in frustration, wanting him to do the same to her clit. Mason chuckled and bit her again.

"I guess you are turned on all the time. Do you need some relief?"

"Yes!"

Mason licked her clit and thrust his finger harder into her. She flinched and tensed, then let the release come as he sucked on her clit once more, sending her blissfully over the edge.

"Oh, God, yes! Mason! Yes, yes, yes!"

"Fuck," Mason growled with her, pumping his finger into her as he drew back. Their eyes locked together. Mason stood and reached for the condom. He withdrew his finger and rolled it on, then slammed into Megan.

"Oh, God," Megan moaned.

"Shit." Mason tried to back out, but Megan wrapped her thighs around him and held him still.

"Don't stop. Please."

"But, the baby…"

"I'm fine in this position. You're not as deep. Unless it doesn't feel good."

"Trust me, that's not the problem at all."

Megan smiled, then moaned when he moved back slightly then stroked inside. His strokes were slow but deep.

She felt every single inch of him as he stretched and filled her. He grabbed one of her feet and lifted it over his shoulder, turning her slightly.

"Oh, God," she moaned again.

"Good or bad?"

"Good," she panted. "So good."

Mason kept going, his strokes speeding up as they both crept closer and closer to release. His other hand slid between her thighs and caressed her still sensitive clit.

"Oh, yes," Megan cried. "Yes!" She came quickly, her body unable to hold back, and Mason was right behind her, giving in with her.

He stood at the edge of the bed, panting, his gaze locked on hers. When their breathing finally slowed and he shifted to move out of her, Megan smiled and fell right back to sleep.

10

———

Mason tried not to make too much noise so Megan could sleep. He wanted to curl around her and sleep also, but his mind was racing.

Braden Wright hadn't called Wray Allen by the time Mason left work for the day. They thought he'd take the bait and demand answers from his friend so they could find out what was going on, but he never did.

Mason felt like they were missing something. Like there was a big piece of the picture they weren't seeing. He hated the feeling, and this case was full of it. Not knowing was always a problem in situations like the ones they were in. If they missed something important, people could get hurt, or worse. They had to figure it out.

Mason leaned back on the couch and closed his eyes. He ran through everything he knew about the case and tried to find what was missing. Wray Allen owed money to someone, but they didn't know who yet. He was kidnapped, but they didn't know how. He was returned, but they didn't have anything on that either.

It was all dead ends. Getting Braden Wright to think the

family was still in danger and that he was thought to be involved was a long shot. Yes, there was an account set up in his name, but he'd never put money in it. What English wasn't sure of was if the account existed to bring Wright into the fold or if it was a secondary account for Allen.

And they still had no idea who the controlling party was.

Too many questions. Too many things unanswered. Wray Allen could answer all of it, but he wasn't willing to share. Why?

Mason sat upright. "They threatened his family," he whispered into the darkness. It was obvious, but that had to be what happened. Whoever he made the deal with had to have threatened his family if he spoke to anyone about what was going on. Otherwise, they wouldn't have returned him, and he would have been sharing what he knew.

It made sense to Mason, but what he didn't get was how was Wray Allen going to get the money to pay these guys back? If he already got into debt, he had no money. What terms did he have to agree to to get out of debt?

Megan groaned in her sleep and drew Mason's attention. The questions still bounced in his head, but he didn't have any answers. If he was lucky, he'd be able to get some sleep and answers would come in the morning.

He took off his shorts and slid into bed with Megan. She rolled over toward him and tucked her hand under her chin. She was adorable like that. Mason smiled and kissed her on the forehead. She twitched but didn't wake up. Mason watched her for a few minutes, thankful when his eyes began to close on their own.

The alarm woke Mason up for the first time in years. He always set it just in case, but he couldn't remember the last time he needed it to wake up. Megan still slept soundly next to him, blissfully unaware of the shrill alarm that pierced through Mason's mind.

He got up and showered, then packed a change of clothes in a bag. He was working at the animal shelter that evening and hoped to get in a run during the day since he was off his normal routine. He kissed Megan's forehead and slipped out the door to head into the office.

Mason was halfway to his Jeep when the hair on the back of his neck stood up. Someone was watching him. He glanced around the small parking area and saw no one. Cars appeared to be empty. No one was walking around. The place was silent.

He took a deep breath and convinced himself he was losing it. He'd been paranoid most of his life, and while it served him well most of the time, letting it get into his mind was not good.

Mason looked around one last time, then got in his Jeep and left for work.

He couldn't shake the feeling all day that someone was watching him. There was no way someone could get into the F-BOMB offices, but something was there, in the back of his mind.

"Any new thoughts?" Dex asked, walking into Mason's office late in the afternoon. "Think we need to try talking to them again?"

Mason shook his head. "I don't know. I figured he'd call by now. What is he waiting for?"

"Maybe we were wrong about him?"

Mason leaned back in his chair and stared at the ceiling. It felt easy the day before when they went to see Braden at the fire station. Piss him off a little and get him to call his buddy. After that, they'd have more to go on.

"English hasn't heard a thing?" Mason asked.

Dex shook his head. "Nothing. Complete silence."

"Complete silence?"

Dex tilted his head. "That's what he said. Why?"

"You don't find that odd?"

Dex shrugged. "I didn't until now. Let's go see what English has."

Mason followed Dex down the hall to English's cave. He had so many computers running that his office was like an icebox.

"You said you've heard nothing from the Allens, is that right?"

English nodded.

"Does that mean nothing important or nothing at all?"

English froze and looked up at Mason and Dex. "Shit."

Mason and Dex exchanged a glance that said they were right.

"They must have found another way to communicate."

"If they were in person, we still would have heard them. Have we seen either of them going anywhere?" Dex asked.

Mason waited while English searched the men's phones. They didn't have a warrant, and the taps were technically illegal, but all they were looking for was information about who'd taken Wray Allen. Mason knew it toed a line they shouldn't be crossing, but he also knew if whoever took Wray came back for his family, there were no lines.

"Their signals are both coming from the Allen's house right now. Braden's been on shift since you spoke to him. This might be the first chance they've had to see each other. Go over there. Do a wellness check or something. Anything to find out what's going on," English said.

Dex and Mason nodded and went for the door. English would fill in Dunn and the others on what was going on.

Dex drove fast through the streets of the city and ducked

into the neighborhood early to get off the main roads. He slowed as they traveled through the residential streets and past rows of houses lined up close together.

Mason leaned forward when they pulled onto the Allen's street. Braden Wright's truck was parked in their driveway, behind an undamaged truck that was registered to Wray Allen.

Dex and Mason exchanged a glance and got out, circling the truck before heading to the door.

Before Dex could ring the bell, a crash inside had them both freezing.

"You're the worst friend in the world! This is the thanks I get for keeping your secrets? Being dragged into your fucked up world is not what I wanted. What the hell, Wray?"

"I didn't know they were going to do that. When they told me my debts would be forgiven, they didn't say they'd be passed on to you instead."

Mason glanced at Dex. He had his phone out, recording the conversation. He slid it into his pocket and stepped to the side of the front door so their shadows weren't visible through the privacy glass.

"Well, what did you think? The thugs you've been playing cards with and losing to for months were just going to forgive and forget after losing twenty grand?"

Mason closed his eyes and drew in a breath.

"I didn't think. I was just happy to go home. To be able to see Stacey and the kids again. I never thought I'd see them."

"And now I get to pay for your poor choices. Probably my sister, too."

"Why would they bring her into this?" Wray asked.

Braden scoffed. "Where do you think I'm going to get that kind of money? I don't have twenty grand plus interest lying around. This is why I never joined you on your getaways."

Dex caught Mason's eye and nodded toward the truck. Mason nodded and walked off the porch with Dex. They got in the truck and drove around the corner before either of them spoke.

"Now we have proof that Braden Wright knows more than he's telling us. He might not know who's behind this, but it sounds like he's about to find out."

"Any idea who his sister is?" Mason asked.

Dex shook his head. "No, but it doesn't matter. We need to shut down whatever is going on before it involves more innocent people."

"And how are we going to do that?"

Dex sighed. "I have no idea."

MEGAN INVITED herself to dinner with Kyra and Slade. She hadn't spent much time with them since she arrived and she really did want to get to know Kyra better.

She sat on a chair in the dining room, sipping a glass of water and pretending not to drool over the glass of wine Kyra was drinking while they chatted.

"Are you sure you don't want a glass of wine?" Kyra asked.

Megan shook her head. "Thanks, but I'm good. I had a headache earlier today and know the wine will bring it back."

"Sorry to hear that. Is everything okay?"

Megan smiled and tried to play into her lie. "Yeah, just stressed about work." Not a lie. "My boss is a crappy manager, and it makes my life more complicated."

"I've been there. It amazes me the people who end up in charge sometimes. I've had some bosses that shouldn't even be working as employees. One of my old bosses couldn't even figure out how to use a spreadsheet to create one of his weekly reports. He had another employee do it, send it to him, and he forwarded it on as though it was his own work. There's a special place in hell for people who do things like that."

Megan chuckled. "I've had bosses like that. My current one is more the type who can't handle someone else being better than he is. I had an old client call and request an appointment with me. He put it on my schedule but never told me about it. When I called him on it, he said I didn't need to worry about preparing because I know what I'm doing."

"That doesn't sound so bad," Kyra said.

Megan shook her head. "He did it because he was hoping I'd mess up the meeting and he could take over the client. It's a huge contract, one that brings in more than my entire salary. And since we work on salary plus commission, this is a huge contract. My boss wanted it for himself."

"Seriously? What an ass."

Megan nodded, happy Kyra believed her and didn't try to convince her she was wrong. Too many people thought they knew the truth and that Megan was being paranoid. She appreciated Kyra not trying to do that.

"I couldn't work with someone like that. I have, but it's painful. Have you thought about finding another job?" Kyra asked.

Megan nodded, deciding to answer that question with some truth. "I have. A lot. My skills are very transferrable so I could go to just about any company I wanted to, but starting over is tough."

"That's very true. I was terrified to take the job at F-BOMB. I had no idea what I was getting myself into. Even after the interview, I wasn't really sure what they did. Obviously, I understand why now, but at the time, it was a leap of faith that it would be a good move for me. I was seriously considering leaving the area before I got the job."

"Really? I didn't know that," Megan said.

Kyra nodded. "Yeah. I didn't really have anyone here. My roommate and I weren't friends, and I didn't get along with my coworkers. I felt really alone. Like it wouldn't matter all that much if I disappeared, and that scared me. Especially after the bank. I could have disappeared. I could have just..."

Justin hugged Kyra from behind and kissed the side of her neck. "You didn't. You're safe."

Kyra nodded. The pain and fear in her eyes didn't fade right away. Megan had never been through anything like Kyra and Justin had. It made her feel silly for worrying about her situation.

"We all have our struggles," Kyra said after a minute with a tentative smile for Megan. "I try to remember that. All the women in our little group have had something happen. None of us are immune to fear. And we've had each other to lean on to get through it."

"You're lucky," Megan said softly. Her throat was tight. "I don't have a group like that."

Kyra reached over and put her hand on Megan's. "You always have us. Even if you're not here, you can always call or visit or anything. I was really looking forward to getting to know you, so I'm a little disappointed you didn't want to stay, but I get it. It's hard being a third wheel. I'm sorry we made you feel like you were in the way."

"You didn't. I promise. I just wanted to spend time with my friend, too."

"Tell me about this friend," Kyra said. "Male or female?"

"Male," Megan said. The fewer lies the better. Maybe.

"Is it a romantic type of friend?"

Megan laughed. "Not exactly. We both agreed we're going to be friends first."

"Your brother and I had that same agreement. Now we're a few weeks from getting married."

"I'm not interested in getting married anytime soon. I have a lot going on."

"If there's one thing I've learned since I met Slade, life comes at you whether you think you're ready or not."

"That's definitely true," Megan agreed with a secret chuckle.

"What are you doing this weekend?" Kyra asked.

Megan shrugged. "I don't really have plans. Why?"

"I have my final dress fitting tomorrow. It's not glamorous or exciting, but if you're free, I'd love to have you come with me."

Megan smiled and nodded. "I'd love to. Thank you."

Kyra grinned. "Good. It'll be fun. My bridesmaids will be there, but having you join us will be great."

"I'd like that." She was happy she could say that honestly.

"For now, let's eat dinner," Justin said, bringing a large serving bowl to the table. He set the salad down in the center, then went back to the kitchen for the rest of the food he prepared.

"Wow," Megan said. "I didn't think you were serious when you said you know how to cook."

Justin scoffed. "Hey! I'm not opening a restaurant anytime soon, but I can keep food on the table."

"He's pretty good," Kyra agreed. "With so many friends around, we end up cooking a lot. A few months ago, the guys had a chili competition to see who made the best chili."

"Who won?"

"Mason," Justin grumbled. "Cheater."

Kyra laughed. "Mason's chili was by far the best. Slade's mad because his was too spicy so no one could taste the flavor he insisted was better than Mason's."

"It was better," Justin argued.

"Maybe, but you burned off all our taste buds before we could find out," Kyra said with a laugh.

Justin wrapped an arm around her waist and tickled her until Kyra squirmed and screamed. Megan laughed at them, wondering if she'd ever have someone like that in her life.

"I'll get him next time," Justin finally said when he sat down. "Mason won't know what hit him when I come after him."

Kyra chuckled and shook her head. Megan just hoped he was still talking about the food. She didn't think her brother knew where she was staying, but she also hid it for a reason. She didn't want to cause problems with his friends, but she was definitely enjoying her time with Mason.

"Maybe you guys can do another competition for the rehearsal dinner. We're having it here, and we said we'd do dinner. What do you think?" Kyra suggested.

Megan was surprised they were doing something casual like that. She liked Kyra more and more as she learned about her. She wasn't surprised at all when Justin said, "That's a great idea. That'll be my wedding gift. A victory."

Kyra laughed and ran her hand over Justin's head. "Then I guess we better make sure we pick something you can cook."

"Hey! I'm a good cook!"

Kyra nodded solemnly. "Yes, honey. You're amazing."

Justin's eyes went wide at her stoic face followed by her laughter. "What are you saying?"

Kyra laughed again. "I'm just picking at you. But if you lose, you still have to marry me."

Justin pulled her onto his lap and kissed her sweetly. "You're the only thing I ever want to win."

"You already have me."

"Which means I won. So, I'm good. The rest is just for fun."

"Until you lose," Megan teased him.

Justin lifted his head and glared at her. "It's a good thing you have a place to stay because I'd put you out after a comment like that."

Megan laughed when Kyra swatted him. "How dare you say that! Megan, you are always welcome here."

"Thank you, Kyra," Megan said, sticking out her tongue at her big brother.

He stuck his out at her, and Kyra started laughing. "This is what I missed not having siblings. I never thought I'd get to witness it at this age."

"Be careful. You might get roped into the middle of it," Justin said.

Kyra smiled. "I'll take my chances."

Megan smiled as they kissed sweetly. She never had a relationship like that, and maybe it was the hormones, but she wanted one. She wanted someone who was going to share her good days and bad. Someone who would make her laugh. Someone who would be there for her, no matter what.

Maybe one day.

11

———

MASON FELT BETTER BEING AROUND THE ANIMALS AT THE shelter. None of them expected anything from him. They'd all been let down by people and the fact that they were indoors and well-fed meant more to them than who was taking care of them.

Mason was grateful to the owners of Best Friends Forever for giving him a chance years ago. For seeing past the beaten down man he was to the person he used to be and could become again. Mason doubted that man was still inside more than a few times, but working with the cats and dogs taught him more than how to exist in the real world. It taught him compassion and understanding and how to take care of others.

The dogs barked loudly when they heard Mason walk into the pen. Every spot was full with some divided up for the smaller dogs. He wondered how Megan felt about dogs and if she would want one when she had the baby. He shook his head and reminded himself she would make those decisions on her own and he had no say.

Mason spent the next hour cleaning out the dog pens

and taking his time to play with each of the dogs. When he was done with one-on-one time, he let the first group out into the yard to run around together.

"What are you doing here?" he heard from the doorway as he whistled for the dogs to run back in.

"Heads up!" Mason shouted back to Kelsea.

Kelsea laughed as the dogs rushed into the room and swarmed her. She dropped to the floor and rubbed all of them, letting them crawl all over her and lick her face.

"Need a hand?" Mason offered.

Kelsea shook her head. "Nope. I'm good. I'll help you get them back in, though. How are you?"

Mason nodded and avoided her gaze. Kelsea was good at sniffing things out, and he was sure she'd have some pointed questions for him if he wasn't careful about everything he said around her.

"Jaymes said you guys are working on a few cases right now. Sounds busy."

"It is. It's tough not having everyone focused on the same thing, but it's good to have more work. Dunn's talked about hiring some new help, but they're all still talking about it."

"You're not talking?" Kelsea asked.

"Nope. I'm the hired help, not one of the decision makers."

"You should say something. Buy in or whatever."

Mason shook his head again. "No. That's not what I want."

"You're still funding the scholarship?"

Mason nodded without meeting Kelsea's eyes. She was the only person who knew Mason donated most of his income to a scholarship in Megan's name. Her maiden name. Bernadette insisted the scholarship be set up using Megan's maiden name and not Mason's last name. It went to children who were victims of domestic violence, most of them children who ended up in foster care. The scholarships helped them pay for whatever they needed help with and offered access to a counselor once they turned eighteen and were no longer eligible for state supported aid.

"You should tell Dunn and the others about the scholarship. I bet they'd all want to help."

"There wouldn't be a scholarship if it weren't for me. They shouldn't have to donate. Bernadette would be so mad if she found out I was one of the donors. It would be worse if the company I worked for was also."

"I still think it's shitty that she set it up in Megan's maiden name. And that you can't tell her."

"Nope. But this year's recipients are all great kids, so it's worth it. I'm not doing it for the recognition. I do it because it's what would make Megan happy."

Mason took a deep breath and smiled to himself. He knew his wife well. He knew her every thought, sometimes before she was aware of it. He could have predicted how she would be as a mom and the kids she would have wanted to help with a scholarship.

He loved her. But she was gone. And another Megan was in her place.

"You okay?"

Mason forced a smile and nodded. He was far from okay, but he wasn't going to tell Kelsea.

"Jaymes and I were wondering if you wanted to come over for dinner. Maybe tomorrow. If you're not busy."

Mason's first thought was of Megan. Would she be okay with him going? Would she want to go with him? What would she do if he went alone? He didn't like the idea of not being with her over the weekend when she was heading back home in a few weeks, but Kelsea and Jaymes were his friends. He enjoyed getting together with them.

"You don't have to. Do you have a date or something?"

Mason shook his head. "No. Not really. I just…"

"Not really? What does that mean? You've always been emphatic that you aren't ready to date. Are you seeing someone?"

"No. She's a friend. It's not anything serious at all."

Kelsea took a step back and stared at Mason with wide eyes. Her dark ponytail swung with her sudden movement and her dark eyes stared him down until Mason squirmed. She could have had a career in interrogation.

"Do I know her?"

"No," Mason said quickly. Too quickly. Dammit.

"Who is she?"

"Kels. Don't."

"Why don't you bring her over tomorrow night. Come at six."

"I can't. She can't. It's not a good idea."

"Please tell me you aren't sleeping with someone's wife or girlfriend. Mason…"

"Seriously? Is that what you think of me?"

"No, but you're being really cagey here. If she's not someone's wife or girlfriend, what's the problem. It's not like any of the guys have a sister or something. Or any… one… No. Oh, Mason." She looked up at him with those big, brown eyes like the whimpering dogs all around them. "Slade's sister?"

"We're friends."

"Are you the friend she's staying with?"

"She showed up at my door."

"And you let her in?"

"No. She let herself in. I was… I was having a bad night,

and she caught me off guard. I didn't want to, but it happened. And afterward... I can't turn her away."

"Why not? It's not like you'd be sending her out into the street. She can go back to Slade's."

"There are things he doesn't know. Things she wants to keep private for now. Please, Kels. Trust me on this one right now. And don't tell anyone. I know you'll tell Jaymes, but don't say anything to anyone else."

Kelsea drew a breath and blew it out slowly. Mason watched as the wheels spun with questions, but she reined it in and nodded. "I'll keep your secret, but you have to promise me you will let Slade know at some point before the wedding."

Mason nodded. "I will. Megan told me he knew she was at my place when she showed up. I didn't realize he didn't until a few days later."

Kelsea snorted. "I think I might like her. You should bring her for dinner. She sounds like she's keeping you on your toes."

"She definitely is." Mason said with a laugh.

Kelsea studied him for a minute. "I've also never seen you smile like that. I think she's good for you."

"She has a life in Kentucky. She's going back to it after the wedding."

"But her brother lives here. And you're here. And—"

"When her brother finds out that she's been staying with me, I might not be here anymore."

Kelsea laughed, but Mason meant it. He had no idea how Slade was going to take the news that he'd been sleeping with his sister. Or that she was pregnant. He was fairly sure he'd get blamed for that one, and he'd take the blame, but he didn't want to see Megan hurt. No matter what happened, she was the one he cared about.

MEGAN WALKED into the bridal shop and looked around for someone she recognized. She was excited to say yes when Kyra asked, but she second guessed agreeing once she left. Megan debated canceling right up until Mason escorted her to his Jeep and drove her to the shop. He sat outside and waited for her to go in with a look in his eyes that promised he would walk her in himself if she pushed back.

He was starting to grow on her.

"Megan," Kyra called from the right side of the store.

Megan smiled and headed toward her, sure Mason was still watching her and would see her walking toward Kyra and leave. She knew if she glanced back, Kyra would ask who dropped her off. Megan wasn't ready for that yet. Plus, it was Kyra's wedding. She wasn't going to mess it up by admitting where she was sleeping every night.

"Have a glass of champagne and sit. I was just about to get dressed," Kyra said when Megan made it closer.

"Thanks," Megan answered with a smile. She looked at the others and thanked Kelsea for making space for her to sit.

"It's great that you're here. I was hoping to see you again soon," Kelsea said with a wide grin.

"Kyra wanted me to come. I'm still a little of an outsider, though."

Kelsea shook her head. "You don't have to be. Stick with us and we'll make you feel awkwardly inside everything. Too much at times."

Megan laughed and wondered about Kelsea. Was she that friendly, or was something else going on?

"How are you enjoying your visit?" Lily asked.

"It's nice. I've done some sightseeing and worked. I've been staying pretty busy."

"That's good. It's hard to sit around and be bored. Although with Howler there, I doubt you're too bored," Lily said with a smile.

"Megan isn't staying with us," Kyra said from the dressing room. "She's staying with a friend. I think we made her uncomfortable."

"No, you didn't," Megan argued.

"You two make me uncomfortable and I'm pregnant," Lily said with a laugh. "When Slade issues orders that using our keys is at our own risk of seeing something we don't want to see, it's hard to imagine staying under the same roof."

"Just wait until you have kids," Nikki called out. "That'll change. You'll have to get much more creative about your naked time."

"You and Ashleigh are going to need to give me some tips," Lily said. "I'm not sure how I'm going to survive six weeks after this one comes. If we have to take things down a notch, I might die. Of course, these days I feel so huge that it's getting harder to do anything."

Nikki chuckled. "The pregnancy hormones wear off once the baby comes. I don't think the six weeks are going to be an issue. You'll be so sleep deprived you'll be lucky if you know when you last showered let alone feel sexy enough to want sex."

"I always want sex," Lily said. "I mean, have you seen my husband?"

The others laughed with her.

"What about you, Megan? I'm guessing you didn't leave anyone behind in Kentucky, did you?" Nikki asked.

Megan forced a smile and shook her head. "Nope. I'm definitely single."

"We should get you a date for the wedding," Kelsea said. "Dex, English, and Mason are single."

"Leave the poor girl alone," Kyra said. Her voice was louder. "Let Megan enjoy single life. Not all of us are ready to run down the aisle. I mean, I am, but I wasn't before I met Slade."

Kyra stood up on the pedestal and smiled at her reflection. Megan's emotions got the better of her and tears filled her eyes and overflowed onto her cheeks.

"Wow," Megan whispered.

"Right?" Kelsea said. "The first time we saw her in that dress, we knew it was the one."

"My brother isn't going to be able to keep his hands off you," Megan said with a chuckle.

"I was hoping for that effect," Kyra said. Her dress had a satin and lace bodice with thick lace straps that stretched over her shoulders. The entire back of the dress was open to her waist. It was like an optical illusion where the dress looked like one tug and the whole thing would come off. Maybe it would.

"The dress is gorgeous. And you look amazing in it," Megan said.

"Thanks. I never thought something like this would look good on me, but it hits in all the right places to hide my belly and make my boobs look really good. Jenn needs to take up the hem just a little now that I have my shoes. They were the hardest thing for me to pick out."

Kyra lifted the skirt of the dress and showed off her purple lace sandals. They had three-inch heels and were definitely the kind of shoes a woman on a mission wore. Like a woman on her wedding night.

"Where did you get those?" Lily asked. "I need them to be my push present. For Archer."

Nikki and Kelsea laughed. "I don't think those would look good on Archer," Nikki said.

"Oh, she's not talking about Archer wearing them. She's talking about wearing only those when her six weeks are up," Kelsea said.

"What she said," Lily agreed. "If I think I'm bad, he's going to lose his mind. Six weeks. He won't last. Especially knowing it's going to be that long."

"Oh, my God," Megan laughed. "I've never had friends who talked like this."

"Sorry," Lily said. "Does it offend you? We can try to stop."

Megan shook her head. "No. You guys are great. I love it."

"Phew," Lily said. "I wasn't sure I'd be able to stop. I would try, but it was a tough promise to make."

Megan laughed. "I'm glad I came here."

"To the shop?" Kelsea asked.

"No. To visit in general. I wasn't sure about it, but I wanted to know the people Justin has been talking about. He loves it here. I miss him like crazy, but I get why he's here. Why he's not coming back to Kentucky."

"I moved up here from Tennessee last year. It's different, but it's a great place to live," Nikki said. "I can't imagine living anywhere else now."

"Have you thought about moving here?" Kelsea asked.

Megan wasn't sure how to answer the question. If she said no, she'd be lying, but if she said yes, they'd likely push for her to move. Not that she wasn't leaning that way, but she wanted to make the decision that was best for her and her child without anyone else's influence.

"I—"

"Hello, ladies," Archer said, walking into the bridal shop and looking freakishly comfortable in there. He looked comfortable no matter where he went.

"Hey, sexy," Lily said, standing to kiss him.

"How is everything going?"

"Good. Kyra is finishing up, and then she needs to change. Do we need to go?"

Archer shook his head. "Slade asked me to walk in and see how much longer. He's in the parking lot."

"Can he see me?" Kyra asked in a shrill voice.

"Nope. He doesn't want to. I told him it's even better when you wait to see what your bride looks like in the dress she chose to knock you on your ass." Archer grinned at Lily and leaned down to kiss her gently.

"She picked pretty well, didn't she?" Lily asked.

Archer looked at Kyra and smiled. "Definitely going to knock him on his ass."

"Good. Now go back out there and keep him outside. We'll be done soon. I love you," Lily said.

"I love you." Archer winked at her, then waved at the others and walked outside again.

Megan was getting sappy. All the couples around were making her want things she had no business wanting. Things she wasn't going to have anytime soon. She knew what she was giving up, but it didn't feel like a sacrifice. Not for a child. She'd hoped to have a family one day. This wasn't the way she planned to do it, but plans changed. She was going to love her child with every piece of her heart, and she was okay with that.

It was just her hormones that were making her wish she wasn't alone through it all. That she would have someone to share her child's life with.

Kyra went to change out of her dress, and Kelsea turned

to Megan again. "I don't want to put you on the spot, but if you did decide to move here, we'd love it. I've never had friends like these ladies before, and at first I was a little unsure about Lily, but she's one of the kindest people I've ever met. And everyone else... we met everyone else after Lily and I met and our group just gets better and better all the time. We have amazing friends."

"Are you thinking of moving up here?" Lily asked, catching the end of Kelsea's statement. "Because you totally should."

"You're in trouble if she's trying to talk you into moving," Nikki said. "She's the one who convinced me."

"You wanted to. You just needed a little push," Lily said. She leaned over and hugged Nikki.

"I've—"

"Oh, my God, what the hell?" Kyra asked as she walked out of the dressing room. "Why did Slade take a swing at Mason? Why is Mason even here?"

Megan turned in time to see her brother's fist connect with Mason's nose. She winced and turned back to the women. "I think that might be my fault. I've been staying with Mason."

"You what?" Kyra asked. "Megan..." She glanced at the others. "I..."

"Mason is an amazing man," Kelsea said. "I didn't know you two were friends before."

Megan shook her head. "We weren't. But when everyone came over, I met him and I... I was intrigued by him and one thing led to another and I've been staying with him."

"Doesn't he live in a studio apartment?" Lily asked.

Megan nodded.

Lily grinned. "Good for you. Mason's hot."

"Guys," Kyra said, drawing everyone's attention to her. "We have to tell her."

"Tell me what?" Megan asked.

Kyra looked at Kelsea, Lily, and Nikki, then back to Megan.

"Tell me what?" Megan repeated.

"Mason was married before. Years ago. Before any of us knew him. His wife... her name was also Megan, and she died. He killed her."

"He what?" Megan asked. "No. That's not possible."

Kelsea put her hand on Megan's arm and said, "It is. It was an accident, but it's true. But he's served his time, and he's a good man. He's one of us. Mason is one of the best people I know. Trust me."

Megan looked into Kelsea's eyes and knew she believed her words. But Kelsea wasn't sleeping with him. She wasn't sharing an apartment with him. She wasn't trusting him with her body, and her baby.

Megan knew there was a darkness to him, but she never expected it to be that dark.

She turned toward the window and saw her brother take another swing, and every fiber of her being told her exactly what she needed to do. Without question.

12

———

Mason parked at the back of the lot and tried his best to stay out of sight. He didn't want Megan calling for a ride back to his place, or for Slade to offer her a ride, so he showed up. But he wasn't sure how he was going to get her to his Jeep without drawing the attention of the others.

Slade parked near the front of the bridal shop and turned off his engine. Mason couldn't see what he was doing, but he kept an eye on the vehicle. With any luck, when Kyra was done, they would leave before either of them noticed Mason.

Archer pulled up next. He went to Slade's truck and spoke to him before going inside. Mason breathed a sigh of relief and slunk down in his seat even more. He kept his gaze on the door to the shop with an occasional glance toward Slade. So far, so good.

Archer walked back outside and looked around. Mason knew the exact moment Archer recognized his Jeep. He lifted a hand and waved, and Mason had no choice but to wave back.

Fuck.

Archer went over to Slade's truck and spoke to him. After a minute, Archer nodded toward Mason. He was done. He could either hide in his Jeep or try to do some damage control. If he wanted to keep his job, and his friends, damage control was a better option.

Mason got out and walked toward Slade's truck. Archer stepped back, letting Slade out of the driver's door.

"What are you doing here?" Slade asked in a voice that said he already knew but needed confirmation.

"We both know why I'm here."

"Humor me and answer the fucking question."

"I'm here to pick up Megan."

"And why would you be here to pick her up?"

"Because she's been staying with me."

Mason didn't have time to move before Slade swung at him. The first blow he avoided, but the second connected solidly with Mason's nose. Pain radiated across his face. Mason stumbled, but he refused to swing back. He should have been honest with Slade from the beginning, and he'd take whatever was coming to him.

Slade swung again, and Mason dodged the next swing. He moved around, not defending himself, but not willing to get his ass kicked, either.

Archer stood to the side, watching the entire thing. He wasn't helping either of them, which Mason took as a good sign. If Archer wasn't holding him down so Slade could beat the shit out of him, he knew Archer was willing to hear him out, even if Slade wasn't.

Slade's next blow grazed Mason's shoulder. He was using his anger, but he was sloppy. Mason was sure he could wait Slade out and avoid more damage. If he was lucky, Kyra was almost done and would drag him away.

"Justin!" Megan screamed.

Her voice drew Mason's attention enough that he turned to look at her. Almost immediately, the side of his face exploded with pain. He dropped to his knees and clutched his face. Blood seeped between his fingers.

"Stop it right now!" Megan shouted. "What the hell are you doing?"

"Him? You've been staying with him? You told me you were staying with a friend."

"He is a friend," Megan said firmly.

Mason could tell she was standing between him and Slade. She was protecting him from her own brother. Putting herself on the line. No one had ever done that for him.

"Megan. You should go home with your brother," Mason said. His voice was rough, the pain getting to him. He pushed himself to stand, ignoring the blood dripping down his face.

"No," Megan said, still using herself as a shield. "I'm staying with you. I want to stay with you."

"You need to come with me," Slade argued. He grabbed her arm.

Megan shook him off. "I'm an adult. I make my own choices. I don't know why you think you can still treat me like a child—"

"Because you're acting like one!" Slade shouted. "You don't know him. You don't know anything about him. And yet you're staying at his place. You didn't even know each other until the first night everyone came to my place. And you..." Slade leaned around Megan to glare at Mason. "I trusted you. I talked to you about my sister. I asked you if you thought she was doing okay. And you what? Took advantage of her? Decided to manipulate her into your bed?"

"I showed up on his doorstep," Megan answered. She walked forward with each statement, getting in her brother's face. "I went to him. When we met, I liked him. I was interested. He refused me. He told me no. But I wasn't willing to take no for an answer and showed up at his apartment. I convinced him to have sex. I talked him into letting me stay there. I did all this. So if you're going to get mad and punch someone, punch me, big brother. I'm the one to blame for all of this."

Slade glared at Mason, then slid his gaze to his sister. His eyes softened, and he reached for her. She swatted his hand away and crossed her arms.

"Megan, I want to protect you. I don't want you to get hurt. You're only here for a few weeks and then you're going home. Living with someone is going to make it harder to say goodbye. Harder to accept that whatever is happening is casual."

"Casual is all I want," Megan said firmly. "I'm not looking for permanent right now. I'm not a child, Justin. I'm a grown ass woman. And you don't get to tell me who I can and can't sleep with or spend time with or anything."

Mason stayed behind Megan, hoping she knew she had his support. He had a lot of regrets, but letting Megan inside that night wasn't one of them. She was smart and funny and clever. She made him laugh and brought him back to reality when he got inside his own head. The sex was amazing, but having a friend, someone to spend time with, that meant more to Mason than anything else. He hadn't had a friend like that since his wife.

Slade glared at Mason again and said, "You better not hurt her."

Mason nodded once, holding his friend's gaze. He understood what Slade wasn't saying. He would have been right there backing him up if he wasn't the one the words were directed at.

Slade turned around for the first time since Megan ran out and realized the attention they'd drawn. Kyra was on the other side of his truck, watching. His shoulders relaxed when he saw her. She nodded, and they both got in and left.

Mason didn't want anyone taking his side, so he walked toward his Jeep before anyone said anything. Megan spoke to the others before she joined him and held her hand out.

"You need to go to the hospital for stitches," Megan said.

Mason shook his head and immediately regretted the decision.

"Yes, you do. Maybe a CT, too. Nikki said so."

Mason glanced toward the others. Kelsea, Nikki, Lily, and Archer were all watching them. Archer had his arm around Lily's waist and whispered something in her ear. Lily nodded. Kelsea's face was pinched with worry. Nikki looked like she was about to walk over and demand he listen if he didn't hand his keys over to Megan.

Mason dropped the keys in Megan's palm and walked around to get in the passenger side. Megan started up the Jeep and waved to the others as she pulled out of the lot and drove toward the hospital. Mason was quiet on the ride. He wasn't sure what to say to her. He didn't mind that Slade got upset. And after almost a week of Megan staying with Mason, he had just as much of a responsibility to tell Slade as she did. Neither of them chose to do it.

"You and I might not be good together," Mason finally said as they pulled up to the ER.

"Why do you say that?" Megan put his Jeep in park and stared straight ahead, not looking at him. Her voice betrayed the calm exterior.

"Because we've barely known each other a week and been in the ER twice."

Megan breathed a laugh. "Both are my fault. I can get a ride and leave your Jeep here if you want me to go."

Mason stopped her before she got out of the Jeep. He held her wrist and waited until she looked up at him. "Thank you for driving me here. I'd really like it if you stayed with me. And not just for now, for as long as you'd like to stay."

Megan's eyes filled with tears, and she nodded. She wiped them away quickly before they fell, but Mason knew the whole thing was emotional for her, too. He didn't know where he stood with his job, but he had Megan. At least for now.

THE WAIT in the ER was long. The man at the desk gave Mason something to press against the cut on his cheek, but otherwise, they just had to sit and wait.

When someone finally called his name, Megan asked if she could go with them to the exam room. The nurse looked at Mason and said it was fine with him. He laid down on the hospital bed and told the nurse all the information she asked for. What happened? When did it happen? Did he fall or get any foreign matter in the wound?

When she was done with the documentation, she told Mason she wanted to take him up for a CT scan to rule out any other injuries. Megan could wait in the exam room.

She watched as Mason was wheeled out of the room and around the corner. Only then did she take a deep breath.

The adrenaline that was racing through her body since her brother took his first swing finally stopped flowing.

Megan was happy she was sitting down as the crash overwhelmed her. Her hands shook and the tears she was holding back streamed down her cheeks. A sob ripped free from her throat. She clamped her hand over her mouth, but not before someone heard her and walked in.

"Are you okay?"

Megan looked up and forced a smile. "Yeah. Sorry."

"You look familiar. Were you in here before? Are you doing all right?"

Megan finally recognized the nurse from the last time. The one who knew Mason. "Yeah, I am. Sorry. I didn't mean to bother you."

"You're fine. Do you need anything?"

Megan shook her head. She couldn't have the nurse sticking around. Mason would be back, and if the nurse was still there, it would not end well for them. "No. I'm good. Thank you, though."

She smiled and said, "If you do, let me know. I'll be here for another hour."

"Thanks."

The nurse left, and Megan drew in a breath. She wondered about her. And about Mason. And about his wife Megan. Did the nurse know his wife? Was she involved somehow? How did he kill his wife?

Megan didn't know anything about him. She liked that at first, but now she wondered if she was being reckless with her decision to show up at a stranger's door and demand he let her in. He was supposed to be safe because he was a friend of her brother's. But was he?

Megan was still trying to answer that question when Mason was wheeled back into the room. The nurse with him said he was all clear. She needed to stitch up his cheek, but otherwise, everything was fine.

Mason winced when she injected his cheek, but otherwise, he was still and quiet. Megan wondered what was going through his mind. She wondered if he would tell her the truth about his wife. She wondered if she really wanted to know.

"All set," the nurse said. "These are your discharge papers. You're good to go. Be careful."

Mason nodded and eased himself off the hospital bed. Megan stood and reached for his hand to help him. Mason looked at her and smiled. He wrapped his arm around her shoulders and thanked her for being there. He leaned on her the entire walk to his Jeep. She helped him inside and got into the driver's seat. She started the Jeep, then turned to him.

"We need to talk when we get home. To your place."

Mason nodded. "I know. I'm sorry about what happened with Slade."

"I don't need to talk about my brother. I need to talk about your wife."

Mason drew in a ragged breath, but he didn't deny anything. He held Megan's gaze and nodded. He knew.

Megan didn't believe she had any right to ask him personal questions, but she was putting her life in his hands. It was time she started asking.

She put the Jeep in gear and backed out of the space. She needed answers. She deserved answers. She just wasn't sure she was going to like them.

I WATCHED them walk out of the hospital together. The way he looked at her said she mattered. She was important to him. They got in his Jeep and talked for a minute before she drove off.

I needed to know what he knew, but I had no idea how to find out. It wasn't like we were friends or he would talk to me. But she mattered to him.

She parked in front of his building and went around to help him get out. She was big, but clearly strong if she could help hold him up. She wrapped her arm around his waist and he leaned on her. The stitches in his cheek and the bruising on his face said he'd been on the wrong side of an argument. If I knew anything about Mason, it was the other guy always looked worse.

Or girl.

Rage boiled through me, and I fought the urge to get out of my car and end him. He shouldn't be allowed to be happy. Not when others weren't. He was a killer. He admitted it. But he was free.

He looked at the woman he was with and smiled. His happiness grated on me. I imagined taking her from him. Bringing him to his knees. Taking away everything he had the way he'd done to others.

My phone buzzed with an incoming call. I checked the screen before I answered. "Yeah."

"Hey, boss. We have a problem."

I groaned. "Telling me we have a problem doesn't help anything. What is the problem?"

"Braden Wright isn't willing to play."

"What?" I barked.

"Braden Wright. The one who took Wray Allen's place?"

"I know who he is. What the hell do you mean he isn't willing to play?"

"He's refusing. Said he's not showing up. He wants nothing to do with it."

"Then we'll find another way to get the money Mr. Allen owes us."

"Like what?"

"I don't know what," I growled. "But we always have evidence that needs to vanish."

"Are you saying—"

"I'm saying there are ways to make people pay that have nothing to do with money. Get everything set up for the next game. I'll be there later."

"Okay, b—"

I hung up. I wasn't in the mood to listen to him any longer. I wanted to see what Mason and his woman were doing. And with the pictures I took, I could find out exactly who she was and what she was doing with him.

And how to get her to pay his debts.

13

Megan supported Mason as they walked to his apartment. She hated that he was hurt because of her. If she'd told her brother from the beginning, he might have handled it better. Instead, he figured it out and was hurt and pissed and took it out on Mason.

She was also a little surprised Justin didn't say anything about Mason's wife. She assumed, when the women told her, that would be Justin's biggest argument, but he never mentioned it.

Megan helped Mason to the couch and eased him onto it the best she could. He dropped and let his head fall back. He closed his eyes and pinched the bridge of his nose.

Megan busied herself getting him medicine for his pain and glasses of water for both of them. She tried to think about what they might eat for dinner since going to Kelsea and Jaymes's seemed out of the question after the day. In truth, she didn't want to sit and ask the questions she needed answers to because if she didn't like the answers, she was going to have to leave. And she didn't really want to leave.

"Megan, sit down," Mason commanded softly.

"I'm just—"

"Stalling," he said, opening one eye to meet hers.

She blew out a breath and nodded. Next to him on the couch was the only place she could sit. She wanted to look at him. To see his face while he told her about the woman he loved, and killed. If there was a chair, she would have chosen that instead, but—

"Get a chair from the table. Or I will. You sit on the couch. It's more comfortable." Mason got up and trudged to the table. He turned a chair around to face her and sat in it.

Megan hesitated, then sat on the couch. She leaned forward and clasped her hands in front of her. She had no idea how to start.

"I met Megan when I was in training," Mason said. Guess he knew how to start. "She was amazing. Bright and funny and smart. She always had a smile on her face. What she saw in me, I never knew, but I was thankful for it."

He smiled a private smile that had Megan feeling more than a little jealous.

"Training was tough, to say the least. She was out there for college and we ran into each other regularly. We talked and got to know each other, but we said we were friends because it was temporary. I was only there a few months and then I'd be sent wherever the Navy needed me."

Megan nodded. It sounded a little like their situation.

"We met on the beach one night. I was out for a run and she was upset about something. I don't even remember what it was now, but she was crying. We talked. For hours, it seemed. When we finally left, she kissed me, and I was done. I'd already started liking her, but when she first kissed me, I knew I'd never be able to see another woman." He winced and met Megan's gaze. "Sorry."

Megan shrugged as though she understood. Her throat was tight with jealousy and pain for what he'd lost.

"After that, we met up whenever we could. It wasn't much, but we tried. When I was done with training, I was sent to Florida. We kept in touch for another month while she finished her semester, then she transferred so she could live near me. I was deployed a few months later, but before I left, we got married. It was quick. We'd only known each other about six months, maybe less. We were young and dumb and in love, and we weren't willing to let anything or anyone stand in the way of our happiness."

Megan sucked in a breath and smiled. She wanted love like that. Love that was so powerful the idea of not being together hurt.

"My first tour was rough. I didn't really know what to expect, but it was hard on me. I tried to be normal when I came back, and for a while I was, but one tour became two and then three and by the time I was home for good, I barely knew who I was. I believed in what I was doing, but it wasn't easy. And coming home was harder."

Megan nodded. She really did understand that. She'd known enough vets to know they were asked to do things they wouldn't do under any other circumstance. Like Mason said, it was the right thing, but that didn't mean it was good.

"The night Megan died, I had a nightmare. I was exhausted from not sleeping and took a sleeping pill. The next thing I remember is the gunshot. It pulled me out of the numbness. It was loud. Loud enough that it broke through my nightmare or sleepwalking or whatever it was. I must have gotten my gun, and Megan found me. I think she might have tried to wake me up, but I didn't know she was there until the gun went off."

"Oh, God," Megan breathed. Tears streamed down her face. Her breath rushed in and out in stilted, shaky breaths.

"After the shot, I looked around, trying to figure out where I was. The gun was the first thing I saw. I stared at it. I remember wondering why it was in my hand. Then she said my name, and I realized she was lying on the floor in front of me."

Megan closed her eyes. She wasn't sure how much more she could listen to.

"I looked at her and wondered why she was on the floor. As I moved closer, I saw the blood. So much blood. I kneeled next to her and dropped the gun and tried to put pressure on the wound, but the blood didn't stop. I called nine-one-one. Megan shook and realization set in. Her eyes... God, I can still see the look in her eyes when she knew she was going to die. She still loved me. Even in that moment, when I took her life, she still loved me. She pulled me to her and kissed me. She was gone by the time I pulled back. I held her, and when the police showed up, I didn't want them to take her. Watching them put her on a stretcher and wheel her out of our home was... She was my best friend, and she was the best person I've ever known, and I'm the reason she's no longer here."

Mason finally looked up and met Megan's gaze. She wiped at her tears and tried to draw in a deep breath. Her hand rested on her belly. She hated herself for having a sliver of grateful that the first Megan was gone so she could be there with Mason. It wasn't fair. It wasn't right. But it was the truth. She... cared about him. She was more herself with him than she'd ever been with another person. She wasn't ready to let that go. And she didn't want to let him go.

Mason was a good man. She knew that from the

moment she met him. Sure, he had a past, and it was dark, but Kelsea said he paid his dues. Which meant...

"Did you go to jail?"

Mason drew a shaky breath and nodded. "The police questioned me. I told them what happened. At first, they let it go. But Megan's sister... do you remember the nurse? Bernadette?"

Megan nodded.

"She's Megan's sister. She showed up at her funeral with the police and insisted they arrest me. They said they didn't have a choice for whatever reason and brought me in. A different detective questioned me and determined I was aware enough of the situation to have been conscious of what I was doing. I was so... raw and hurt that I didn't care what happened to me. The only person who mattered was gone, so I was no longer important. I pled guilty and was sentenced to forty years to life."

"Are you... How did you...?"

"I was required to see a therapist. I hated it, but after a few years, some of the rage and pain eased and I started talking. A few more years and my therapist went to court for me. He said I was not of my right mind that night. That I had PTSD that caused me to detach from reality. He argued that I was serving a sentence for something I had no recollection of committing and I would likely never remember it. That I was mentally unstable at that point, and that in the years since, I'd worked on myself and I was at a point where I should be released."

"And they let you out?"

Mason shook his head. "No. The judge didn't agree. But my therapist kept arguing. He went back time and again and worked with a new lawyer and they got my sentence reduced."

"Wow."

Mason nodded. "I haven't had an episode in years. I still talk to my therapist regularly. I know what sets me off and avoid alcohol and stress. I would never have let you stay here if I thought I might hurt you. I should have told you about Megan, though. I should have given you all the facts so you could make the decision for yourself."

"The night I came here. You had a bottle of scotch."

Mason nodded slowly.

"I haven't seen you touch it since."

Mason shook his head.

"Was that... What happened?"

"I saw Bernadette at the grocery store that night. She was behind me in line and tried to get the manager to call the police on me. She brought back a lot."

"So, you bought a bottle of Scotch?"

Mason drew a breath and nodded. "I dumped it down the drain the next morning."

"You did?"

He nodded again.

"Why?"

He shrugged. "Because I knew drinking it would be bad for me. I knew if you hadn't shown up when you did, I could have ended up in jail again. Or dead. I didn't want that. And I didn't want to hurt you, or the baby."

Megan knew trusting her gut was always the right move. It never steered her wrong. She trusted it when she went to Mason's that first night. When she told him about the baby. When she stood between him and her brother earlier that day.

And she trusted it again as she got up from the couch and walked over to him. He leaned back in his chair and watched her. He barely moved as she got closer. She reached for his hand, and he closed his eyes. He finally put his hand in hers and she tugged him to his feet.

Megan took his face in her hands and tilted it down so he had to look at her. She waited until he opened his eyes and then said, "You're a good man, Mason."

He closed his eyes again.

"Look at me."

He drew a breath and looked at her.

"You're a good man. Megan wanted to share her dying breath with you because she knew that. She didn't blame you or hate you. She loved you. And you've beaten yourself up for years because of one moment. One painful, heart-breaking, world-crushing moment. But it was one moment. All the moments before that one told Megan who you were. And all the moments after have helped shape who you've become. And you're a good man."

He shook his head.

"You would not have killed her on purpose. And you've done everything you can to help me since I've been here. I didn't give you a choice, but you've taken care of me. You could have dropped me off on my brother's doorstep on the way back from the hospital and avoided me for the rest of my trip, but you didn't. You took care of me, of us. Because you're a good man."

"I didn't deserve her, and I don't deserve you."

"Probably not, but that doesn't change that you're a good man."

He chuckled, and she slid her arms around his neck and pulled him closer. He wrapped his arms around her waist and held her tight. Shoulder to hip, their bodies pressed against each other. Megan needed to feel him, to hold him, to know he was there with her. She stroked the back of his neck and smiled against his chest when he took a deep breath and his body finally relaxed into hers.

Megan tilted her face up and kissed the exposed edge of his neck. His fingers tightened on her lower back. She licked his collarbone, and his cock twitched against her stomach. She nipped at his Adam's apple, and he groaned.

"Megan."

"I trust you, Mason."

He pulled back from her and stared into her eyes. She stood still and let him look at her. She wanted him to know the words weren't just empty words. She meant them. She knew it would hurt when things ended between them, but not because Mason was anything less than a good man. She knew it would hurt because she let herself care about him. She let him into her heart. She thought of him as a friend, but he was more than that.

He was important to her. He was special. And he was someone she could see herself falling for if she wasn't careful.

Mason leaned forward slowly, giving Megan plenty of time to back away. She didn't move, she just let him come to her. She let him close the distance between them and press his lips to hers. They both sighed at the contact and parted their lips to taste each other.

Megan couldn't remember the last time she made out with a man like she was with Mason. They stood together and kissed like teenagers first figuring out how much fun kissing could be. They tilted their heads one way, then the other. They licked and sucked each other's tongues. They teased and tested each other.

Their hands stayed put, hers around his neck and his on her waist. They focused on their kiss. Gentle pecks when they pulled back to catch their breath, then deep, passionate kisses when gentle wasn't enough. With each kiss, Megan knew walking away from Mason was going to be nearly impossible. She wanted someone like him in her life, but more than that, she wanted him in her life.

His hands slid lower on her waist and teased the edge of her pants. His fingertips caressed her skin. Megan loved the feel of his rough hands on her body. She couldn't get enough of him.

Mason walked them toward his bed, keeping their lips together the entire time. Megan couldn't remember the last time she was so turned on from just kissing a man. Usually they rushed to the endgame, skipping over a few steps. Kissing was quickly becoming her favorite part of sex. Kissing Mason was like having sex. It was sensual and passionate. He knew how to make her thighs clench with need and her pulse race and her heart pound. Megan was going to hold on to the memories of Mason for years as she turned herself into a nun while she raised her child alone.

They stopped before they made it to the bed, and Mason took a step back. He looked at her and licked his lips. "Megan..."

"Mason."

He smiled. "I don't want you to feel like anything has to happen. I will take you to Slade's right now if you want. Or the middle of the night. Tomorrow. Any time. I don't ever want you to feel like you're stuck here. Or that anything has to happen. I—"

"Mason, I know. And I appreciate you saying all that, but I want to be here. I'm the one who showed up. I'm the one who forced my way in. I'm the one who didn't give you a choice. I want to be here."

"There was a lot you didn't know about me when you came here that night. I don't want you to think I'm going to get mad if you want to leave. I don't know what you read or heard or whatever—"

"What do you mean?"

He shrugged. "You obviously found out about Megan from somewhere. I don't want you to worry—"

"Kyra and the others told me when we saw you and Justin fighting. Kyra saw it and asked why you two were fighting, and I said it was my fault. She told me, but Kelsea insisted you're a good man. They all did. But they wanted me to know the whole story. They wanted me to know about Megan."

"I wondered," Mason admitted. "I should have told you, but I haven't been involved with anyone since, and I didn't plan on this. I—"

"Mason, stop. I trust you. I'm not here because I think I can't leave or because I worry you're going to do something if I do. I'm not here because of some misguided sense of respect or whatever. I'm here because you're a good man, and because we're friends, and because I like you. A lot."

He met her gaze, and a smile quirked up the edge of his lips. "You do?"

Megan chuckled. "Yes, I do. I like kissing you and touching you and feeling you inside me. I like watching movies with you and having dinner with you and talking to you. I like being here because I like you."

He moved closer and slid his arm around her waist. "Well, that's good because I like you, too. A lot."

Megan grinned and reached for him. He went willingly toward her and wrapped her in his arms again. Right where she wanted to be.

14

MASON WASN'T SURE WHAT HE DID TO DESERVE HER IN HIS life, but he wasn't going to question it. It was temporary, and he was going to enjoy every minute of it. Megan was a beautiful woman who wanted to spend time with him. He was a lucky son of a bitch, and he was not going to complain.

She laughed as he nibbled on her neck. He pressed the flat of his tongue over her collarbone and she moaned softly. He loved that sound.

Mason lifted her shirt up and trailed his fingers over her round stomach. He wondered what it would be like when he could tell she was pregnant. He wanted to feel her baby move, to hold her hand while it kicked.

He brushed his hand around to her back and pushed the thoughts from his mind. He wouldn't be around for that. He wasn't the baby's father, and he wasn't going to see Megan when she was that far along. Their relationship was temporary, and he needed to remember that.

Megan grabbed his shirt and pulled it up, exposing his entire torso. She pressed her body to his. He groaned at the feel of her bare skin on his. He reached back and yanked his shirt off, then lifted hers off her also. He leaned down and buried his face between her breasts, breathing in her scent and kissing the soft mounds.

"Are you going to let me taste you again?" Mason asked.

Megan moaned softly. "Maybe."

"I hope so. I enjoyed that. I love licking you and sucking you. I love tasting your come and watching your body move."

"Me, too."

"Good. What else do you like?"

"I like feeling you inside. And feeling you let go. I like knowing you can't hold back with me."

"You make me feel too damn good."

"Me, too," she said with a smile.

"Then I think we're both wearing far too many clothes."

"Me, too."

He chuckled and hooked his thumbs in her waistband. He slid her pants and panties to the floor, kissing her mound and her belly as he stood back up. He dropped his jeans and briefs and stepped out of them. She unhooked her bra and added it to the pile of discarded clothes before they both moved to the bed.

"Lay down," Mason commanded.

She did as he asked.

"Spread your thighs for me." He licked his lips as she quickly followed his instructions. "Can I taste you?"

She nodded.

Mason growled as he laid on the bed and positioned himself between her thighs. He licked her skin and loved the way she squirmed. He pressed her legs wider and parted her folds so he could watch as her body tightened, already begging for him.

"Please," she whispered.

"Don't worry, I'm not going to make you wait long." He trailed one fingertip through her wetness and sucked it into his mouth. She moaned, and he looked up to find her watching him. Mason grinned, then lowered his mouth to lick her, keeping his eyes locked on Megan's.

Her moan was long and loud. Her eyes rolled back and her head fell to the pillow. She arched her back.

Mason used his tongue to build her up slowly. He wanted her orgasm to last as long as possible. He licked her with the flat of his tongue, only sucking on her enough to make her entire body tight. Every time he released her, she sighed with frustration. He grinned against her flesh, waiting for the right moment to send her over the edge.

Mason slid one finger into her channel and stroked her slowly, his pace matching that of his tongue. She wiggled and writhed on his bed, her body begging for her release. His cock pressed against the mattress, as ready as she was, but he ignored himself and focused on her. He wanted to watch her come apart.

"Please," she said again, the desperation in her voice clear.

Mason increased his pace, earning a skip in her breath and a tightening of her body. He sucked on her clit a little longer and added a second finger. She was close. He could feel the ripples inside her, the tension building as she rushed closer to losing her mind.

Her breath pulsed out of her as quickly as the muscles of her channel pulsed around his fingers. He waited until she was panting to push. He added a third finger, stretching her body wider so she was ready for him. He flicked her clit, then sucked hard and sent her screaming over the edge.

Mason didn't let up as Megan flooded his hand. He licked and sucked and groaned at the flavor of her on his tongue. He needed more from her, and he was going to get it. He bit her gently, testing her body, and she nearly came again. He curled his lips back and let her feel his teeth as he sucked hard on her once more.

"Oh, God. Mason! Yes. Oh, fuck, yes!"

Her body shook and flailed with the power of her orgasm. She was barely aware of what was happening, the glazed look in her eyes unfocused but blissful.

Mason felt like a god. He was the king of orgasms. He removed himself from between her thighs and grabbed a condom. He had it rolled on and was back between her legs, ready to slide into her, before her eyes met his.

"My God, that was amazing."

"Yes, you are," he said. Every day, she amazed him. Her strength and confidence and the person she was. She was stunning. And with her blonde hair spread on his pillow and her body wrapped in his sheets, he wondered how he would ever sleep in his bed without her.

He wasn't ready to think about that. Not yet. Not when he still had time with her.

"Come here," he said, encouraging her to lift up to kiss him. She propped herself up on her hands and let him meet her halfway. She groaned when he pressed his tongue into her mouth, giving her a taste of herself.

Mason moved next to her and laid on his back. She looked at him like he was crazy. "What are you doing?"

"I want you on top. I want to watch you. Take what you need from me."

Her face softened. "I just need you."

He leaned over and kissed her again, stuffing down the emotions her words brought up. He needed her, too. She was healing him, something he never thought was possible. She was letting him be himself, letting him be a man again.

She pushed him back as they kissed and climbed on top of him. She laid down on him to keep kissing him, but shifted after a minute and sat up.

"I don't think my body liked that," she said, staring at her stomach. "I felt something weird."

"Are you okay?" Mason asked. "The baby?"

Megan nodded. "I don't hurt or anything. It was like my body was saying not to do that. Sorry."

"We can move if you want to. Or stop."

She shook her head. "I don't want to. Let's see if this works. Help me line up."

She lifted up on her knees and leaned to one side. Mason reached between them and slid a finger into her. She moaned and shook her head. He grinned, then grabbed his erection and eased her onto it.

They both groaned when her body met his. Her eyes closed. "Holy shit. You feel so damn good."

"God yes," Mason agreed.

Then she moved, and his eyes rolled back in his head. Every lift of her body had her tightening around him, grabbing hold and not letting him go. When she slid back down, the friction of their bodies and the wet press of her against his had him ready to blow.

With each stroke, she moved faster, the sensation sending her spiraling as quickly as he was. Her hands slapped onto his chest so she could use him for support. She leaned over, unable to hold herself up.

Mason grabbed her hands in his and lifted her up. The change had her body tightening around him. She moaned loudly and fucked him harder. Faster.

He clenched his jaw and did everything he could to hold back. She was close, and he was going to make sure she got there before he did. He didn't matter. Only she did. He needed her to feel good. He needed to know he gave her something, even if it was only sex.

She whimpered, her strength fading as her orgasm slipped away. Her movements were jerky, her body tense.

"Touch yourself," Mason said roughly. "Finish yourself off."

She shook her head.

"Let me see you, Megan. Let me watch how you like to come. Let me feel you come with my cock inside you."

She sucked in a breath, then released his hand. She eased it between her thighs, like she was afraid of what he would think.

"That clit needs you. Touch it. Rub it hard. Yes, there you go," he said. His eyes were glued to where her fingers spread her apart and brushed over her clit. She was tentative for a second, then she moaned and forgot all about him watching.

"Yes," she said softly. "Oh, God. Fuck me."

Mason thrust up into her while she held herself still. Her strength was all but gone. Her forearm twitched with her movements. Mason couldn't stop watching her rub her clit. His cock was full, ready to burst, but he was mesmerized.

Her fingertips brushed his cock, and they both moaned. "Fuck, Megan."

"Yes," she moaned. "Oh, yes."

Her strength left her, and she whimpered. Mason took over, using his free hand to press hard against her clit. He held her fingers there and rubbed fast, not letting slow happen again. Neither of them could take slow. They needed fast. They needed now. They needed—

"Oh, fuck, yes!"

Her channel locked around him and pulsed as she came

hard. Her body shook as her orgasm claimed her. He thrust hard into her, finally letting himself go, and followed her right over the edge.

"Megan!" he shouted, every cell of his body knowing for the second time in his life he'd fallen for a beautiful, curvy woman named Megan.

She collapsed onto him, and he immediately rolled them so she wasn't lying on her stomach. They faced each other, their bodies soaked with sweat. Their breath panted together. She had a blissful, sleepy smile on her face. He kissed her forehead and watched her as she drifted to sleep.

Mason didn't want to get up, but he did anyway. He got rid of the condom, then sat on his couch and watched Megan sleep. He told her about his wife, and she said she trusted him. She wasn't willing to walk away. She didn't want to walk away. She was still there, in his bed, sleeping off the amazing orgasms they shared.

Mason didn't set out to fall for her. He thought that part of him was broken, shattered. But she put all the pieces back together. She made him feel whole again. She showed him that there was still a man inside who was worthy of love. Maybe even worthy of her.

He drew a deep breath and debated telling her what he was thinking, but he shook his head at himself. She was clear from the start that she had no interest in anything outside of sex and friendship. They were good. And she was leaving after Slade's wedding. He wasn't going to mess up her life.

Mason sent Kelsea a quick text that Megan was sleeping and they probably would not make dinner. He promised to reschedule with them. She asked if they were okay, and he assured her they were.

Then he put his phone down and crawled into bed with

Megan. She curled against him and wrapped her arm around his waist. She settled her head on his shoulder and threw her leg over his. Before he knew it, he was snoring. Blissful. Sleepy. With Megan at his side.

MEGAN IGNORED her brother's calls and texts for the rest of the weekend. When Kyra sent her a text asking her to let them know she was okay, she replied and said she was fine, just needed a day. Kyra thanked her, and her phone went silent after that.

Monday morning was different. Mason got up and headed into work, which left Megan alone in his apartment. She'd been there alone so much that it didn't phase her. Until there was a knock on the door.

She wasn't sure if she should open it or not. She didn't live there. Whoever was there was not there for her. But she felt guilty not answering the door. There was no peephole for her to check who was outside, and finally, she just opened it.

To her scowling big brother.

"What are you doing here?" Megan asked. She crossed her arms and leaned back.

"I need to talk to you."

"About what?"

Justin ran a hand over his jaw and took a breath. "Can I take you to breakfast?"

Megan tilted her head and studied her brother. He was the knock down doors, punch the bad guy, kick ass and take names type. He wasn't the out to eat and talk type.

"Why?"

"Because I want to talk to you, and Kyra said I have to be nice if you're going to listen to me."

Megan breathed a laugh and shook her head. "I think I might love my soon-to-be sister-in-law."

Justin scowled. "Me, too, but unless we talk, I don't think she's ever going to be your sister-in-law."

"Why? What did you do?"

Justin kicked the ground and shook his head. "I didn't do anything."

"Uh huh. Just like you didn't break my doll when I was four?"

He looked up at her with a glare. "I apologized for that."

"After Mom and Dad forced you to admit you did it."

He groaned. "If you won't come out, I'm going to come in."

Megan grabbed her purse and ushered him out. The last thing she needed him to see was how tight the apartment was and how impossible it was for her and Mason to not share everything. Especially since she wasn't entirely sure where her panties ended up the night before.

Justin drove them to a small diner not far from his office. He didn't say much until they were seated and had both ordered. Then he met her gaze and asked, "Why Mason?"

Of all the questions, that was one Megan didn't expect. And one she didn't have an answer to. She shrugged. "Why not?"

Justin shook his head. "I don't have anything bad to say about Mason. Kyra told me she told you about his wife. Honestly, that never crossed my mind. He's a good guy."

"But?"

Justin shrugged. "You're my little sister."

Megan gestured to her figure. "I'm not exactly little."

Justin scowled at her. "I hate when you talk about yourself like that."

Megan's cheeks warmed. "I... Jeez, we can either talk about how fat I am or talk about Mason. Is there a door number three?"

Justin chuckled. "Well, I don't want to talk about your weight because I don't think it's a problem."

"Which means you think me being with Mason is a problem. Good to know."

"Megan, you came up here for a few weeks. To visit. And after a few days you tell me you're going to stay with a friend, then I find out you're not staying with a friend, you're screwing one of my teammates."

"And I'm not allowed to?"

"He's almost fifteen years older than you. Aside from the fact that he's been married before, and he killed his wife, he's a lot older than you. He's a friend of mine. He's someone I have to trust with my life. And you're sleeping with him and standing between us to defend him."

"Because you were being an ass. You have no right to tell me I can or can't sleep with whomever I want. You never did. I love you, big brother, but I'm not turning over my life choices to you."

"I've made a lot of mistakes," Justin said quietly. He leaned forward and rested his forearms on the table. He folded his hands in front of him and looked up at Megan. "I have regrets. Lots of them. The biggest one was leaving when you were so young. I wanted to protect you from everything, and I wasn't around to do that. But I am around to protect you from this."

"From what?" Megan asked. Was there something else she didn't know about Mason? She tucked her hair behind her ear and bit the inside of her lip. She wasn't sure she could take more surprises.

"I don't want you to get hurt. Mason isn't a forever kind of guy. He's never dated anyone. I've never even seen him with a woman. He's private and isolated. I trust him with my life, but he's not the kind of guy I'd want you involved with because he's going to hurt you."

Megan drew a breath and blew it out slowly. She wasn't sure how to respond to her brother without making him mad.

The server gave her an extra minute when he brought over their breakfast. Justin dove into his without noticing that Megan was sitting there, unmoving, debating her next words.

"When you left, I was crushed. I thought I'd done something wrong. I was hurt and upset. That first year, school was hard. Kids were always mean to me, but everyone knew you were my brother and it would mean bad things if they messed with me. When you were gone, I got picked on even more. I learned to make jokes before they could. I taught myself to hold back my tears until I was in the bathroom alone. I stopped trying to make friends."

"Megan..."

She shook her head and straightened her shoulders. "I hated it, but I survived. The shittiest part was I thought things would be better when I left high school. That people would accept me in college, and when that didn't happen, I thought maybe when I had a job. But it's never happened. People take one look at me and see fat. They see a woman who doesn't care about herself, has low self-esteem, and is an easy target. I don't have friends. I don't have people I can turn to. I don't have anyone in my corner."

Justin opened his mouth, but she held up her hand.

"Not in town. Mom and Dad are great, but they're not going to tell my coworkers to stop being mean to me. And I wouldn't want them to. And I know you're always here for me, but it's different when you're here and I'm there. I wanted to come up here because I wanted to spend time with you and get to know Kyra and—"

"Mason?" Justin spat.

Megan groaned and resisted the urge to slap her brother. "Mason... I didn't plan on Mason. I didn't plan on meeting him or being with him. That night at your house, he saw me. He looked at me. He didn't immediately dismiss me because I'm not skinny. I wanted to feel attractive. I wanted to be desired. I'm thirty years old and I haven't been a virgin in a long time, but I never had a man really look at me like he couldn't wait to be with me until I met Mason. That's why I went to his apartment. And that's why I haven't left. And I don't really give a shit if you're mad about that."

15

MEGAN LEANED BACK ON HER SIDE OF THE BOOTH AND GLARED at her brother. She had no idea what he was going to say. She half expected him to drag her to the airport and put her on a plane home.

"I'm sorry," he said instead.

She narrowed her eyes at him, not understanding.

"I should have been there for you. Then and now. And men... men suck. Many of us can't pick a decent woman to save our lives. A few of us luck out and end up with amazing women who kick our asses and don't let us walk away. Things weren't easy for Kyra and I. I fucked it up over and over again, and I still do all the time. But I'm one of the lucky ones because she hasn't given up on me yet." He drew a breath. "I still think you're too young for Mason, but I'm not going to tell you you shouldn't be happy. I want that for you."

Megan shook her head. "I'm not falling in love with Mason. He's a good guy, but I'm... I don't live here. I like him a lot, but I'm not kicking his ass and holding on tight. We're enjoying each other for now. I guess we both needed to know there's someone out there who sees us for who we are."

Justin reached for her hand and squeezed it. "Good. And for the record, I really do like Mason."

Megan nodded. "I know. And I think he knows, too. Although the black eye you gave him might not have him agreeing to that statement right now."

"How bad is it?"

Megan shrugged. "It's bruised, but he doesn't complain. You know how he is."

Justin nodded. "Yeah. He never says anything bad about anyone, and he doesn't ever bitch. The rest of us are always moaning about something, but Mason just goes with it all."

"I think he feels like he's an outsider. He told me you were going to fire him when you found out."

"Why would I fire him?" Justin asked.

"Because of me. I lied when I went to his house and told him you knew where I was going. When I showed up for lunch and he realized you didn't know, he told me I needed to tell you or you were going to fire him. He's still an outsider in his mind. He's not one of you. And you might not think of him that way, but he does."

"Mason is one of us. He's a part of the team. None of us see him as someone different."

"I think you need to tell him that."

Justin drew in a breath and nodded. "Thanks. I will. And no more secrets."

Megan forced a smile and nodded. She wasn't ready to tell him about the baby or that she was thinking of moving, but she'd get there, eventually. Aside from those two pieces of news, she could promise not to keep anything from her brother.

They finished their breakfast and talked about less

emotional topics, like Justin's upcoming wedding. He rolled his eyes when she asked him about the whole thing, and she laughed when he told her all he cared about was the bar.

"And Kyra?" Megan asked.

Justin's face softened. "Always Kyra."

After breakfast, he dropped Megan back off at Mason's apartment. She waved as he drove out of the parking lot, then turned to go to Mason's apartment. She was about to reach for the handle when someone said, "Excuse me. Do you live here?"

Megan turned toward the man and smiled. "No, I'm visiting a friend."

"Oh, I'm sorry. I was wondering if— Wait, don't I know you?"

Megan shook her head and backed up toward the door. "I don't think so."

"No, I do. You were with Mason O'Connor one night. I saw you getting pizza. I'm Leo."

Megan vaguely remembered him, but she definitely remembered the cold reception Mason gave him. And the creepy feeling she got from the man. "Oh, yeah. Nice to see you again."

"You are?"

She raised her eyebrows at his outstretched hand. She debated with herself, but his smile never faded and his hand never faltered. "Megan."

"Really?" Leo rubbed his chin and studied her. "I thought his wife died."

"I'm not his wife. And she did."

"So Mason found himself another beautiful Megan. What are the odds?"

"I guess pretty good. Listen, I need to run, but it was good to see you again, Leo."

"Tell Mason I said hello, will you?"

Megan smiled and let herself into Mason's apartment. She closed and locked the door, then peeked out the window to see if Leo was gone. She breathed a sigh of relief when she saw him walking to a white truck in the parking lot.

She needed to find out who he was, and stay away from him.

MASON WAS SITTING in his office when Slade walked in and closed the door. He straightened and waited. It was what he'd been waiting for. Slade would tell him he was fired, and Mason would have to find a new place to call home. Maybe he could go back to Kentucky with Megan. No one knew him there. He could start over.

He nearly laughed at himself for the thought. Megan didn't want him hanging around. Guess brother and sister were of the same mind.

"You thought we would fire you," Slade said. It wasn't a question.

Mason nodded once.

"Why would we fire you?"

"There's a code, and I broke it."

"What code?"

"Don't fuck with a teammate's family."

Slade took a breath and shook his head. "When we went after Williams, he broke the code. He kidnapped Jaymes and then Lily. He tried to blow up an entire city. He killed one of our own while we were still serving. He broke the code. I'm not thrilled you're with my sister, but I don't think it would matter who she was dating, I wouldn't like him."

Mason wasn't sure if that was a compliment or not so he sat still.

"Megan hasn't had it easy. Especially with men. She said you... you make her feel like she's special. Thank you." Slade held Mason's eyes as he said the words.

Mason nodded. "She is special."

"I know that, but I'm her brother. I'm supposed to think she's special. Most men aren't as smart as me."

Mason chuckled with Slade.

"It'll take me a little while to accept it, but I'm not going to stand between you."

Mason nodded. "Thank you. And I know she's going back to Kentucky. I'm not going to do anything to mess with her life."

Slade nodded as he got up. "You know your past has nothing to do with my hesitation, right?"

Mason shrugged. "It's hard to imagine it wouldn't, but I was surprised you didn't tell her the other day."

Slade shook his head. "I know that was an accident, and I know you'd never hurt my sister, or anyone else, on purpose. But you are what, thirteen, fourteen years older than her?"

Mason nodded slowly. "Almost fourteen, yeah. But she doesn't seem that young. She's an amazing woman."

Slade narrowed his eyes and nodded. "Yes, she is."

Someone knocked loudly on the door. Slade turned and opened it, stepping back when Dex nearly ran into him.

"Sorry. I need Mason. I got a call from Captain Patrick. We need to go. Now."

Slade stepped out of the way as Mason hurried after Dex. It wasn't until they got into the SUV before Dex took a breath and told him what was going on.

"Allen's back to work today. They went out on a call and

he was driving. He made a wrong turn and got to the scene late. Two firefighters ended up trapped inside the blaze. Both are headed to the hospital."

"Okay? Why does this matter?" Mason asked.

"Because if these firefighters die, they could charge Allen with murder."

"For making a wrong turn?"

"If he did it on purpose? Yeah."

"Oh, shit," Mason said.

"Exactly."

Mason was quiet as Dex drove to the scene. His mind was racing with everything Slade said, but kept bouncing to what Dex said. Could Allen really have made a wrong turn on purpose? Would he have risked the lives of other firefighters? And why?

Dex couldn't park close to the fire, so he pulled over on a side street and they walked around the block. There was a barricade up with an officer stopping anyone who tried to go through.

"Captain Patrick called and asked for us to come. Ryker Hamilton and Mason O'Connor."

The young officer spoke into his radio and waved them through after confirmation from the captain. Dex walked like he knew where he was going, so Mason followed behind him and he took in everything they went by.

The fire still blazed in a large warehouse. Several others nearby had trucks parked in front with hoses pointed toward the exterior that faced the one on fire. Thick, black smoke filled the air above them and blocked the sun.

Dex headed straight for Captain Patrick. He was off to the side, speaking to Wray Allen. They were almost there when Braden Wright stepped in front of them.

"We need to talk," he said, staring at Dex.

Dex nodded.

"Not here. I'm working."

Dex handed him his card. Wright stuck it in his pocket and turned back to the fire. He jogged away, leaving Mason and Dex to exchange a glance.

"Gentlemen," Captain Patrick said, drawing their attention. "Thank you for coming."

Mason hung back just enough to be able to observe what was happening while Dex spoke to Captain Patrick and Wray Allen. Patrick explained that two of Allen's teammates accused him of taking the long way on purpose. A firefighter has the responsibility to go the most direct way to a fire, unless it is absolutely out of the question. They're saying he made a bad call and cost the other stations valuable time. This is a four alarm blaze, and when it's this big, time can't be wasted."

"I didn't waste time. But I am sitting out here with you instead of in there taking this thing down," Allen argued.

"Your teammates don't trust you right now, Mr. Allen. They don't want you in there with them."

"Then let me work with Braden. He knows me. He knows I'm not going to do anything that will risk someone's life."

Dex and Patrick exchanged a glance. Patrick shook his head. Mason took that to mean they couldn't let him go, but after Braden approached Dex, he wasn't entirely sure. It could mean Braden was one of the firefighters who reported him.

Every group had their own code. Rules for the group to make sure everyone was safe. When lives were on the line, it was necessary, even if the rules weren't always spelled out. Allen broke one of those rules. Maybe more than one. What Mason was trying to figure out was if Wray did it on purpose, if he was aware of it, or if he was just off his game after being away for so long. The man's bruises had faded but were still visible. He moved like his other injuries were healed, although that was a surprise after only a few days. Mason figured Allen would be out of the game for at least a month, but he was driving the truck and ready to fight a fire.

If he could find a partner.

"Have you been to this area before, Mr. Allen?" Dex asked.

"Yeah, sure. We get called here every so often."

"Have you ever been down here when you weren't working?"

"No," he said with a chuckle. "Why would I come down here?"

Dex shrugged. "I don't know. I've never been down here. I'm just asking about you."

"No," he said firmly. He glared at Dex. "I've never been down here."

"What route did you take from the fire station?"

Wray scoffed. "I thought I took the best one. No one said anything. We got here, and they went nuts. Two guys were trapped, but how was that my fault?"

"I don't know. How would that be your fault?"

"It's not," Wray said. He continued to glare at Dex, arms crossed.

Confrontational. Defensive. Angry. Mason studied a lot of people, especially when he was in jail. He learned to read body language. It got him out of more than one mess. Wray's body language said he was hiding something. Mason didn't know what it was, but something wasn't right.

"What is the building used for?" Mason asked Patrick.

"I'd have to look it up. I'm not entirely sure," Patrick said.

"Will you let us know?"

"Of course."

Mason watched out of the corner of his eye as Wray fidgeted. He didn't like the questions, and he didn't like the idea that someone might find out who worked there.

Dex asked a few more questions of Captain Patrick while Wray watched his teammates work. The firefighters got control of the fire with multiple stations working at different points. Mason was impressed with how quickly it went from blazing to manageable.

"Looks like you don't have anything to do," Dex said to Wray.

Wray scowled at him. His Adam's apple bobbed as he swallowed roughly. Mason saw one group of firefighters turn off their hoses and back away. There was still a fire, but it was clearly contained and only active in the center of the building.

"I'd rather be in there," Wray said.

"Well, hopefully you will be, but we have to investigate, and considering the circumstances around you are already in question, your captain wanted you on the sidelines for this one," Captain Patrick said. "I think he made the right call. You should know that if one part of the team isn't working well with the others, the whole team falls apart."

Wray glared at him but eventually nodded. Patrick let him go back to his truck as his crew loaded up their gear to head back to the station.

Another man in turnout gear walked over and shook hands with Captain Patrick. "Thanks for holding him. The guys are a little twitchy right now. Hopefully it was nothing, but when they pulled up, late, and saw two guys being dragged out right after a beam collapsed, they started pointing fingers."

"Understandable," Patrick said. "I would have wondered

the same thing. Especially after him being off the job for a few so long."

The firefighter nodded. "We're heading out. Thanks again."

Patrick nodded and waited for the trucks to leave before telling Mason and Dex the man was the captain for Wray's fire station.

"Did he tell you who questioned the turn?" Dex asked.

"No. I didn't ask. I was just holding Mr. Allen from going into the fire. They have their own internal division that'll look into it."

Dex nodded. "If you hear anything, let us know."

"Will do. Thanks for the assist. I wasn't sure how this was going to turn out, but I figured you guys would want to see the man in action. Have you found anything concrete about what happened?"

"No, but something tells me it won't be long before new information comes out," Dex said.

Patrick tilted his head. "Saying something like that to a cop makes it sound like you're going to plant something. Tell me you aren't going to do that."

"No, of course not," Dex said. "Braden Wright said we need to talk."

Patrick's brows shot up. "Really? Well, that's interesting. He hasn't been very forthcoming with information."

"Nope, but something has changed. It appears as though he's getting dragged into whatever is going on, and maybe he's not sure how to get out of it."

"Be careful."

Dex and Mason nodded. "We'll keep you posted when we have something we can work with."

"Thanks."

Patrick went deeper into the foray, but Dex and Mason

headed back to the barricade to head out. Mason listened for anyone talking and nearly tripped over his feet when he heard, "Allen's fucked up. He's in deep and he's covering his ass. He won't be behind the wheel again."

Mason nudged Dex. "Did you catch that?"

"Catch what?"

Mason paused and pulled out his phone. "Guys over my left shoulder were talking about Allen. Made it sound like they know what's going on. And said he won't get behind the wheel again. Sounds like they think he did it on purpose."

Dex nodded and grabbed his phone. He snapped a few pictures. "We'll find out who they are and what they know. Good ear."

Mason nodded, then followed Dex away from the scene. They had a lot of work to do. And somehow everything always led back to Wray Allen. Mason was really starting to not like the man.

16

MEGAN TRIED TO MAKE HER DAY FEEL NORMAL. EVERY SOUND outside the apartment had her heart racing and her body on high alert. She tried turning on the TV to drown out the noises outside, but that only made her more anxious because then she couldn't hear.

She was a mess by the time Mason got home and cried with relief when he opened the door.

"Thank God," she breathed.

"Are you okay?"

She shook her head and glanced past him to the empty hallway outside. "I had breakfast with Justin this morning, and when I got back, the guy we saw at the pizza place was here."

"What?" Mason asked. His entire body was rigid, and his voice left no room for Megan to think her fear might not have been warranted.

"Leo, he said his name was."

"You spoke to him? Are you okay?"

Megan shook her head. Tears streamed down her cheeks

as the adrenaline and fear mixed together and took over. Mason wrapped an arm around her and led her to the couch. He held her close and let her cry all over him. He didn't ask her anything until she was out of tears.

"Did he hurt you?"

"No, but I remembered the way you spoke to him. I knew he wasn't someone you wanted around."

"He's not. He... Leo was my cellmate. He got out before me, but I thought he left the area. I didn't realize he was still local. He had a reputation for being someone you don't cross. He wouldn't hesitate to hurt someone if he felt it was warranted. He was serving time for aggravated assault, but he told me that was just because they hadn't caught him for all the other crimes he committed. I never asked what else."

"Were you in touch with him after you got out?"

"No. Never. Which means he looked me up after he saw us. What did he say to you? Where did you see him?"

"He was outside. Justin dropped me off, and I came up here. He was right outside the door. He pretended it was a coincidence that he ran into me, but I don't think it was. He left right after we spoke."

"What did he say to you?"

"He said it was nice to see me again and to tell you he said hello."

"Nothing about why he was here?"

Megan shook her head. "He started out by asking if I lived here. Almost like he was wondering if it's a decent place. I told him I was visiting a friend, and then he said he recognized me. He asked my name. He thought..."

"He thought what?" Mason asked.

"He said he thought your wife was dead."

Mason sucked in a sharp breath. Megan hated telling him that part, but he needed to know everything Leo said.

"I'm sorry."

Mason pulled her closer and kissed the side of her head. "I'm sorry. If you weren't staying here with me, he never would have approached you. He's a master manipulator. He knows how to get people to do whatever he wants. And he's good at it. I saw him talk one guard into handing over his phone so Leo could make a phone call. The guy was smiling and laughing like they were buddies. He can convince people to do just about anything."

Megan rubbed her hands up and down her arms. She still felt like he was watching her. "Every sound the rest of the day had me on edge. I thought he was going to come back and break down the door or something."

Mason shook his head. "He's not a blunt force kind of guy. He's like a surgeon. He'll slice and dice you, and he won't let anyone know he did it. The fact that he showed up here..."

"What?"

Mason drew a breath. "I don't know. It feels like he wants me to know he's watching. Like he's hoping I'll figure something out, but I don't know what."

"What makes you say that?"

"Because Leo likes the shadows. He likes to have other people do his dirty work. He could have had someone else bump into you if he thought he could get info out of you, but he came himself. He wanted me to know he was here. Why?"

"He's letting you know that he knows you're here."

"Yes, but why? That's what I'm missing. He's never looked me up, as far as I know. But now... what's changed?"

Megan thought about it for a minute, but she had no idea. She'd never spent much time trying to get into the mind of a criminal, and she didn't like the idea of starting now.

"Why do you smell like smoke?" she asked.

Mason groaned. "I was at a fire today."

"You were in a fire? Are you okay?"

"No, I was *at* a fire. The case Dex and I have been working on is investigating the disappearance of a firefighter. He vanished for ten days, showed back up, and today he made a wrong turn that delayed his team from getting to the scene. Two firefighters were injured, and some people are saying he made the wrong turn on purpose so they got there late."

"That seems so small. What would making a wrong turn buy him? And why would it matter?"

Mason shook his head. "That's what Dex and I are trying to figure out. When the guy reappeared, he had bruising that made it seem like he was beat up, but they still wanted something from him. We think he owes someone money, but English hasn't been able to trace the money back to anyone. Accounts are set up with corporations in countries that don't care if it's legit."

"If he owes someone money, how is making a wrong turn going to pay them back?"

"I don't know. Maybe insurance for the damages, but there were other companies there, and the building was a total loss, anyway."

"Do you think he knew those other firefighters were going to get hurt?"

Mason sucked in a breath. "I hope not. He has a wife and a couple of kids. If he got himself involved in something shady, and then adds a few lives, I'm not sure any of them will survive."

"Survive?"

Mason shrugged. "If the people he owes money to aren't afraid to kill two firefighters, why would they be worried about a family of four?"

"Wow. I forget how messed up the world is. Sometimes I wonder what I was thinking bringing a child into this. Then I remember I didn't exactly plan for it."

Mason chuckled. "Yeah, but you're going to be a great mom. This is a lucky kid."

Megan smiled. "Thanks. I hope so."

"Definitely."

Megan leaned over and kissed Mason. She intended to pull back quickly, but one taste and she got sucked in. The man was impossible to resist. Especially when he moaned low in his throat and made every cell in her body vibrate with need.

Nope, that was just his phone.

Mason pulled back with a groan and answered it with, "What?"

Megan couldn't hear the person on the other end, but from the look on Mason's face, it wasn't take-off-your-clothes-and-have-sex-all-night news.

"Okay. See you in a few." Mason hung up the phone and sighed heavily. "We need to go."

"We?"

"Yep. But this is definitely to be continued."

Megan smiled. "I like the sound of that."

WALKING into Slade's house with Megan rose more than one eyebrow. Mason assumed Slade filled the rest of the guys in on where Megan was staying, but clearly they didn't all get the message. If the whispered questions Megan got were any indication, the news hadn't made it through the women, either.

But Mason didn't have time to worry about everyone's judgement about him and Megan. He had to focus on the conversation Dex was relaying to the group. The one he said they all needed to know about because the investigation the two of them were handling was sounding like it needed more firepower behind it.

"Start from the beginning and tell us what this case is about," Archer said.

"Firefighter got kidnapped. Gone for ten days. Shows up with bruises on his face and apparent rib and collarbone injuries. Says he was in a car accident and had no memory. Claimed his car was in the shop from the accident. His buddy covered for him with his station. English found an account in the first guy's name that looked like a debt account. That one is now gone, but there's one in the buddy's name. Today, Patrick called us to a fire where guy one made a wrong turn that delayed their truck getting to the scene. Two others were injured, and the blame went on the driver for not getting them there. Guy two said he needed to talk to me. That's who I met up with an hour ago," Dex said.

He looked around the room at the others. They all nodded their understanding for Dex to continue with the conversation he had with Braden Wright.

"I didn't realize he called you," Mason said.

"He did," Dex said, holding his gaze. "And I didn't call you because he asked me not to."

"Me specifically?"

"Yes, which is when I knew it was going to get complicated."

"What did he say?" Dunn asked.

"When he asked to meet, I told him I'd give you a call," Dex said, nodding toward Mason. "He refused. He said he didn't want me calling you or anyone else, but he specifically said your name. I asked him why, and he said he didn't know who he could trust and asked me to come alone. He gave me an address near the water."

"You met with a suspect alone?" Dunn growled.

"He's not a suspect. We haven't thought he was involved since the beginning. We think he knows more than he's telling us, but we agreed he's not a suspect."

Dunn was not happy, but he nodded for Dex to continue.

"Okay, so I met Braden, and he's all twitchy. He asked if anyone came with me or if I called anyone or anything. I assured him I followed his instructions. He said he isn't sure who he can trust, again, and that he needed to talk to me. He told me he found the bank account, but that he didn't know about it when we spoke. Then he confessed that Wray Allen has a gambling problem. Not an addiction, he doesn't think, but he played cards in college and thinks of himself as good. He got an invite to a game from another firefighter about a year ago. Wray went and won. It was decent. A few grand over a couple of months. Then he started losing. He was only playing once a month or so, but as he started losing more and more, he started playing more and more. Now, he goes almost every time he's off, but the debts kept climbing. Braden doesn't know for sure how much debt Wray is in, but Wray confessed that if he can't pay, he's supposed to recruit someone else to the game who'll end up paying his debts."

"What does that mean?" Jack asked.

"I think it means Wray was the other guy's payment. He got Wray into the game, then stopped going. Wray ended up in debt even though he was good to start with. Now, they want Wray to bring someone else in to transfer the debt," Dex explained.

"So, he's in the middle of a ring who shuffles the debt around to avoid getting caught. They bring one guy in, let him win some until the debt is paid for the first guy. Probably tell him it's a cut for the house. Then they put him in harder games so he starts losing. The wrack up his debt and start all over again with another recruit. They can probably pass it off as transactions and loans to get around any red flags with banks," English said.

"I would guess," Dex said. "But here's the problem. Braden won't do it. He refuses to go to the game. He told Wray he has no interest and that the only risk he wants to take is the one he takes with his job."

"What did Wray say?" Mason asked.

"He got pissed and looked scared is what Braden told me. He said if he doesn't recruit someone new, they're going to force him to do other things," Dex said.

"Like making that wrong turn?"

Dex nodded to Mason's question.

"How in the hell does that do anything?"

"We don't know that yet, but first thing tomorrow, I'm going to put a call into Patrick to see if he found out who that building belongs to. A fire is a great way to destroy evidence of all kinds of things."

"Yeah, but it was a few minutes. And there were other engines on the scene. Was it really that big of a deal?" Mason asked.

Dex shrugged, but Jaymes was the one who answered.

"It might have been a test. Williams did that. He had little things, small changes, that he wanted me to do. Tests to make sure I actually did what I needed to do. It could have been as simple as a test to see if he'd follow orders."

The rest of them exchanged glances.

"If that's the case, we need to find out what else they're asking him to do," Dunn said.

"And now. Braden is worried. He thinks Wray is in over his head, and he's afraid he can't get out of it," Dex said.

"He might be right," Jack said. "What do we need to do?"

"The first thing we need to do is find out who's behind the money and the game. Then we need to figure out what they need Wray to do for them," Dex said.

"And we need to make sure his family is safe. If they're asking him to do things, chances are they're threatening his family," Mason said.

"He's right. We'll head over there in the morning and try to talk to them," Dex said.

"Guys, you all need to eat," Lily said, sliding her hand around Archer's shoulder. "Take a break and get some pizza."

Mason hadn't even noticed the boxes of pizza on the counter when he and Megan got there. As soon as he saw them, his stomach growled.

Everyone found seats and sat to eat. Megan was with Kelsea and Kyra and looked like she was content. Mason took a seat next to Dex and asked if he thought Braden Wright had a personal issue with him.

"Why do you ask?"

Mason shrugged. "If he knows who I am or knows my past, he might not be willing to talk if I'm around. I could make this case harder. I don't want that. If you need to take

Jack or someone else with you, I won't stand in the way of that."

Dex shook his head. "I don't think he has an issue with you. I think he has an issue with everyone. I think he's worried about everyone."

"But he called you and not me."

"I'm the one who gave him my card. I can't explain it any other way. I don't know him. But I feel for the guy. He's been dragged into something he never wanted to be a part of. He's in the middle now, whether he likes it or not, and he can't change it. He probably feels trapped. Maybe a little scared."

"These guys run into fires. Do you really think anything scares them?" Mason asked.

Dex shrugged. "He looked scared. He's spooked. The whole situation has him on edge. And after today…"

Mason nodded. "It's different when it doesn't touch you. When it does, it's hard to ignore the issues right in front of you."

Mason's gaze slid to Megan. She was smiling at something Kelsea said.

"When did that happen?" Dex asked.

Mason shook his head. "That woman is a force. I don't think she knows what *no* means. She certainly doesn't like to hear it."

"She's been staying with you?"

Mason nodded. "I didn't set out to fuck things up with Slade or anyone else. She told me he knew where she was, and I was… it was a rough night when she showed up. I tried to say no, but—"

"Oh, my God! Are you pregnant?" Kelsea shouted.

Mason turned as the whole room swung their gazes to look at him. Megan's eyes went wide. She opened her mouth to say something, but no sound came out.

Mason wanted to explain, but it wasn't his news to share. He would support whatever Megan wanted to tell the others, but he wasn't going to be responsible for whatever it was.

"You son of a bitch! You knocked up my sister! I'm gonna fucking kill you!"

17

———

It was like slow-motion replay. Her brother swung for Mason and knocked him down with one hit. Megan was frozen, unable to move, as Mason pushed himself to his feet.

"You get one. That was it. Don't come at me again."

"I think I might have to fire you. I should have done it before."

The room went silent. The tension was thick enough that Megan felt like she had to swim through it to get between the two of them. She faced her brother and stuck a finger in his face.

"How dare you? Just this morning, you told me you were going to be okay with this. That you weren't going to stand in the way of us. And that you weren't going to fire Mason."

"That was before I knew he got you pregnant. What the fuck?"

Justin tried to push past Megan, but she stomped on his foot and punched him in the stomach. "Don't make me get dirtier."

He glared at her but backed up.

"Mason is a good man. You told me so earlier today. I

didn't tell you I'm pregnant because I didn't want you to know. I didn't want anyone to know. And you're a dumbass if you think he's the father. I've been here for like five seconds."

"He's not… who is? Why isn't he here with you?"

"Because he's a non-issue. And my pregnancy is a non-issue. You don't get a vote on what I do. I told you not to tell me who I could sleep with, and I'm not interested in your opinions about what I should do about my child."

"Megan—"

"Unless the next words out of your mouth are *you're right*, I don't want to hear it."

Justin sighed and reached for her. He pulled her into a tight hug and said, "I'm going to be an uncle?"

Megan nodded against his chest and finally felt like she could breathe. "Mom and Dad don't know. Please don't tell them."

"You know you're not going to be able to hide this from them, right?"

Megan pulled back and shrugged. "I know, but I'm not really ready to talk about it yet."

"I'm so sorry," Kelsea said. "I just sort of blurted it out, loudly. That was really wrong of me."

"It's okay," Megan said. "I know you weren't doing it to be mean or something." Megan realized everyone was staring at her. "Um, can we all go back to talking about other things so I'm not the center of attention?"

Justin turned and glared at the men until they all turned away. The women started chatting immediately, watching Megan out of the corners of their eyes. She was sure they'd have a million questions, but she could answer them later.

Megan turned to Mason and reached up to touch the swollen part of his cheek. "Are you okay?"

Mason glared past her at Justin and said, "Fine."

"I'm sorry," Justin said. "Why would that not be my first thought?"

"And what if it were my kid? You really think firing me and kicking my ass are the right way to handle things?"

Megan looked back at her brother and had to force herself not to laugh at his scowl.

"Justin, I love you, but you are not my white knight. You were for a long time, but I can take care of myself."

"I don't want anyone taking advantage of you."

"Well, you threw your punches at the wrong man. The father is a guy I work with who made me think we were friends. We've slept together a few times over the years, but usually when he's been drinking. When I told him I was pregnant, he said it couldn't be his because we were sleeping with other people and he always wore a condom. This child would be better off if Mason was their father."

Justin winced and nodded. "You're right. I'm sorry. I shouldn't have threatened to fire you and I shouldn't have hit you."

"You ever want a ride to Kentucky, let me know," Mason said.

Justin growled. "Same."

Megan looked between the two of them and her pregnancy hormones went crazy again. Tears filled her eyes and her throat was thick with emotions. She loved these two men.

Wait. Not like that. Slade was her brother, but Mason... it was affection. Care. Adoration. Appreciation. Love was different. Love was deeper and more.

Wasn't it?

"Are you okay?" Mason asked.

Megan nodded. "Yeah. I'm just going to sit with Kelsea so she knows I'm not upset."

"Okay. If you're tired or want to go, let me know."

Megan nodded and skirted around her brother. She took a seat next to Kelsea again. Kelsea immediately apologized.

"It's fine. I promise. I didn't want Justin to know because I figured he'd react exactly how he did. I didn't see him blaming it on Mason coming, but I knew he'd be pissed."

"He worries about you," Kyra said. "He feels like he let you down."

"He's never let me down. He's always been my best friend and my biggest fan."

"He still is," Kyra said with a smile. "He misses you."

"I miss him, too. A lot."

"We should come visit you sometime. Especially once the baby comes. How far along are you?"

"I'm only ten weeks. It's still early."

"Have you been to your doctor yet?"

"I called when I found out I was pregnant, but it was too early for me to come in. But we heard the heartbeat last week."

"You did? How?" Lily asked.

"Um, well, there was an incident the first night, and I was bleeding and Mason took me to the hospital," Megan said.

"Is incident code for rough sex?" Ashleigh asked quietly. "Because we had the same thing happen once. Scared the hell out of Daniel."

"Seriously? Is that it?" Kyra asked.

"Um, yeah. He felt really bad, and that's the only reason Mason knew about it. I wasn't going to tell him. Hell, I wasn't going to stay with him, but he was really sweet and he took care of me, and I just stayed."

"That's so sweet," Lily said. "Over the last few days, things have changed for me and I feel so uncomfortable. I barely let Archer get close enough to touch me. Rough sex sounds like a fantasy. Any sex sounds like a fantasy."

"For me, it was early. We didn't realize it could happen. I mean, it can happen even if you're not pregnant, but since we knew I was, we freaked out when we saw the blood. But sex in general is tough. Have you tried being on top?" Ashleigh asked.

Lily shook her head. "I don't usually like that."

"It's good," Megan said without thinking. She slapped her hand over her mouth. "Sorry," she said through her fingers.

"Nope. No sorry here. We talk about everything, and you're Slade's sister and Mason's whatever, so you don't get to be shy," Lily said. "Plus, if I can find a way to have sex with my husband, he might still be my husband after this baby comes. He's getting cranky."

"You'll make it work," Ashleigh said. "Try on top. Yes?"

Ashleigh looked right at Megan and waited until she finally agreed. "I'm not as far along as Lily, but I look like I am. It was good. So, so good."

"Nice. I have a mission for tonight," Lily said with a wide grin. "Thank you, ladies."

"Any time. I wouldn't have survived my pregnancy without a few tricks. We'll all help each other," Ashleigh said.

Megan smiled at the women around her and wondered why she'd never found friends like them before. They were amazing. Funny and smart and sassy. She loved them.

The reasons to stay were quickly adding up. She just wasn't sure if Mason needed to go in the pro column or the con. Maybe she needed to decide how she felt about him.

MASON RUBBED his jaw and glared at Slade. He got why he was pissed, but to immediately jump to Mason being the father pissed him off. Especially after he thought they were fine just that morning.

But Mason had a job to do. He needed to focus on Braden Wright and Wray Allen and whatever they were involved in. They needed to find out who was behind the whole thing.

"What do we need to do about Braden and Wray?" Dex asked as he took a seat next to Mason.

Mason dragged his gaze from Slade to focus on Dex. "That's not what you really want to ask me."

Dex held his gaze for a long minute, then nodded. "Do you know what you're doing with her?"

Mason sighed and shook his head. "Not even a little."

"Look, I'm not an expert with women, but getting involved with someone who's so close doesn't seem like a good idea," Dex said.

"I didn't set out to get involved with her. I told you that."

Dex drew a breath and avoided looking right at Mason.

Mason leaned back in his seat and crossed his arms. "What?"

"She's pregnant?"

Mason nodded slowly.

"I know you wanted kids. Is this... I mean, are you...?"

"Am I with her because I think it's a ready-made family?" Mason growled.

Dex shrugged.

"No, okay? No. I didn't know when I first... And after... She's not staying here. She's going back home. I'm not trying to jump in and be something I'm not."

Dex held Mason's eye. He finally nodded. "Okay, then we need to figure out how to handle this situation we're in. Braden doesn't know more than what he told me. I think he's staying at the fire station. He doesn't feel safe at home."

"Shit," Mason said. "I wish we could figure out who's behind all this. Get rid of them so we can put a stop to all this."

"Yep. If Wray won't tell us, hopefully English can figure it out."

Mason nodded. "Yep."

"Are you ready to go?" Megan asked. She slid her hand around his shoulder and smiled.

Mason stood and nodded. If she was asking, she either wasn't feeling well or was upset about something. Whatever it was, Mason was going to get her out of there.

"We can talk tomorrow," he told Dex. "Let everyone else know we had to go."

Dex nodded and waved as Mason led Megan toward the door. Once they were outside, he wrapped an arm around her and asked if everything was okay.

"Yes," she said. "I just couldn't wait another minute to finish what we started earlier."

Mason groaned and pulled her in closer. "I love the way you think."

"Drive fast."

"Yes, ma'am."

MASON PUT his fist through the bag and blew out a breath. He repositioned himself and swung again. Shift, hit, shift, hit. He had gotten used to letting out his aggression with his hands. It was a way for him to think, to let his mind wander while he moved his body. And it usually worked.

But he was dripping with sweat and no closer to an answer.

Mason grabbed the bag and stopped the swing of it. He held onto it for a minute, then let go and unwrapped his boxing gloves. He dropped them to the floor and reached for his water bottle.

Mason sat on the bench and drank his water. He wiped his face with a towel. His mind raced still, even after the workout. He couldn't wrap his head around what was going on and it was starting to make him a little crazy.

Mason finished his water, then went to the bathroom for a quick shower. He changed and walked down the hallway to his office. While his computer powered up, he checked his phone to see if Megan was awake yet. He asked her to text him when she was up so he knew she was safe.

Megan: I'm awake. Nothing going on here. Going to do some work. I'm not leaving today.

Mason: Thanks for letting me know. If you need anything, text me.

Megan: I will. It sucks feeling like a prisoner, but I know it's better this way. He gave me the creeps.

Mason: He's like that. He can be charming when he wants to be, but mostly he's manipulative and vindictive. He'll do anything to get what he wants from someone.

Megan: I just wish we knew what he wanted from you.

Mason: Yeah.

Megan: Stay safe. I need to get on a call. Talk soon.

Mason: You too.

Mason stared at the texts and smiled. He was about to lock his phone and put it away when he stopped.

Megan said she felt like a prisoner.

She couldn't leave.

She had no choice.

She was trapped.

Just like Wray Allen. And Braden Wright.

"English!" Mason shouted as he hurried down the hallway.

English looked up as Mason pushed into his office. "You bellowed?"

"Leo Knapp. I need you to do a deep dive on him."

English tilted his head. "Why? Who is he?"

"He's my old cellmate. He was bad news. But he's out. He's a free man. I ran into him last week. It doesn't feel like it was a coincidence."

English typed as he listened. "And you think he's after you or something?"

Mason shook his head. "No, but I think he wants me to know he's watching me. I think he might have something to do with our firefighters."

"Who has something to do with our firefighters?" Dex asked from the doorway.

"Where's Slade?" Mason asked.

"In his office. Why? He's working with Archer on the drug case."

"Tell him to go get Megan. Right now. If I'm right, she can't be alone."

Dex's eyes widened before he turned and raced down the hall. Mason focused on English knowing Slade would take care of his sister.

"Holy shit," English said. "This guy is in everything. He has a hell of a rap sheet, but he's also a suspect in a bunch of open cases. There's an FBI file on him, and something with Homeland. He was your cellmate?"

Mason nodded. "He told me he was in there for something small because they couldn't ever prove he was involved in the big stuff. He made it sound like he was guilty of everything, but he was too smart to get caught. I think he has a network that carries out most of his dirty work."

"It looks like he might."

"Are you finding any connection between him and Marzette Corporation?"

English shook his head. "Unfortunately, no. I don't see anything that ties him to them, or anything that ties him to gambling."

"Dammit," Mason swore. He took a deep breath. "I was sure that was it."

"The building was owned by Marzette Corporation," Dex said. "The fire was likely a coverup for something else. It might have even been where they were holding Allen."

"Seriously?" Mason said.

Dex shrugged. "It's possible. A fire destroys all physical evidence of him being there and it destroys whatever else they had in that building."

"Can we search for any other buildings the company owns?"

English nodded and clicked a few buttons. "Three. All warehouses, all near the water, all previously vacant."

"Likely all used for their games," Dex said.

"I think we need to go ask Allen and Wright some questions. We need to know what they know," Mason said.

Dex nodded. "Yep. And we need to talk to them together. I get the feeling Wright is ready to roll on his buddy."

Mason agreed. "Any chance they're both still on shift?"

"Let's check and go pay them a visit."

"Thank, English. Keep digging into Leo. See if there's a connection anywhere. Or something else. He's involved in something we're looking into. He wouldn't have shown up if he wasn't."

English nodded and continued staring at his screen. Maybe they would figure this out.

"Megan! Megan!"

Megan apologized to her client and asked if he could hold on for just a minute. She hit mute and went to the door to find out what in the hell was wrong with her brother.

"Why are you here?"

"Mason sent me. He said to get you out of here."

"What? Why? I was just texting with him thirty minutes ago and he didn't say anything."

Justin shrugged. "I don't know, and I don't care. If he thinks you're in danger, we're leaving. Now."

"I'm talking to a client. I need to finish this call. Can you give me a few minutes?"

Justin glared at her, but Megan didn't back down. He finally sighed and nodded.

Megan watched as he peeked through the blinds outside. She unmuted her phone with a shaky hand and apologized for the interruption.

"Where were we?"

"We were talking about the extra support," the customer said.

"Yes, of course. So, if you sign with us, we have a customer service center that's open twenty-four/seven. There is always someone available to answer questions because we know our customers don't always work nine-to-five. If you sign up for the gold tier service, we guarantee delivery for orders under a hundred dollars in two business days. Anything under a thousand dollars in one business day. Certain orders above that can be delivered in eight hours or less. You can select items you want to have available for that kind of turnaround. We have scheduled ordering for items that you use regularly, and you would have one dedicated rep to answer your calls and questions. That would be me."

"And these prices you sent me are typical prices?"

"Those are current prices for all the items. We have multiple options for each item, depending on what you need, but these are actual prices." Megan watched Justin as he looked around the apartment, not watching her but looking.

"Wow. Really?"

"Yes. We work with our suppliers to ensure we have some of the lowest prices for our customers."

"This is amazing. I think this is the best thing for us. We've been considering making a change for a while, and it sounds like this is the right move. What are the next steps?"

"I'll send you some paperwork to sign, and once you get it back to me, we can set up your first round of orders."

"It's that simple?"

Megan smiled and prayed it came through in her voice instead of the anxiety she was feeling. "It's that simple."

"Okay. Well, then, this is perfect. Thank you. I look forward to hearing from you again."

"Sounds good. We'll talk soon."

Megan hung up the phone and faced her brother. "You have no idea what's going on?"

Justin shook his head. "No."

"Do I need to pack my stuff?"

"I don't know. But if it's not safe for you to be here, maybe you should. Maybe you should come back and stay with Kyra and me."

"If I'm not safe here, what makes you think I'm any safer at your house? I'm still alone all day."

Justin sighed heavily. "Fine. Don't pack your stuff. But let's go. Mason will have to fill us in when we get back."

Megan glanced around the room and decided to take her computer with her. If nothing else, maybe she could borrow an office or conference room and get something done.

If she could stop shaking.

18

———————

DEX PARKED TO THE SIDE OF THE FIRE STATION. MASON stared up at the large building and wondered if their plan was going to work.

"Do you think they'll actually hand over information about these people?" Mason asked.

Dex shrugged. "There's only one way to find out. Let's go."

They walked inside the station and up to the desk. Instead of finding the firefighters outside, they had to request to speak to Allen and Wright. Mason didn't love that, but it was the only way.

The good news was, they knew both men were there.

"They'll be right down," the guy behind the desk said. Dex nodded as the man eyed them. Mason could only imagine what someone wondered when they saw him and Dex walk in. Especially when they came in asking for not just one but two firefighters.

"What are you doing?" a voice said from inside the fire station. The doors were open and with the wide open space indoors, sound echoed through the entire building.

"I was called."

Mason was fairly sure the first voice was Braden's and the second Wray's. It sounded like they weren't together when they each were notified to meet a visitor.

"Why?"

"How the hell do I know? Where are you going?"

"I was called, too."

"Do you know who it is?"

"Nope. I'm on my way. Just like you are."

"Wait—"

"Get the hell off me!"

Boots stomped down a set of stairs before Braden Wright turned the corner and saw Mason and Dex. He stopped, then glanced past them to the guy behind the desk. "Can we use the office?"

"Yeah, sure. These guys are here for both of you, though." The man nodded to Wray Allen as he appeared behind Braden.

Braden sighed and nodded, then pointed to the office behind the desk.

It was a small room, but it had a door, and hopefully, no ears inside. Mason stood near the door while Dex, Braden, and Wray took the other walls.

"What are you doing here?" Braden was the first to speak.

"We need some information about Marzette Corporation. Who they are, what they do. That kind of thing." Dex crossed his arms and looked at both of them.

Braden shook his head. "Never heard of them. Why are you asking us?"

"Because your partner has heard of them," Mason said.

Wray looked at Mason and shook his head. "I don't know what you're talking about."

"Are you really going to do this?" Mason asked.

"I still don't know what you're talking about."

"Do you think these men are going to let you make wrong turns to forgive your debts? Do you really think that's going to be the worst of it?" Dex asked.

"I didn't make that turn on purpose. I got turned around and confused."

"That's convenient, but it's also a lie. The people you owe money to aren't worried about how they get their money. They only want to know they can control you. Why do you think they wanted you to bring in more firefighters?"

"How do you...?" He turned to Braden. "You told them?"

"You might not be worried about your family, but I am. This has to stop. I'm not willing to pay the price for you. And I'm not willing to walk away and see your family killed because I don't want to put myself up as collateral."

Braden got in Wray's face. Wray shoved him back. Braden hit a desk and shoved the furniture against the wall. Mason looked at Dex, but he waved him off. Guess they were going to fight it out.

Mason knew there were times when that needed to happen. When men needed to throw their punches and yell and then they could move on. He'd done it more than a few times. It helped get that anger out, and if he had to guess, Braden was carrying a shit-ton of anger.

He swung at Wray and landed a solid blow on his cheek. The bruise from his 'accident' was still yellow and healing, and the new blow likely hurt like a bitch.

Wray stumbled backward but caught his footing after a few steps. He shook his head as he opened his eyes and went straight at Braden. Braden sidestepped the hit and punched Wray in the back. Wray shouted and dropped to one knee.

"Are you two done?" Dex growled. "Because we didn't come here to watch you kill each other."

Both men breathed heavily. They stood and glared at each other. Braden was the first to speak.

"I want this to end. What do we need to do?"

"First, we need to know what we're dealing with," Dex said.

"And who," Mason added.

Dex nodded. The four men stared at each other. Wray Allen clearly had no interest in helping, which meant Mason had to watch him for any sign. They figured that would happen and were prepared for it. Dex was going to do the talking. He would focus on Braden, ask him questions and find out everything he knew. They were sure Braden had already told him everything, but they wanted to use Braden to trap Wray into admitting something. Mason was going to watch Wray. If he had any reaction, Mason was going to call it out. Force the issue. Make him admit to anything and everything he knew about what he got himself into.

"First, there was another firefighter, is that right?"

Braden nodded. "Yes. He's retired now. Left the area, actually. He's the one who invited Wray into the game."

Wray scowled at his friend.

"Do you have something to add?" Mason asked him.

Wray glared at Mason but kept his mouth shut.

"And these games bring in someone new, someone who doesn't know anything about what's going on, and then they set the person up to take the fall for the guy who brought them there."

Braden nodded. "That's the way it appears. I haven't been to a game. I don't gamble."

"So, how do they make their money back? How do they get to where they actually earn anything?"

Braden shook his head and glanced at Wray. "I don't know. I'm guessing by getting firefighters or whoever to do things like Wray did. Take a wrong turn so a fire burns a little longer, maybe even give them information about things. I guess it depends who owes the money. An inspector could rule a death an accident. A cop could shoot first and ask questions later. I mean, it depends."

"But it's subtle, right?" Dex asked.

"I would guess, but I don't know. I don't know who's involved with this group. I don't know anything about them—"

"Then why are you talking like you do?" Wray spat.

"Because you're not," Braden shouted back. "Do you want to go to jail? Is that really what you're after? Do you think Stacey and the kids will be happy to find out you went to jail protecting the men who kidnapped you? She was terrified. When you disappeared, she was so scared. I've never seen her so scared. And I helped create that. I covered for you. I told her you were fine when you disappeared in the past. And now, you go away for ten days. I know they had you. I know they wouldn't let you come back. I know they kicked your ass for a week. And still... still, after all that, you're still protecting these assholes."

"I'm protecting my family," Wray shouted.

"By not saying anything? How is that protecting your family?" Braden yelled back. His arms were thrown to the sides in frustration. A vein on the side of his neck bulged.

Mason cleared his throat, and the other three men looked at him. "What did they say they'll do to your family if you talk to the cops?"

"They'll kill them. All of them. And they'll kill me last so I have to watch my family die."

"We need them in custody," Dex said, pulling out his phone.

"No!" Wray shouted. "If we disappear, they'll know. They'll come after us. We have to pretend everything is normal. Eventually, I'll pay off my debts. And then we'll be free."

"No, you won't," Dex said calmly. "Men like this... they don't let you off the hook. They know you have no choice. They have the means to disappear. If they want to run, they can. Easily. But if you try to, you won't be able to make it. You're ordinary people. You have family and friends. You have a life here. Leaving, cutting all ties, never returning, it's almost impossible for most people to do. And they know it."

Wray Allen's hands shook. He leaned against the wall and sank to the floor. He dropped his head and gripped the back of his neck.

"What do we do?" Braden asked quietly.

"We find these people. We take them down. We make sure they can't hurt anyone else ever again. But that means we need to know who they are. We need to know everything. Are you ready to talk?"

Wray Allen looked up at Dex and nodded. "Yes, I'll talk."

"Good. First, do you know Leo Knapp?"

Wray shook his head. "No. Why?"

"Now is not the time to lie to us," Mason growled.

"I'm not lying. I've never heard of him. Who is he?"

"Well, we thought he was the man behind the curtain. We figured you would recognize the name, even if he wasn't the one who personally held you," Dex said.

"No. I was held by a man named Eli. He was the only one I ever saw or spoke to."

"Is he the one who gave you your injuries?" Mason asked.

Wray hesitated for a minute, then nodded.

"You didn't encounter anyone else when you were being held? Ten whole days and he was the only person you saw?"

Wray nodded. "I was in a room that was like a prison. A cot, a bucket, and a door. I couldn't see outside my room. I couldn't even hear anything."

"And there wasn't anyone named Leo there?" Mason clarified.

"It wasn't like they gave me a directory," Wray snarled.

Mason resisted the urge to slam the man into the desk.

"What can you tell us? Do you know where you were?"

Wray shook his head. "When you go to a game, they give you an address. You meet at that address and a car comes and gets you. They blindfold you so you can't see where you're going. When you get to the building, someone gets you out of the car and takes you inside. I never saw the exterior of the buildings or the interior. When they took me, it was the same. I thought I was going to a game."

"Where do you meet?"

"It changes every time. I've met them in downtown, north of the city, neighborhoods. Wherever they tell me."

"I have to ask you something," Mason said.

Wray turned his focus to him.

"You sound like you might be a smart guy. Why in the hell did you get messed up in this?"

Wray sighed and closed his eyes. "When Stacey and I got married, we planned kids one day. Eventually. She got pregnant right away. She was still finishing her masters, but we knew we wanted kids so we said we'd make it work. We both wanted our kids close together, so after our oldest, we started talking about a second. Stacey was on maternity leave, but when her degree was finished, we knew she'd be making a lot more money. My mom was watching Joey, and we said we'd just see what happened. A month after Joey turned two, we found out Stacey was pregnant with Evan. We were in a two-bedroom apartment, so we decided to buy a house. Then my mom fell and couldn't watch Joey anymore. And Evan was coming whether we were ready or not. Sam, the other firefighter, told me the game was a good thing. He said he was going to retire because of how much he'd earned playing. He brought me in, and it was easy to win at first. I was paying off bills and we were struggling a little less. It was a thousand a month, maybe a few hundred, but it helped. Until I started losing."

"So, you won back what the last guy owed, then they turned things on you and you lost," Dex said.

Wray nodded. "I didn't know it at the time. I thought it would turn around. That I'd get back to it. That I would start winning again. I started going more and more. I'd win one day then lose twice as much the second."

"Why didn't you walk away?"

"They kept loaning me the money to play. I couldn't walk unless I could pay them back."

Mason and Dex exchanged a look. Mason shook his head. He knew how easy it was to stand on the outside and judge another person, but damn. Wray should have come to his senses a whole lot earlier than he did.

"You owe twenty grand?" Dex clarified.

Wray nodded.

"And they want you to bring in Braden to pay off your debts?"

"Yeah," Wray admitted. "They said he's single and his sister has money so they figured he'd be good for it."

"You son of a bitch," Braden growled.

"I'm sorry. They knew all this. I didn't tell them."

"No, but you went there. You thought you could win free money from people like this. You thought it would be so easy."

"I'm sorry, Braden."

Braden glared at his friend and crossed his arms. His scowl made it clear there wouldn't be any family barbecues anytime soon, but Mason hoped one day they could look back and forgive the mess.

First, they needed to live through it.

"We need an invite to that game," Dex said.

"What? No. Why?" Wray asked.

"If you need someone to forgive your debts, why not us?"

Wray shook his head. "These men don't accept strangers. They know who they're looking for. They told me to bring in Braden. It's not like I wanted to."

"Why don't you ask them? Maybe they'll be open to someone else. Someone who's actually willing to play. Someone with money to throw around."

Wray's gaze flipped between Mason and Dex. "Why are you doing this for me?"

"Because we can't walk away any easier than Braden can. We might not know your family, but that doesn't mean we want to see them dead," Dex said.

"I don't know."

"Try. How do you get in touch with them?"

"I have a burner," Wray admitted. "I keep it in my locker. It's always off unless I want in for a game. Then I turn it on, send a message, and turn it off again. An hour later, I turn it on to get a text with more info. If there's a game that night, I'll have the location to meet and the time. If not, they send me the date of the next game and text the meeting info that day."

"Good. Go get it. Send the text. And give us the number you send the text to," Mason said.

Dex nodded.

Wray got up and left the room. Mason and Dex looked at Braden. He looked defeated. Like he just found out his best friend was, for all intents and purposes, a criminal.

"I can't believe he kept all this from me."

"Money makes people do stupid things."

"He could have gotten himself killed. Or his family. How could he have done that?"

"The same way you're willing to talk to me even though you have no idea if you can trust me," Dex said.

"Stacey is like a sister. Wray has always been like my brother. I couldn't sit back and let this all happen without at least trying to help it. It seemed like you guys knew what you were doing."

"We do," Mason said. "We're going to take care of this."

Braden nodded as Wray walked back into the room. "What do I say?"

"Say you have a replacement player and need a game," Dex said.

"Say you have two," Braden said.

"No. Mason can't go with me. The guy we think is behind all this knows Mason. We can't take the chance," Dex said.

"I'm not talking about him. I'm going with you. You can't go in there alone. And from the sound of things, it won't be possible for your team to have your back. I'm going with you."

"Bray—"

"No, Wray. You don't get to control this. You've held back too much already. I'm not letting him walk into this alone, just like I wouldn't have let you if you told me what was going on. We're going to end this."

Wray nodded. He looked like he wanted to say something, but he just sent the text. He turned the phone to Mason to record the number, then powered it off.

"And now we wait."

Mason nodded. "We wait."

19

MEGAN WATCHED THE DOOR WITH ONE EYE WHILE SHE struggled to focus on work. If Mason was worried about her safety, she was going to be worried about his. She had to believe it had something to do with Leo, but that was just a feeling.

Kyra walked into the conference room Megan was using and set a mug in front of Megan. "It's tea. I know you can't have a lot of caffeine. Of course, I don't know if you like tea."

Megan nodded. "I do. And thanks."

Kyra smiled when Megan looked past her toward the hallway. "I know how you feel. Every time they go out, I get so nervous. I watch the door and listen all the time. It's terrifying. They've been shot, blown up, chased. They go after dangerous people who don't want to be caught."

"How do you handle it?" Megan asked. She took a sip of the tea and let the warmth spread through her. It didn't chase away all the chill of her fear, but it helped.

Kyra shrugged. "Most of the time, I don't handle it well. I've spoken to a therapist, which helps, but she's also made me see that the fear is mine and mine alone. Nothing is really going to make it go away. I have to trust that they know what they're doing."

"And you think they do?"

Kyra nodded and smiled. She leaned forward and drew a breath. "I do. They're smart men and they don't take unnecessary risks. They never go into a situation alone. They always have each other's backs."

Megan nodded and sipped her tea. It made her feel better to hear Kyra say all that. Justin would never offer up a weakness, but Kyra made it sound like there might not be one to share.

"Tell me how you and Justin met."

Kyra chuckled and leaned back. "You haven't heard our story?"

"Nope. Did you meet after you started working here?"

"Um, no. I was supposed to interview here, but I stopped at the bank on the way and it was robbed while I was there."

"Are you serious?"

Kyra nodded. "Slade was there at the same time. He tried to help me, but he was drugged, too. He stayed the night at the hospital with me. I rescheduled my interview and by the time I went in, he'd figured out I was supposed to be here and tried to talk them into hiring me. They wouldn't hire me unless I was the best candidate, but thankfully they thought I was. After that, it was impossible to resist him."

"Are you serious?"

Kyra laughed. "I am. How did you not know all that?"

"I don't know. I thought something happened, but I thought you were kidnapped or something."

"That, too. It was a rough start to a new job, but it was worth it to see what these men do. I was able to experience the coordinated efforts of their talents first hand. Not that I want to again, but it proved I was working for an amazing organization. I don't doubt them because I know what they're capable of."

Megan smiled. "I've always been impressed by my brother, but I don't know much about his life after he joined the Navy. I think he wanted to protect my parents and me from the fear. And he was probably right to do it, but I feel like I don't know him that well."

"It's hard when you don't live close to each other. And our time off here is usually not planned. When we have a slow schedule, everyone takes a few days because when we're busy, it's all hands for a while. They'll sometimes go weeks without even taking a weekend off," Kyra confessed.

"That's insane."

Kyra shrugged. "It's part of the job. When someone is missing or hurt or in danger, these guys aren't going to put their personal lives ahead of that. They're protectors."

"They're saviors."

Kyra smiled and nodded. "They are."

"What are you two talking about in here?" Justin asked. He walked over and kissed Kyra, then winked at Megan and sat next to Kyra.

"You. It sounds like you guys are pretty badass," Megan said.

"Well, it is in the name. Foreign Borders Overseen by Military Badasses. Lily came up with it."

"Tell me you're joking," Megan said.

Justin shook his head. "Nope. Our first mission was to save Jaymes. Our old CO kidnapped him and he ended up in Canada. We stuck around to help keep the borders safe, but have taken whatever cases come our way. Dunn's built a relationship with the local PD and FD and we help out with all sorts of things."

"Like a missing firefighter?" Megan said.

Justin nodded. "Yep."

"Are Mason and Dex back yet?" English asked from the door.

Justin shook his head. "I haven't seen them. Why?"

"I think Mason might be right about the name he gave me. I still can't find anything concrete, but the deeper I dig, the more shady it gets."

"Are you talking about Leo?" Megan asked.

Three heads swung to look at her.

"How do you know that name?" Justin asked first.

Megan shrugged. "I've met Leo. We saw him last week at a pizza place, and he approached me at Mason's apartment just yesterday."

"That's why he wanted you out of there," Justin said. "He gave English that name today. He must have figured something out, or suspected something. That's why he sent me to get you. In case Leo comes back."

"The guy is creepy," Megan said. She rubbed her hands up and down her arms, feeling a chill again.

"Can you ID the guy?" English asked. "If I show you pictures, can you tell me who he is?"

Megan shrugged. "Yeah. Anything to help."

"I'll be right back." English ran down the hallway and was back in a few seconds with a laptop. "Is this him?"

Megan looked at the man in the photo and shook her head. "No. Leo has a bigger nose."

"Okay, what about him?" English showed her another picture.

Megan shook her head again. "No. His eyes are too wide set. Leo has dark hair, too, but the eyes get me."

"This guy?" English asked, pulling up yet another picture.

Megan nodded as soon as English showed her. "That's

him. That's the evil look in his eyes and the manipulative smile. He's..." She shivered. "He gives me the creeps. I know that isn't him live, but just looking at his eyes makes me feel like he's watching me."

"Can you do a scan of the area for this guy?" Justin asked.

English chuckled. "Sure, if I have a few years. It's nearly impossible to just scan every camera in the area for someone. I have to have an area to start with."

"What about the area around the fire the other day?" Justin suggested.

English nodded and tapped a few keys. "There aren't many cameras in that area, so it might not take long. I'll start with the twelve hours before the fire and go from there."

English carried his computer out of the room as he typed something.

"Do you think he'll find something?" Megan asked.

"If there's something to be found, he'll find it," Kyra told her. "Hopefully, all this is over soon. This is always the hardest part for me. When it feels like they've figured out what's going to happen, but they have to move in and stop the bad guys."

"This is when it gets fun," Justin said. He leaned back in his chair with a smile and linked his fingers behind his head. "We love this part."

"Aren't you worried about the police? Isn't this something they should be handling?" Megan asked.

Kyra chuckled. "I've asked the same thing so many times."

"And?"

Justin shrugged. "We always talk to the cops. Dunn updates everyone. He won't ever do anything unless he has the full support of local law enforcement. If we didn't do that, we could be arrested. We're not cops, but because we operate with their authorization, we are within the law."

"This is all just—"

"Meeting!" someone called from down the hallway.

Megan looked at Kyra and Justin. Justin stood and looked out into the hallway. "Dunn?"

"Bring her," another voice shouted back.

Justin turned back to Megan and said, "You're coming, too."

Megan stood and followed her brother and Kyra down the hall to the large conference room at the front of the building. When she walked in and saw Mason, she nearly cried with relief. He was okay.

"Hey," Mason said with a smile. "You okay?"

She nodded, unable to speak.

Mason tilted his head. "You sure?"

She sucked in a breath and nodded again.

Mason chuckled like he understood, then winked at her.

Megan sat next to Kyra and gave Dex and Mason her full attention.

"Wray Allen finally told us everything. He said all the same things Braden Wright said, so we believe it was the truth. Allen had some new insight since he's actually been inside. The games are invite only. They want people like him who can get sucked in and will either invite others back or will do them favors to pay off their debt. Allen does not know Leo's name. Said he was held by someone named Eli. The games are set up by text using a burner. He got us an invite to the next game, happening in two days," Dex explained.

"Us? Both of you? Is that a good idea?" Archer asked.

"Even if we don't have proof Leo is involved, if he is, your cover will be blown the second Mason walks in the door," Jack said.

Dex shook his head. "Mason isn't going in. Braden Wright is going with me."

"You're taking a civilian?" Dunn asked.

"He's a firefighter, and he already knows the risks. He was invited in, anyway. Allen set it up, told these guys we want in. We have the burner he uses to communicate with them." Dex held up a phone, then slid it across the table to English. "Tomorrow we turn it on and get an address to meet them. They will blindfold us and take any and all weapons and communication devices."

"No," Dunn said firmly. "I can't authorize this."

"We have no choice," Dex said. "These guys aren't going to let Allen's family live. They're going to either rope someone else into this or kill them. They need freedom. And we need to catch whoever is behind this."

"I don't like it."

Dex shook his head. "I don't either. I'd rather go in with all of you behind me, but Mason is going to watch the meeting spot. He'll follow us to the game. When we get inside, he's going to relay the location so you guys can come and we can take these guys down."

"You two have this all figured out?" Dunn asked.

Dex and Mason exchanged a glance. "We tried. I know it isn't ideal, but neither is letting whoever this group is continue to threaten and intimidate the local FD. We have no idea who else they've gone after. It has to stop."

Dex looked around the room and met the gazes of everyone there. Even Megan felt the strength of the others sitting around her. She was ready to fight, to grab a gun and go eliminate some bad guys.

For the first time since she got there, she knew the men

her brother had surrounded himself with were stronger than any threat that could come at them, and she understood what Kyra was saying. The fear would always be there, but so was the confidence that they would be okay. Because they were badasses. All of them.

I SHOULDN'T SMILE, but I really couldn't help it. I don't think I could have planned the whole thing better if I tried. And as much as I tried to make everything work out, I didn't even try for this one. It just fell into my lap.

"I thought you didn't want Allen coming back here," Eli said.

"I don't, and he's not coming back here. He's sending his replacements. He thinks that's going to be enough to get himself out of debt."

"He doesn't know you well."

I chuckled. "No, he doesn't."

"Who are the new recruits?"

"Braden Wright is one of them."

"He refused. That's why Allen gave us time for the evidence to burn. Because Wright wouldn't play."

"It appears as though his mind has been changed by an old friend of mine."

Eli looked more than a little confused, but it didn't matter to me. Eli didn't know anymore than the rest of them. He thought he was on the inside, but he wasn't. I knew better than to trust anyone. People turn on you in a heartbeat, and criminals have zero loyalty. The only way to inspire loyalty was to threaten people. I had no problem doing that either.

"Allen is trying to set us up. He thinks he is smarter than

we are. He's bringing in Braden Wright, but the other man isn't a firefighter. He's a former SEAL. They're coming here to take down our organization."

"Then we can't let them in. Why did you agree to invite them?"

"Because revenge is fun."

"What?"

I turned and looked at Eli. He was a large man, but all his brains were in his biceps. He couldn't follow a trail laid out for him. He was good as a front man because his face was the one people saw. No one knew I was even a part of the games, but Eli was too dumb to realize he was the only one anyone knew. If the whole thing went down, he would take the fall for it.

Of course, that was my plan the whole time. Eli thought I was watching out for him since he was my cousin, but that didn't mean I wouldn't sell him down the river to save my own ass.

"The new guy, the SEAL, he's going to have to play by the same rules as everyone else. He's going to be coached by Allen. He knows what he's getting into. And chances are, he'll have a tail so the rest of his team knows where we are."

"What? They'll call the cops."

I shook my head and laughed. "No, they won't. They want the glory. They want to take us down themselves. They're going to try to take control of the situation, but they won't have any idea what they're getting into."

"What do you mean?"

"I mean, Allen can tell them anything he wants. He can lay out the whole situation. But we know what they know. We know he'll tell them about our meeting location and not having bugs or weapons. He'll tell them they won't see the outside or inside. But there are things Allen doesn't know.

These guys... they have tech. High tech. Advanced tech. They have things that most of us can't get our hands on. So, they're going to try to get inside. We'll be ready for them. And we'll have some insurance, just in case."

"What kind of insurance?"

I smiled. "The kind that guarantees success."

20

Megan sank onto Mason's couch and sighed. She felt like it was the first real breath she'd taken since Justin knocked on the door that morning and told her she had to come with him to the F-BOMB office.

"Are you doing okay?" Mason asked. He hovered near the kitchen like he wasn't sure if he should be near her or not.

Megan reached out her hand for him to come closer. He took it and let her pull him to the couch next to her. "I'm better now."

"Did Slade give you any issues today?"

Megan shook her head. "He was fine. Everyone was. It was just a lot for me to absorb. The whole day was... I didn't really understand what you guys do, and seeing it firsthand was a little overwhelming."

"We do it to keep people safe."

"I know. And I think it's great. I'm really proud to know all of you."

Mason didn't respond. He just sat there with her hand in his.

"Can I ask you something?"

"Sure."

"Would you be okay if I decided to stay here?"

"You mean tomorrow? No. I think Slade would kill me if I didn't bring you in, and I'm not sure it's a good idea for you to be here alone. Not until all this is over. And until we know what's going on with Leo. If he isn't the one behind all of this, we still need to find out what he's doing."

Megan shook her head. "I don't mean tomorrow. I mean move here. Stayed in Niagara Falls."

Mason leaned back and stared at her. She wasn't sure if the look on his face was a good one or a bad one.

"I'm not asking to move in with you or anything. I don't want to change our situation. I mean, I don't expect anything of you. I wasn't asking you that. I love what we have, but I also love being here. Being near my brother and Kyra, and the rest of the group. I like the area and I have never known people like this before. And yes, I mean, you are part of the reason I want to stay, but I'm not going to try to build a family with you or anything. This is fun, and... I'm sorry. I shouldn't have said anything." Megan moved to get up, but Mason grabbed her hand and kept her on the couch. She looked at their joined hands, then up at him.

He smiled. "I think it would be more than okay if you decided to stay here."

"Yeah?"

He nodded. "Absolutely."

She smiled. She really wanted to kiss him, but she didn't want to make him think she was only staying because of him or that kissing meant sealing some deal they hadn't actually made. Or—

He leaned in and pressed his lips to hers. She sighed again, letting herself melt against him. His hands slid down her sides and back up again, cupping her breasts and using them to guide her onto his lap.

Megan straddled him and gasped when she felt his hard length between her thighs. He groaned and thrust up against her.

"Bed," they murmured together. They pulled apart with matching grins.

Mason's hands stayed on her body as she got up. He hooked a finger in the band of her jeans and lifted her shirt. He kissed her stomach, licking her exposed skin. He pushed her shirt up until she took the hint and pulled it off. Mason went to work on her jeans, unbuttoning and unzipping them as he continued to kiss her body.

She kicked her jeans to the side and stood before him in her bra and panties. She felt exposed after telling him she wanted to stay in New York. More exposed than she'd been since she admitted to him she was pregnant.

Mason leaned back and took his shirt off, then went right back to kissing her. His tongue circled her belly button, then he moved to stand, kissing his way up her torso until his lips met hers again.

They moved toward the bed together, hands exploring and lips sealed together. Megan's thighs ached, the waiting already making her crazy. She wanted to imagine being able to do this again, even after the baby arrived. It was a lot to hope for, but she was starting to accept that she was falling for Mason. He wasn't just a fling anymore. He was someone she wanted to spend more time with. Someone she wanted to explore a relationship with.

She had no idea if he felt the same, but she was pretty sure he did. The way he looked at her and the little things he did to show her she mattered stuck in her mind all the time.

"I need you," he whispered against her lips. "I'm not sure I'm going to be able to wait long."

She shook her head. "I want to feel you inside me now. I can't wait."

"Are you sure?" he asked.

Megan nodded and reached for him. She cupped him through his jeans and moaned at the feel of him in her hand. They both fumbled with his zipper to free him. She wrapped her hand around him as he shoved his jeans off his hips. He groaned and thrust into her hand. He shoved at his briefs, his jerky motions ineffective at getting those down while she stroked him.

"Fucking hell," he growled. "We need a condom."

Megan moved with him to the nightstand. She let go of him and opened her palm for the condom. He gave it to her and dropped to his knees while she opened the package. He kissed her stomach again and trailed his tongue lower while he nudged her thighs apart. He drew her panties down her legs and made himself space between her legs. One long lick had her knees buckling and her falling onto the bed behind her. Mason knelt at the edge of the bed and pressed her thighs wide, taking another taste.

"Let me have one."

She wasn't sure she could stop it if she tried. He slid two fingers into her and groaned with her when they slid in without any resistance.

"You're ready for me. Let go, Megan. Don't hold back."

He wasn't slow with his movements. His fingers pressed thick and long into her and his tongue made quick work or her clit. The orgasm came up on her so quickly she lost all control of her body and flailed on the bed as it took over.

"Fuck. Yes. Mason. Oh, God. Yes, yes, yes!"

She screamed and cried and whimpered when he pulled

his fingers out. She didn't notice him taking the condom from her hand and barely processed anything until he slammed into her in one smooth motion.

"Oh, God," she moaned, her body tightening around him as another orgasm raced toward her.

"Fuck, Megan."

She couldn't say anything. Her brain was mush and her insides were locked up. The only thing that worked was the parts Mason had control over.

He pressed his thumb to her clit and sent her back over the edge. She screamed and cried as he let go and slammed hard into her. He backed off almost as soon as he pressed in so deep. Megan wanted that back, but she knew he was thinking about the baby. The last thing they needed was another trip to the hospital.

"Look at me, Megan."

She pried her eyes open and watched him as he stared at her. His gaze strayed from her face to where their bodies met and back up again. His jaw tightened and his eyes started to close. Then his muscles jumped, and he held himself still inside her. She felt him pulse and come, their bodies linked.

He brought their joined hands to his lips. He kissed the inside of her wrist, then lowered their hands to his chest and held them there.

"Did I hurt you?"

Megan shook her head. "It was perfect. You were perfect."

He smiled faintly. "I think we were perfect."

She smiled back.

He pulled out and went to the bathroom to clean up. She took her turn after he was done, then they climbed into bed together.

"Are you sure you are okay with me staying in town?"

He kissed the top of her head and squeezed her tighter. "Yes. I'm very, very happy to hear that."

MEGAN WENT into the office with Mason the next day. She decided to start looking for jobs right away so she could secure something before she got too much farther along in her pregnancy. It was a risk to change jobs when she was pregnant, but since she decided to move, she wanted to make it happen as soon as possible.

There was a chance she could stay on with her current company and manage her clients remotely, but Megan wasn't sure she wanted to do that. If she had other options, she wanted to explore them.

A quick search showed a few companies looking for sales agents. She tried not to be too excited. She knew a lot of people worked in sales, and it was easy to get passed over for a job. Especially if they thought she would need moving expenses.

Megan went to talk to Kyra. She needed a favor. "Do you have a minute?"

"Of course," Kyra said. She hit another key on her keyboard, then looked up with a smile.

"I don't want to tell Justin yet, but I've decided to move here."

"What? You have? Because of Mason?"

Megan shook her head. "No. Not because of Mason. The whole reason I came up here when I did was to see if this was a place I might want to move. I feel like I need a change. I don't have people in Kentucky. I don't have a best friend or a group of friends or anyone, really. I have my parents, but they do their own thing. I have my work, but I can sell office supplies from anywhere. Hell, I can sell anything if I really want to."

"Okay. I can respect that. And understand. Why don't you want your brother to know?"

"I'll tell him, but I don't know how long it'll take me to find a job. I was updating my resume and thought about applying to a couple, but I don't want them to see Kentucky and dismiss my application because they aren't willing to pay relocation. I really don't have much stuff that I would bring, so I'd fly home and drive my car up here. Relocation would be mostly a waste. But I know companies get funny about stuff like that."

"Okay?"

"Can I use your address?"

"Our house?"

Megan nodded. "Yes. I know it's a lot to ask."

"No, it's not. Of course you can. You didn't even need to ask something like that."

"Are you sure?"

"Absolutely. And let me know how the search goes."

"I will. Thank you."

Kyra nodded. She was smiling, so hopefully that meant she was okay with Megan moving to town.

Megan updated her resume and applied to two of the jobs she found. She didn't think anything would come from either of them, but it was good to put herself out there.

DEX AND MASON parked near the casino in downtown Niagara Falls. It seemed like a good meeting spot since they were supposed to be blending in. How the four of them were going to blend in, Mason wasn't sure, but he was going along with the plan.

Mason still believed Leo was the one pulling the strings on the card game happening the next night, but even if he wasn't, they all had to be careful. Whoever was behind it could be watching them. Which was why they needed to blend in.

Mason and Dex walked through downtown trying to pretend they were casually out for a walk like the tourists in the area. Parking near the casino was easy because people frequented it as much as they did the waterfall that brought the majority of visitors to town. It was a walk to get from one to the other, but on a weekday, it was busy enough for them to not stand out.

As they got closer to the Falls, the crowds picked up. Mason and Dex exchanged a glance and focused straight ahead on their destination. There was no way of knowing who could be watching them.

"Two please," Dex said when they finally made it to the front of the line. Braden and Wray were two spots behind them.

Dex took the tickets, and they walked to the side. They pretended to be looking around. Braden and Wray joined them a minute later and asked, "Do you know which way we need to go for the next boat?"

"Yeah, it looks like we're on the same one as you. It's just up here. Ever been?"

The men exchanged meaningless small talk while they got in line with everyone else going to the ferry. They accepted their raincoats and pulled them on as they found a spot at the back. They figured the ride was out in the open enough that they might not draw attention to their actions but busy enough that they could blend in. Dex and Mason agreed having Wray and Braden to the office was a risk, and for them to show up at the fire station or their homes again could raise red flags. Someplace neutral and public shouldn't attract attention, as long as no one noticed the four of them were meeting.

"I didn't see anyone," Mason said after a few minutes.

"Neither did I. I think we're good," Dex agreed. "Tell us what we need to know."

Allen nodded and jumped in. "Tomorrow they'll send a text with the location. When they do, reply with Y only. A black sedan will meet you there. They will take your devices and scan you for any bugs or other tech, then put you in the back and blindfold you. When you get to the location, they'll bring you into the game room."

"How many people can we expect to be there?"

"Usually four or five tables of players plus staff. I'd count on thirty to fifty people in total."

"Do you know if any of them are in the same position? It seems like there have to be some people who are just there for the game and not there to pay off a debt."

Wray nodded. "I think some are. They likely have no idea what happens. But I've never seen anyone show up without a blindfold on, so it's not like any of the people there are totally innocent."

"Good point," Mason said. "What happens when you get inside?"

"They'll put you at a table. When I went with Sam, they separated us. I don't know how they determine who sits where, but you don't get to pick your seat."

"We can handle it," Dex said with a nod toward Braden. "You going to be okay with this?"

Braden shrugged. "I'm not sure I have a choice. I can't let you go in there on your own."

"I owe you for that," Dex said. "It takes guts to do what you do every day, but to do this is different. We have no idea what we're going to face." He turned back to Wray. "Do any of the staff carry?"

Wray nodded. "There are guards at the door with weapons in plain sight. The bartenders and servers don't appear to have anything. There are knives at the bar, skewers, stuff like that, but I've never seen guns on them."

"Does anyone walk around as host?"

"Eli will sometimes be there. He isn't always."

"And you're sure you've never seen Leo Knapp?" Mason asked.

Wray shook his head. "Not that I remember. A lot of people have been through there, so it's possible, but if he's there, it's been as a player."

Mason nodded, but the answer still didn't sit well with him.

"Will you take our picture?" a young woman nearby asked Mason.

He forced a smile for her and took her phone. He snapped a few pictures of the friends with the Falls in the background and handed it back.

"Thanks. Hey, can I get your number, too?" she asked.

Mason's brows went up as the other three tried to stifle their laughter. "Sorry, but I'm unavailable."

The woman shrugged. "Worth a shot."

She and her friends laughed and moved to another part of the boat while Mason tried not to toss Dex, Wray, and Braden overboard.

"You could have been her father," Braden said.

Mason flipped him off and growled. "Let's get back to it so we can get out of here. My shoes are soaked."

"He's old man cranky. He sounds more like he could have been her grandfather," Dex said.

Wray and Braden laughed, and Mason just rolled his eyes. Children. All of them.

21

———————

Everyone in the office was on edge the day of the game. Mason could feel the tension in the air. The only thing that eased him a little was having Megan around. She made the guys laugh and brightened up the office a little. Enough that Mason could think straight.

Mid-afternoon, Megan made herself scarce from the rest of them so they could do their last-minute prep, but Mason missed having her around. He was bouncing on his toes when the text came through with the address for the meeting. It was smack in the center of downtown.

"That's perfect," Dunn said.

"Too perfect," Mason countered.

"This isn't outside their norm," Dex said. "Wray said he's met them downtown before."

"It just feels too easy," Mason said.

He hoped he was being paranoid, but he couldn't shake the feeling that Leo was behind the whole thing. There was no proof no matter how deep they dove into him, but he was around, and Mason knew he wouldn't make a point of seeking out Mason, or Megan, if there wasn't a reason.

Mason walked through the offices in search of Megan before he suited up. He wanted a minute to talk to her. When he couldn't find her, he went to Kyra's office.

"Have you seen Megan?"

"She went out for a minute."

"She went out?" Mason asked. "What do you mean, she went out? She was supposed to stay here."

"What happened?" Slade asked as he walked into Kyra's office.

"Megan's gone," Mason said.

"What?"

"She didn't want to tell you guys." Kyra looked between the two men. She got up from her chair and came around her desk. She put a hand on Slade's arm and drew his attention. "Your sister wants to move here. She asked me the other day if she could use our address for resumes. I told her yes, and she started applying for jobs. She wants to get something before she's too much further along into her pregnancy."

"Wow, okay. Um, that's awesome, but what does that have to do with her being gone?" Slade asked.

"She got a call today. One of the jobs she applied for wanted to interview her and had a spot this afternoon. She told me where she's going, but you guys were all so busy that she didn't want to interrupt. Plus, she didn't want to jinx it. She's really hoping it works out," Kyra said. She smiled up at Slade, and he relaxed. He trusted Kyra.

Mason did, too, but he didn't trust the outside world. "So, she left. Without telling us, without anyone watching her, without protection?"

"She's a grown woman," Kyra argued.

"Who could be in danger," Mason said.

"Okay, let's calm down. My sister owes us an explanation, but if I know anything about Megan, it's that she won't sit tight when she gets something in her head. I can't tell you how many times I got in trouble growing up just because she wanted to see what I was doing."

"I hope you're right," Mason said.

"Ready?" Dex asked.

Mason scowled at Slade and Kyra and nodded. He followed Dex out of the building and into one of the team SUVs. Dex was driving his personal car and leaving it close to the location. Mason was going to follow Dex and Braden, then communicate with the team when they reached their destination.

Mason held back where he wouldn't be noticed but could still see Braden and Dex. They talked to each other, but their faces displayed the tension Mason felt. Dunn wanted Dex to wear a vest, but Dex said it would be picked up by the wands. Everything they thought of would be noticed, and then Dex wouldn't make it through the door. If he didn't make it, they had no way of knowing what was going on inside or what happened to Braden or Wray and his family. Dex insisted on playing by the rules.

A black sedan pulled up in front of Braden and Dex. Mason watched as two men got out. He took pictures of them and sent them back to English. The men talked to Braden and Dex, then nodded toward the waiting vehicle.

Nothing seemed out of the ordinary. For the people walking by, it could be two men who were waiting for a ride. Mason realized how easy it was for the entire thing to happen without anyone paying any attention.

Braden and Dex got in the back of the sedan, and it pulled away from the curb. Mason waited until they were half a block ahead before he pulled out and followed them.

The twists and turns the driver took said he was trying to

check for a tail. Mason was careful, taking different turns if he had to in order to not be noticed. He had no clue if it worked, but when the sedan stopped in front of a large warehouse on the north side of town, he hoped it meant he was successful.

Dex and Braden were let out of the car. Both had blind-folds on, but their hands weren't tied. A man walked out of the building in front of them and waved a portable scanner up their fronts and backs. Both men removed their phones and handed them over to one of the men. Only then did they move toward the building.

Mason hit the button on the dash to call the office. Dunn answered. "Did they stop?"

"Yes. Dex and Braden just went inside. It's a large ware-house, very similar to the one where the fire was. A few buildings around the place, but mostly wide open. It looks like there are cameras on the corners of the building, so we'll need some help getting those out of service before we can get too close," Mason said.

"Do you have an address for us?" Dunn asked.

Mason relayed the address and kept his gaze trained on the building. No one moved around it. Everything was still. He wondered where the other players were and how they got there. If they had more than one vehicle transporting people to the site, it was likely someone would be arriving soon.

"Mason, did you say 3649?" Slade asked.

The tension in his voice had Mason shifting in his seat. Maybe it was his imagination. They were all tense. He looked at the building in front of him and confirmed the address. "Yeah. The building has it right on the front. Why?"

"Because that's the address where Megan had her interview."

MEGAN KNEW something was off when she pulled up in front of the building. It didn't look like any corporation where she'd worked before, and she had a hard time believing the job was real. She tried to tell herself she was being paranoid, but the feeling kept sinking deeper and deeper into her.

The man she met first was polite and pleasant. He welcomed her and offered her a glass of water and something to eat. Megan accepted the water but passed on the food. Her stomach was in knots and food would not make it better.

When he left her in the gray office, Megan looked around and tried to figure out more about the company. She couldn't find any details about it online, but she knew there were companies that didn't have websites, even though the concept was ridiculous to her.

It was only when Leo walked in that Megan knew for sure she was in trouble and that the job interview wasn't an actual job interview. She should have listened to Justin and Mason. Now all she could do was hope they found her before it was too late.

MASON WASN'T sure he'd survive long enough to wait for the rest of the team to arrive. Megan was in that building. She was tricked into going there. She was likely going to be hurt. And he couldn't do a damn thing about it.

When the other SUV parked next to Mason, he nearly took off right then. He was smart enough to wait for backup, but he wasn't waiting another second. He had to find her.

"Mason, stop," Dunn said. "I understand you want to get

in there, but we need a plan. This was supposed to be a recon mission to watch Dex and Braden's backs. This is different. We don't know what the building looks like. We don't know anything."

"I know the woman I love is in that building, and that means she's in danger," Mason said.

The others stared at him, their eyes wide, faces shocked.

Mason had no idea why they were looking at him like that until he played his words back. He drew a breath and closed his eyes. When he opened them again, he focused on Slade. "If she gets hurt because of me, I'll never be able to forgive myself."

Slade nodded sharply and focused on Dunn. "We need to save my sister."

"Cameras are looped," English said. "We can get to the building without being detected. I have no way of knowing what's inside. If there is something, it's closed circuit and I can't get into it without an access point, which I don't have."

"We'll take it. Any blueprints?" Dunn asked.

English shook his head. "No. Everything I can find shows an open building, four floors, but no internal structure. We can tell from here that isn't the case."

"How can you tell?" Archer asked.

"The lights in the second-floor window. Third from left. You see the light there, but you don't see any glow in the windows next to that. If there wasn't a wall between them, we would see the light, so the blueprints are shit," English explained.

"What do we do?" Jack asked.

"Jack out here. Anyone comes out that door, take them out. The rest of us are going inside. Mason, you're with me. Slade with Archer. Rocky and English. Circle the building to find other exits, then we breach. Everyone on comms?" Dunn met the eyes of the entire group.

They all nodded.

"Good, then let's go."

Mason's anxious energy pulsed through his body. He was grateful Dunn was his partner. He would keep Mason in check and make sure he wasn't doing something that would make the whole situation worse.

The pairs moved in a line toward the building with Jack watching their six. At the door, they split off with Mason and Dunn going to the left and the other teams going right. Rocky and English were going to head around to the back of the building and try to access it from there. Dunn and Mason moved to the door on their side and waited until the others were in position.

"Ready," Slade said through the comms.

They all waited a few seconds until Rocky repeated the same word. Dunn was last, making sure everyone was set before giving the order to enter the building.

Mason opened the door and stood back so Dunn could go in first. The hallway they walked into was dark. Every other light flickered overhead. Mason strained to hear sounds, but the building was quiet.

Like English said, it also was not a wide open space. The hallway they were in led in two different directions after a few feet. Dunn and Mason traded a glance, then moved toward the front of the building.

Their footsteps were quiet on the vinyl floor. Guns raised, ready to eliminate any threats. Mason's blood pumped hard through his veins, ready to attack. Ready to save Megan. Ready for anything.

"Game. Ground floor. Back half. Two guards at the door. Heavily armed," Rocky said quietly.

"Copy," Dunn acknowledged.

Mason kept his focus on the pathway in front of him. He needed to find Megan.

"Second floor clear," Archer said.

"Heading to three," English added.

"Two good copies," Dunn said.

Mason stopped. He thought he heard something. Dunn froze next to him. They didn't move until a scream had them both turning.

Mason and Dunn ducked around a corner and looked back down the hallway. Leo had Megan with her hands bound. He dragged her out of a doorway just past the hallway they used when they breached the building.

"Megan," Mason breathed. He lifted his gun to eliminate Leo.

"If you miss, it'll ricochet and could hit her," Dunn said.

"We can't let him take her out of here."

"Jack, side door."

"Door is blocked. A van just pulled up."

"A van?"

Mason made a move to follow them, and Leo aimed a gun down the hallway and fired off a few rounds.

"Nice to see you again, my old friend. Sorry I can't stick around and catch up," Leo said.

Megan screamed as Leo shoved her out of sight.

Mason moved to follow them, but Leo reached around the edge again and fired down the hallway. Mason hit the floor and waited for the bullets to stop. As soon as they did, he was on his feet again, running down the hall.

"I can't see the door at all," Jack said.

"Don't lose that van," Mason growled as he raced toward the door. He hit the bar to release it and stopped. The door opened less than an inch. Mason hit it again. And again.

"Van is on the move," Jack said.

"Follow them. Megan is in that van," Dunn said. He caught up to Mason and slammed his shoulder into the door. "Our door is compromised. We need another exit."

"Front door is clear from here," Jack said. "In pursuit now."

Mason and Dunn retraced their steps and made it to the front door in time to see Leo drive by in an SUV.

"What the hell?" Dunn said.

"Did you see Megan?" Mason asked.

"No, but we have to follow him. Jack is on the van, we'll get Leo," Dunn said. He clicked his comms. "Megan is out of the building. We're following. The rest of you watch Dex and Braden's backs."

"Copy."

"Where's Megan?" Slade demanded.

"Leo has her," Dunn said.

Mason felt the words like a punch to his gut. Leo was his problem. Megan was in danger because of him. Leo only got to her because she was someone in Mason's life.

Dunn got behind the wheel and followed Leo's SUV. He headed straight for the highway, getting into the middle of traffic before taking a quick exit.

"Got the van. No one here except the driver. He was delivering food. Has no idea what I'm talking about. Captain Patrick is here," Jack said.

"Fucking hell," Mason said.

"We're behind Leo. He has to have Megan. North heading toward Lewiston on one-oh-four."

"Patrick's calling in support."

Dunn floored it, gaining on Leo. Mason watched as the SUV drew closer. He leaned forward. He couldn't see

Megan, but she had to be in there. There was nowhere else she would be.

Dunn tapped the rear quarter panel and sent the other SUV spinning toward the shoulder. The tires hit the soft gravel and slowed. Leo tried to correct, but Dunn hit them again and the SUV finally stopped perpendicular to the road.

Dunn and Mason were out of their vehicle and approaching Leo's in seconds. The rear of the SUV was in the road, blocking the entire view of the driver's side. Dark tinted windows made it impossible to see movement inside the SUV. Mason and Dunn signaled to each other to move around opposite ends of the SUV.

Mason went to the front. The interior light was on, and the driver's door was open. The seat was empty.

"Mason," Megan whimpered from a few feet away.

Mason looked up and saw her six feet from the front of the SUV's bumper. Leo had one hand wrapped around her throat, the other holding a knife to her stomach. Tears streamed down her face, and the fear in her eyes tore a hole inside him.

It was all his fault.

"Are you okay?" Mason asked.

Megan nodded as much as she could with Leo holding her throat.

"What do you want, Leo?"

"What do I want? What do I want? Let's see. I want to be left the hell alone. I wasn't bothering you. Why come after me?"

"You're the one with a hostage."

"Yes, because you put me in this position."

"So, you're behind Marzette Corporation?"

Leo shook his head and pressed the blade against

Megan's abdomen. She gasped and tried to move back, but he held her in place.

"Please," Megan cried.

"I told you everything would be fine if you did as I asked," Leo said like he was chastising a child.

Megan closed her eyes, and more tears ran free.

"Let her go," Mason demanded.

"Now, why would I do that? She's the only reason you're here and not at the game. If I let her go, then you'll go back there and spoil the fun I have planned for the rest of your team."

"What are you talking about?"

Leo smiled. His eyes blazed with evil. "I'm talking about the fireworks set to go off in less than five minutes. Maybe I should let her go. Then you can go watch."

Dunn and Mason traded a look. They both had their guns trained on Leo, but without a clear shot, there was no way to get rid of him.

"All those people. Your teammates. The firefighters. All the innocent business people." Leo shook his head. "And all on your watch. You were inside the building and never picked up on the explosives. Do you think the city is going to want you around protecting them when an entire block is leveled? I know I don't feel safer."

Dunn moved behind the SUV and spoke to Archer and Slade. "Evacuate the building. Now. Five minutes. Get the hell out of there."

"Well, I guess it's time for me to go." He turned his head and leaned in close to Megan. "I'm sorry, but I don't think you'd be a good fit for the position. Considering you'll be unavailable for a while."

Then he plunged the knife into her stomach.

"NO!" Mason shouted. He ran to Megan and picked her up off the ground. He cradled her head in his lap and pressed his hand against the wound in her abdomen.

He was only vaguely aware of Dunn calling for an ambulance as Leo took off in his SUV. Mason stared into Megan's eyes and hated himself for letting her in that first night. If he'd turned her away, she never would have met Leo and she never would have gotten hurt.

Another vehicle pulled up and stopped. Rocky raced over to Megan and took over. Mason moved away, his body in slow motion. He stared down the road where Leo had taken off.

He was going to pay.

Mason got into the SUV Rocky and English drove and pulled out onto the road. He pushed the gas to the floor. The only thing that mattered was making Leo pay for what he did to Megan.

It didn't take long for Mason to catch up to Leo's SUV. He drove right up behind him and slammed into the back. It spun, but Leo righted it and took off, pulling away just enough that Mason could make another run at him. He hit the back again and Leo spun off onto the side of the road.

Mason got out of his SUV and went to the driver's side. Leo was leaned over the steering wheel, trying to push himself up.

Mason yanked open the door and dragged Leo out of the SUV. He slammed him against the side, and Leo grinned up at him. "Hi, Mason. I didn't think I'd see you again so soon. How's Megan?"

"You son of a bitch," Mason said. He punched the other man, enjoying the crunch of his nose as it broke beneath Mason's blow.

"Maybe I should ask how your friends are. Did they survive?"

Mason punched him in the stomach. Leo doubled over, but he got up smiling.

"This is assault, Mason. Do you really want to go back to jail? Hey, maybe we can be roomies again." Leo laughed.

"You're not going to jail," Mason growled.

"Oh, that's so nice of you, Mason. You're going to let me go free."

Mason laughed and shook his head. "I'm going to kill you."

Leo snorted. "Then everyone else will die. Including you and your bitch."

Mason punched him again. And again. And again. He'd never hated another person as much as he hated Leo in that moment. He wanted the man to die. He wanted him to not ever take another breath. He deserved nothing more than to burn in hell for what he did.

Mason backed up and readied to swing again. Leo lifted his head with a smile and held his hands up like he was surrendering. That was when Mason realized what he was holding.

His phone buzzed in his pocket, but Mason couldn't worry about that. He had to focus on the psycho in front of him.

"What is that?" Mason asked.

Leo choked out a laugh and waved it around. "This? This is the present I had set up for you. Haven't you ever seen a deadman switch?"

Mason closed his eyes and drew a deep breath. An odd feeling of calm washed over him. "Where is the bomb?"

"Oh, it's close, Mason. Very, very close." Leo smiled. His smile turned to laughter that crawled up Mason's spine and made him twitch. The man was truly evil. "See, I knew what you would do. I knew you would come in after your friends. I knew you would have multiple points of entry and that I would be able to get out. I knew you would chase after me with your precious replacement Megan. And I knew I needed insurance. That's what this is."

"Insurance?"

Leo chuckled. "Exactly. Because if you kill me, I kill you. It's almost poetic, don't you think?"

"I think I might still take my chances," Mason growled.

"And leave replacement Megan without a Baby Daddy?"

Mason paused. He hated to admit it, but Leo was right. He didn't want to leave Megan without someone. He didn't want her to have to do everything on her own. He knew he wasn't the father, but he wanted to be. He wanted Megan in his life. And the baby. He wanted all of it.

But he had to survive in order to have it.

"I guess you are going back to jail," Mason said.

Leo grinned at him and shook his head. "That's not going to work for me."

"I'm not letting you walk. You tried to kill Megan and the baby. You kidnapped a firefighter. You ran an illegal gambling ring that was designed to steal from people so they would help you destroy evidence."

Leo raised his eyebrows at the last one.

"Didn't think we knew about that one? We did. We know everything there is to know about you. And we can make it stick. You're not getting away with it this time. There's not going to be a fall guy. We have your cousin, Eli, too. We have everything."

Leo glared at Mason for a long moment. He nodded slowly. "I have to admit, I'm impressed. I didn't think you'd figure it all out." He held up his hands again, indicating he wasn't going to be a threat. "There's just one thing you didn't account for."

"What's that?"

Leo shrugged. "I'd rather die than go back to jail." He opened his hand and released the deadman switch.

Mason watched like it was happening in slow motion. Leo's hand opening. The switch light blinking. It fell from Leo's hand and sailed toward the ground.

Run!

Every fiber of his being said he had one chance to get the hell out of there. That if he was going to get the future he wanted, he had to run.

So he did.

Mason turned. He ran. He only had seconds. The failsafe on the switch wouldn't be long. He heard the rattle of it hitting the ground, but he didn't turn back to look. He hadn't even made it back to his SUV. If he could—

BOOM!

The blast knocked Mason off his feet. It threw him against the SUV. He hit his head. Everything hurt. Smoke, fire, burning flesh filled his nose. His eyes watered. Then everything went black.

MEGAN HEARD voices in her sleep. She tried to place them. Her head was fuzzy. Maybe she left the TV on before she fell asleep.

Megan tried to push herself up, but pain sliced through her stomach. She groaned and reached for the area that hurt. Something dragged across her body.

She pried her eyes open and did her best to focus. She wasn't at home. The beige walls and dark TV had her trying to figure out where she was. She turned her head and spotted Justin. In a chair. His eyes were red.

"What...?"

"You're awake. Do you remember what happened?" Justin asked.

Megan shook her head. "Why am I here?"

Justin looked at the other side of the bed. Megan followed his gaze until she saw a nurse. Mason's sister-in-law. "Bernadette?"

She smiled and nodded. "That's a good sign. You don't remember why you're here?"

Megan shook her head. "I... The baby!" She reached for her stomach as the whole thing rushed back to her. The interview. Leo. Him dragging her out and putting her in the backseat. Getting run off the road, then stabbed. Mason.

"The baby is fine," Justin said firmly. "You need to rest, though."

"Mason? Where's Mason?"

Justin looked up at Bernadette and grimaced.

"Tell me," Megan snarled.

"Mason is upstairs. He has a serious concussion and some burns. He should recover, but he's not awake last I checked," Bernadette said.

Megan closed her eyes and tried to fight her tears, but they wouldn't stop. "I'm so sorry. It's not fair of me to ask you about him, but..."

"You love him," Bernadette said. She nodded. "My sister was the same. Mason has a way of making himself very lovable. Before Megan died, I loved him, too. Not the same way, but he was a brother to me. He was kind, and he adored my sister. I thought he would protect her from anything, but he couldn't. He had demons. Demons I don't think he knew he had."

"I know you hate him—"

Bernadette nodded. "I do. I hate what he did to my family. What he took from us. I don't think I'll ever be able to forgive him for that. But I'm trying very hard to move on. Seeing him again opened a wound. A big one. I will never forget my sister, but she wouldn't want me to punish Mason forever."

"I don't know if I could be as kind as you're being right now."

Bernadette smiled. "You had nothing to do with any of it. I'm sorry for the way I treated you when you were here before. I won't be your nurse, but I wanted to see you and wish you well."

Megan smiled. "Thank you, Bernadette. And I am sorry for your loss."

She smiled sadly and left the room.

"Obviously there's a lot I don't know. First, why were you here before? Second, how to you know her? And third, are you okay?"

Megan took a deep breath and winced at the pain in her side. "I'll be okay."

"And the other two questions?"

"We'll talk about that stuff later. Can you find out how Mason is?"

Megan hoped her brother would leave the room for a few minutes, but all he did was pull out his phone and send a text. "Still asleep."

Megan dropped her head back to the pillow and tried to figure out how she could get rid of Justin. She loved her brother, but the emotional impact of the day was starting to overwhelm her and she was going to lose it. Soon.

"So, do you want to watch some TV? Usually the channels suck, but we can find something." He grabbed the remote and turned on the TV. He flipped for a few minutes, then stopped at a made for TV romance.

"We don't have to watch this," Megan said. She loved the movies, but she knew it would bring out the tears if she watched it.

Justin shrugged. "I don't mind. Plus, it's a good excuse."

"For what?" Megan asked.

Justin smiled at her and reached for her hand. He squeezed it and leaned back in his seat to watch the movie. He didn't let go of her hand.

Megan got it. She settled back on the bed and let the emotions out. She laughed and cried and held her brother's hand until the pain meds did their job and she passed out again.

MASON COULDN'T EVEN REMEMBER HAVING a drink, let alone enough to give him such a painful headache. He groaned and wondered if he could make it to the bathroom without puking or pissing on himself.

"Whoa, whoa. You can't get up on your own."

"What?" he croaked. Who was there? And why?

A beep echoed through his head. Mason turned and sat on the edge of the bed, his eyes still closed against the pain.

"You have to wait for a nurse."

"Nurse? Dex?"

"Yeah. You're in the hospital. You've been out since the explosion."

"Explo—Leo. Is he dead?"

"Yeah."

"Good." Mason forced his eyes to open. "How's—"

"How are we doing in here?" The voice was behind Mason and entirely too happy for him.

"He was trying to get up," Dex said.

"That's a good sign, but after a head injury like yours, we need to help you for the first few times. Where are you headed?"

"Bathroom," Mason said.

"Okay, let's go."

Mason looked up at her. She was shorter than him with gray hair and a kind smile. She was probably great at her job, but there was no way she could actually help him. And no way he was going to use the bathroom in front of her.

"Would you rather I helped you?" Dex said.

Mason growled at him and rolled his eyes. Which only made his head spin. "Fine." Mason accepted the arm of the nurse and was surprised when she held him up without any issues. She told him he needed to sit in the bathroom since he was a fall risk. She was respectful of his privacy and stepped out once he was on the toilet with a stern word to call her when he was ready to stand up.

Mason took a minute alone to put the pieces back together. He needed to know how Megan was. If Dex was there, Mason hoped that meant Braden was okay, too. Too many people were involved in the mess Leo created.

Leo.

Mason should have known something was going on sooner. He should have put an end to it long before he did. Instead, he couldn't figure it out and people got hurt.

The nurse helped Mason back to his bed, and he finally looked at Dex. His eye was bruised, and he sat like he had bruised ribs. "What happened?"

Dex shook his head.

"Tell me. I need to know."

Dex sighed and leaned forward. He winced and straightened. "The whole thing was a setup. They knew we were coming. All the people inside were there to take us out. Braden saved my ass. We had to basically fight our way out. Archer and Slade ended up helping us, but I would be dead if it weren't for Braden."

"Fucking hell."

Dex nodded. "Yeah. They were watching us long before we were watching them. They knew all of us."

"How is... everyone else?"

Dex held his gaze. "Megan had surgery. She's going to be fine, and the baby's not harmed. Leo is dead. Eli is in custody. The rest of the players are rolling on each other. Everyone is trying to cut their own deal so they don't go down for their involvement. Leo had a much bigger organization than we knew. And he was smart. He had it all hidden. We never would have found him if it weren't for you."

Mason shook his head. "He never would have done this if it weren't for me."

"He was running all this long before he got on our radar. It would have kept happening. You were the one who figured out that he was the mastermind."

"It doesn't feel like I figured anything out."

"Hey, get some sleep. You need it. We'll talk more tomorrow."

Mason nodded as his eyes closed and he drifted off.

"What do you want to do?" Justin asked as Megan handed the tablet back to the nurse.

She was free to leave the hospital. Her stitches would come out in a few days, and she needed to schedule an appointment with an OB, but she could go home.

She just wasn't sure where that was.

"I don't know," Megan admitted. "I just need to rest and decide what to do from here."

"Do you want to stay with us for a few days? I can get your stuff from Mason's."

Megan nodded. She hadn't heard from Mason and had no idea if he wanted her at his place or not. She was going to need help getting around for a week or two, so it made sense to go back to Justin and Kyra's.

Justin went to get his truck while Kyra helped Megan shove the rest of her things into the patient belongings bag the hospital gave her. The clothes she was wearing when she got there were evidence, but she was allowed to keep anything that didn't have blood on it.

"Have you talked to Mason?" Kyra asked as they walked out.

Megan shook her head.

"I'm sure you'll hear from him soon."

Megan nodded, feeling a lot less confident than Kyra did.

Justin was parked in front when they made it outside. He helped her into the seat, then drove to his place. He and Kyra were careful about getting Megan inside without Howler attacking her. The dog was clearly worried when Megan shuffled past him. He whimpered, and when Megan sat on the couch, he walked over slowly and put his head on her lap. He stayed like that the rest of the day while Megan watched movies and tried not to stare at her phone.

Megan drifted off at one point. When she woke up, she smelled something that made her stomach growl and heard a whispered conversation.

"We can get married anytime," Kyra said.

"I know. I want to marry you. I don't want you to think I'm trying to get out of this."

Kyra chuckled. "You couldn't if you wanted to. You're stuck with me."

"Best news ever. I'll start making calls tomorrow. I'm not sure if we can get our whole deposit back, but we'll see. Maybe when we reschedule we should plan to host ourselves."

"That's probably a good idea," Kyra said.

Megan heard them kissing. She checked her phone, but she had no missed calls from Mason. No texts. Nothing. Just silence.

She wanted to know what he was thinking, but she was afraid to ask him. If he was done, she would respect that. If not... why hadn't he called?

"You're awake," Kyra said. Her voice was far too bright and happy.

"Yeah," Megan said. She groaned when she shifted her position. "Why are you guys canceling your wedding?"

"Because you had surgery," Justin said.

Megan snorted. "Seriously? You're going to put your life on hold because of me?" They looked at her like there was no other choice. "No. I'm not going to let you do that. You need to have your joy. Celebrate your love. Tell the world that assholes like Leo can't take things from you. No. You're getting married."

Kyra and Justin exchanged a glance and laughed. "Well, okay then. I guess we don't have a choice."

23

MASON DROVE UP THE TWISTY ROAD. THE STONES ON BOTH sides varied from barely visible to towering. Trees dotted the sloping landscape. It almost seemed peaceful there.

He'd never been to Megan's grave. He knew where it was, but he was arrested at her funeral and wasn't present when she was laid to rest. After he was released, he couldn't bring himself to go there. He didn't feel as though he had a right to visit.

But he needed to go now. After everything, he had to see her. To talk to her. To put the past behind him. So he could move forward.

He pulled off the road, careful not to intrude on the graves that lined the street. He got out of his truck and looked up the gentle slope to where her stone stood tall compared to the ones closest to it.

Megan Ruth O'Connor
Wife, sister, daughter, and friend
Gone too soon but always in our hearts

Mason was almost surprised Bernadette didn't manage to get *wife* removed and Megan's name changed on the gravestone. Seeing her name with his last name reminded him of the pain. Of what he did. He tried for years to push it away, but he wanted to feel it. One last time.

Mason sank to the ground in front of Megan's stone. He stared at it, imagining she was there. Sitting on the stone and laughing at him or maybe leaning against it with a scowl on her face. She scowled a lot when he came back. She knew he wasn't okay. She tried to help him, but he couldn't be helped. Not at that point.

He wondered many times how their lives would have changed if he'd gotten the help he needed. If he'd been able to admit what he was dealing with. She might be alive. They might have kids. They would have celebrated twenty years together if she hadn't gotten sick of him and left.

He smiled, picturing her saying she never would have gotten sick of him.

Mason drew in a breath and let his mind talk to her. Speaking out loud felt far too vulnerable, but in his head, he had things to tell her.

Starting with I'm sorry.

He told Megan about Megan. The woman who'd captured his heart recently. About her baby and his teammates. He told her about his life and how he missed her. And he told her he wished things had been different for them.

Then he asked for her to forgive him.

A vehicle parked nearby, but Mason didn't pay attention to it. There were people scattered throughout the cemetery visiting family and friends, and one more car wasn't a big deal. Until he heard Bernadette.

"What are you doing here?"

Mason spun on her and immediately regretted it. His head was still a little wobbly and his legs almost gave out with the quick movement. He stumbled and caught himself on another stone, then steadied himself before he let go.

"I didn't know you'd be here. I'll come back another time."

Mason started to walk past her, but she said, "Wait."

Mason stopped. He struggled to meet her gaze.

"I will probably never be able to forgive you. Adam tells me that isn't fair, but I know I can't. I'm trying, but more than that, I want to. Because I know it's what she would have wanted. She knew you were having trouble. I tried to get her to stay with us, but she wouldn't leave you. She loved you too much to give up on you."

Mason drew in a breath. He worshipped her. He would have done anything for her. If he'd known what was going to happen, he would have gotten help to save her. But he didn't.

"Megan was the best person in my life, and when she..." Bernadette sucked in a breath. "When she died, I lost more than my best friend. I lost my baby, and I lost myself for a while."

"Bernie," Mason sighed. He had no idea she was pregnant. He reached for her, but she stepped back and he let his hand fall.

"I'm sorry. I just... I found out a month ago I'm pregnant again. We'd almost given up. This baby is a miracle baby. But then I saw you in the store. It all came back to me. I've been barely functional. And when your new Megan came into the hospital..."

"I didn't know you worked there," Mason said.

She nodded. "I know. And I know you didn't bring her there to hurt me. I want to be happy for you. And for Megan.

She's a very kind woman, and she obviously loves you. And I hope you two are happy together."

Mason heard the sincerity in her voice and could only nod for a moment. "Thank you. I would never hurt you on purpose. I'll never forgive myself for what happened to Megan, or you. You're wrong about Megan and I, though. She doesn't love me. I'm not the father either."

Bernadette tilted her head. "I thought you said you were the father."

He shook his head. "I lied, and I'm sorry for that. They assumed I was when I brought her in, and I knew I wouldn't be allowed to see her, and she... I was worried about her."

"I understand that. But she does love you. I saw her last week. She told me."

"She did?"

Bernadette smiled. "She did. And I guess that's news to you."

Mason chuckled. "It is. But it's good news."

"Good."

Mason wasn't sure what to say to her. A woman he'd been close enough to that he knew everything about her was a stranger. But she helped him.

"Mason... I hope you'll come back and visit her again. I think she'd like to meet Megan. And your child. If you're willing."

Mason looked back at the stone and swore he saw her grinning at him from her perch on the edge. "I will."

"Goodbye, Mason."

He drew a breath. "Goodbye, Bernadette."

He had a wedding to get ready for.

MEGAN WAS TRYING to brace herself for seeing Mason. It had been a week since she was released from the hospital and she still hadn't heard a word from him. Her brother was unusually quiet about the situation, too. Maybe deciding to move to Niagara Falls wasn't such a good idea.

Megan was still considering her options with that one. She reported what happened to work, and Douglas agreed to give her leave so she could recuperate. It took off some of the pressure so she could think. She definitely needed time to think.

Her parents came in for the wedding a few days earlier and tried to get Megan to move to the hotel with them, but she insisted she wanted to stay with Kyra and Justin. If nothing else, they were good for her mood, and she was never alone. They both took off the week she was home so they could be there if she needed anything. She was finally healed enough that her stitches were out, and she could function normally. Every so often she felt a twinge, but she knew that wasn't just from the knife she took to the gut. It was also from the one in her heart.

Megan drew a breath and forced a smile for her parents. Justin was in one room with his groomsmen, and Kyra was in another with her bridesmaids. Justin was going to walk their mother down the aisle, which meant Megan was going in with their dad. Before the rest of the guests poured in and she had to see anyone she didn't want to see.

Her dad took her hand and looped it through his arm. He smiled at her and started down the aisle. Megan focused on putting one foot in front of the other. If she made it to the end, she would be safe for a little while.

Megan went in first, then her father followed, leaving a space for her mom. Her dad leaned over and said, "How are you feeling?"

Megan smiled. Another smile. Another empty emotion. Another thing she was faking. "I'm good."

"You look beautiful. That color is nice on you."

"Thank you, Dad."

"The hotel is very nice. If you change your mind about staying there, Mom and I will get you a room."

Megan shook her head. "No, thanks. Justin and Kyra are going away for the next week, and I agreed to watch Howler for them."

Her dad chuckled. "He's a good dog. Justin has found a pretty great life here, hasn't he?"

"He has."

"Great friends. A good job. And a wonderful person to share his life with." Her dad sighed. "It's hard not having him home, but your mom and I know he is happy here. That's all that matters to us."

Megan nodded slowly. "Okay."

"You know that's what we want for you, too, right? For you to be happy. Whatever that means to you."

"Um, thanks?"

He chuckled and patted her knee.

Megan smiled again, wondering if something was wrong with either of her parents. Was one of them sick? Were they getting divorced? Why was he talking about happiness being the most important thing? She agreed, but she was also fairly sure some suffering was essential. It wasn't ideal, but she needed money for things like food and diapers, which meant she had to work. And she had to live in a place she could afford. And she had to make decisions based on what was best for not just herself, but for the baby, too.

"Are you and Mom okay?" Megan blurted out.

Her dad turned to her and tilted his head. "Of course. Why do you ask?"

"Because you sound like you're dying or something," Megan hissed.

Her dad chuckled just as the music changed. "Ooh, it's starting."

Kyra's parents were there, but they didn't look overly happy about it. Her dad walked her mother in, and they sat together. Justin walked their mom down the aisle, then took his place next to Rocky, Dex, and Jack. Justin looked over at Megan and winked.

The bridesmaids came in one by one. They all wore pool blue dresses in different styles. When the last of them made it up to the front, the music changed again and Kyra walked down the aisle.

Because she couldn't see Kyra over the rest of the guests, Megan watched her brother. The love in his eyes and the joy on his face were things she'd never seen before. She was happy for him.

Maybe her dad was right. Maybe happiness was the only thing that mattered.

What makes me happy?

She knew the answer as soon as the question whispered through her mind, but it wasn't an option. Mason wasn't hers. He never was.

Megan focused on her brother and Kyra vowing to spend their lives together and to love each other forever. It was beautiful, and the tears that rolled down Megan's cheeks were happy tears. After everything Justin had been through, and Kyra, they deserved to be happy.

Megan followed her parents out of the church. On her way down the aisle alone, she spotted Mason staring at her. Her breath hitched, and she looked away immediately. He was a part of her past now.

Megan stuck close to her parents during pictures, then

rode with them to the reception. She knew eventually she would have to speak to Mason, but she needed more time to heal before she did.

The reception was what any good party was supposed to be. People laughed and drank and danced and had fun. Megan let her brother spin her around the dance floor and did her share of laughing. She was having fun. Even without Mason, she was falling for the rest of the people in Niagara Falls and leaning toward staying.

The music slowed, and the couples around her immediately paired off. Megan started to move toward her chair but was blocked by Kyra and Justin. She changed directions and found her parents in her way. Another change and Lily and Archer blocked her.

She turned again and found Mason standing just a few feet away.

"May I have this dance?" he asked.

Megan drew in a breath and prepared to say no until she realized the others were watching her and smiling. "What...?"

"Find your happiness," her dad whispered.

Megan closed her eyes for a moment, then nodded. She felt Mason before he touched her. He took her hand in his and placed his other one on her waist, keeping a safe distance between them.

"I wanted to apologize."

Megan wasn't sure she could listen to him tell her he was sorry for not calling. She got the message once. He didn't need to spell it out for her. She tried to pull back, but he held firm.

"I wanted to apologize for getting you hurt."

"That wasn't your fault," Megan said. "That psycho is to blame, not you."

"He did it because he knew we knew each other."

"You didn't do anything. You can't blame yourself for it."

He smiled at her, but it was definitely forced. "I thought I lost you."

"So you left?"

Mason shook his head. "I knew Rocky would take care of you."

Megan shook her head. "I don't mean then. I understand why you went after Leo. He'll never hurt anyone again, thanks to you. But that wasn't when you left. You left when you didn't call or text. When you didn't check on me."

"I checked on you every day. I asked Slade about you. I got updates. I knew you were in pain, and I knew I'd only bring more until I got a few things sorted out."

"Like what?"

"My wife."

Megan drew back. She never wanted to replace her. She never imagined she would or could. Loving a person meant giving a part of yourself to them, and you couldn't ever get that part back. It belonged to that person. His wife, Megan, would always have a piece of Mason. She took that with her when she died. And Megan respected that.

"What did you have to sort out?"

Mason drew a breath and met her gaze. "I needed to talk to her about you. To tell her I'd fallen in love with someone else. To ask her to watch over you. I needed to know she forgave me for what happened."

Megan couldn't breathe. Hope bloomed so big inside her that there was no space for air. "And?" she squeaked out.

"She would have loved you."

Megan breathed a laugh.

"Well, maybe not if I was with both of you at the same time, but you know what I mean. She was a special person.

I'll always love her, but we said goodbye. I am hoping I can forgive myself eventually, but for now, knowing that she would have forgiven me, that she did in her way, it gives me hope that maybe things will work out."

"With?"

Mason looked at her. He tucked her hair behind her ear. He smiled and said, "You. Because I love you, Megan. And I love your child. And I want you in my life. You make me happy. This isn't what we agreed to, and it isn't what you said you wanted, but I'm going after what makes me happy. We both came too close to death, and I'm not wasting another minute holding back how I feel about you. And if you don't feel the same... I'll just have to convince you otherwise."

Megan laughed.

Mason shrugged. "I don't know your plans. I don't know what you want to do next. I don't know if you're willing to move in with me or if you want to find a bigger place or if you're ready to tell me to back off, but—"

Megan reached up on her tiptoes and pressed her lips to his to stop him from continuing. Mason growled and eliminated the distance between them. He parted her lips with his tongue and groaned when he licked his way into her mouth.

Cheers and whistles met Megan's ears and had her pulling back. She looked around and found everyone on the dance floor staring at them and clapping. Megan put her head against Mason's chest.

He leaned down and whispered, "They all helped me to get here. They were hoping you'd give me another chance. But I told them all to not say anything to you. I didn't want you to think you had to say yes because they were pressuring you."

"You talked to everyone?" Megan asked. Her gaze landed on her parents, dancing and laughing and looking happier than ever.

"Yes. I told your parents everything. Well, almost everything. And I asked if they would be okay with me asking you to move in."

"Is that why my dad said all that stuff about going after what makes me happy?"

Mason chuckled. "Maybe. I didn't tell him to, though. I wanted you to decide if you were willing to give us a shot. Like I said, if not, I was going to do the pressuring myself."

Megan grinned. "No pressure necessary. I'm right where you are."

"You are, huh?"

Megan nodded. "Yep. There's this guy that isn't my baby's biological dad, but I think he's going to be the best dad ever because I love him, and he's pretty amazing. And I was hoping we might get another chance."

"Oh, yeah?"

Megan nodded. "Absolutely."

Mason leaned down and kissed her again. "I love you."

"I love you, Mason."

The DJ came over the loudspeaker and said, "Well, folks, we can turn things back up since the groom's sister and her man have finally made up. Thanks to all of you for helping push her in the right direction."

Megan gasped and glared wide-eyed at Mason. He shrugged. "Well, physical encouragement is different from emotional. It just gave me the opportunity."

Megan laughed.

"So, what do you folks say to a little dance competition? I hear these men might be a little bit competitive. Anyone up for it?"

Mason and Megan locked eyes and nodded. "Let's win this."

Megan grinned. "O'Keefe's don't like to lose."

"Neither do O'Connor's. I think we can kick some butt."

Megan laughed. "We'll go down trying."

The DJ turned on the first song, and everyone lined up to dance. Archer and Lily bumped around with her belly leading the way. Ashleigh and Daniel totally cheated making everyone cheer for Junior. Megan and Justin's parents shocked them all by spinning around the dance floor and ending with a show stopping dip and a kiss that made Megan blush. Mason twirled Megan around and led her right out of the reception to the cheers of the crowd.

"I needed a minute alone with you," Mason said.

"We were in the middle of a competition."

Mason shook his head. "I already won because I have you."

Megan sighed happily. "You might be too sweet for me."

Mason chuckled. "Then maybe I need to dirty things up a little and tell you how much I missed waking up to you. How hard I've been every night sleeping on the pillow you used. And how desperate I've been to get you back to my bed so we can get in some practice for baby number two."

Megan gasped. "I'm barely pregnant with baby number one."

Mason groaned and slid his hands low on her butt. "So?"

"You want more kids?"

Mason nodded. "I do."

"And you want them with me."

"I do."

"And you want to start practicing now?"

"Hell fucking yes, I do."

"Oh, thank God. I wasn't sure how much longer I was going to last."

Mason laughed and pulled her in close. "Then it's time we go home."

Megan nodded. "Home. I like the sound of that."

DEX SMILED as Mason and Megan disappeared from the reception. He was vaguely aware of the fact that they didn't return, either.

"How are you holding up?" Braden asked him.

Dex nodded. "About as good as can be expected. How are you?"

Slade and Kyra invited Braden to the wedding after his heroics that saved Dex's life and made it so they were able to bring in everyone who was a part of Leo's organization.

"All good."

"Yeah?" Dex wasn't sure he believed it. Braden was by his side, fighting their way out of the middle of everything. He'd gotten in more than his fair share of hits, but he took a lot, too.

"Not my first fight. Usually, it's a little more even, but I don't think those guys were interested in keeping things fair."

Dex chuckled. "No, they definitely weren't. They didn't care at all."

Braden grinned. "Thank you. For saving Wray. I know he fucked up, and I know he didn't deserve your help, but thank you."

"It's what we do. And we all deserve a hand once in a while. He's no different. I hope he gets the help he needs. Give up gambling for good."

"Me, too. I think he's going to. Stacey is a good woman, but she's not going to put up with it. When he came back, she had no idea. Now that she knows the full story, I'm keeping my phone close."

"You think she's going to kick him out?"

"I wouldn't be surprised. And I wouldn't blame her. He put them in a shitty spot."

"True. It sounds like he didn't intend to and anyone would have ended up in the same situation, but that doesn't make it better."

Braden snorted. "Nope. Not at all."

"Listen," Dex started, "I know my situation would have been very different if you weren't there with me. I've been back to the wall before, and the men on my team are the ones I've always counted on. You're on that list. I owe you. Anything, any time, I'm there."

Braden shrugged. "Just doing what we do."

"I know you went in to save your friend, but you saved my ass. Thank you."

"You're welcome. I hope I never need to call in a favor from you, though."

Dex lifted his glass in toast. "Agree, but if you do, we'll all be there."

Braden nodded sharply. "Same goes."

Dex nodded back.

"I'm going to go find a dance partner. I'll see you later."

"Enjoy." Dex asked for a refill of his club soda and went back to his seat. He thought about finding a dance partner, but he wasn't in the mood. Maybe one day.

THANK you for reading Megan and Mason's story! This was a tough one for me. Loss is such a hard thing to process, and loss like Mason experienced is that much more painful. Megan was just right to heal him, and he healed a piece of her, too.

Up next is Dex's story. When he's called in to work as private security, Taylor is less than interested in his assistance. Until it's clear her life, business, and employees are in danger. He doesn't let her out of his sight, and he doesn't mind the duty one bit. Read Future now!

ARE YOU READY FOR MORE? Newsletter subscribers get *exclusive* bonuses like short stories, bonus scenes, and a first look at everything new. Sign up for my newsletter today so you never miss a thing!

BEST FRIENDS ADALINE and Rosienna need a break and take off for the beach. All they want is sun, sand, and time away from their lives. Blake and Hayden are not part of the plan, but plans don't always work out. Check out Finding Home now.

ABOUT THE AUTHOR

USA TODAY Bestselling Author Mary E. Thompson spent most of her childhood wishing she had a few less curves. She hid between the pages of books because her favorite characters never cared what size her clothes were. Now, neither does Mary, and she writes stories about women like her. Real women who have curves, chase dreams, and find love, because we should all be happy, no matter what size we are.

When Mary's not reading or crafting stories, she's playing with her two kids or living out her own real life romance with her amazing, curve-loving hubby. She has a weakness for chocolate and will fight you for the last peanut butter cup. Unless you trade her for a glass of wine. Then everyone can be friends.

Visit https://MaryEThompson.com/subscribe/ to sign up for Mary's newsletter, **Romancing the Curves**. You'll get free ebooks and other fun stuff, like exclusive, members only content and giveaways, plus be the first to know about new releases and sales!

For even more great stuff, find me at:
MaryEThompson.com